ROSINA'S CHOICE

ROSINA'S CHOICE

Pamela Edgar

This first world edition published in Great Britain 1995 by
SEVERN HOUSE PUBLISHERS LTD of
9–15 High Street, Sutton, Surrey SM1 1DF.
First published in the USA 1995 by
SEVERN HOUSE PUBLISHERS INC of
595 Madison Avenue, New York, NY 10022.

British Library Cataloguing in Publication Data
Edgar, Pamela
  Rosina's Choice
  I. Title
  823 [F]

  ISBN 0-7278-4817-8

Typeset by Hewer Text Composition Services, Edinburgh.
Printed and bound in Great Britain by
Hartnolls Ltd, Bodmin, Cornwall.

To my beloved mother, Dorothy Brunette,
who accompanied me so enthusiastically on my trips
to the locations in the book for research.

Chapter One

The stranger was first seen crossing the rocks by Rosina, on a cold winter afternoon, where low-hanging clouds to the north dribbled fine droplets of moisture over the one long, low-lying hill, effectively cutting the small settlement off from the outside world. She was at first dismayed, then, with her apron full of herbs, she ran swiftly and silently in her soft veldschoen-boots, along the promontory set above the rocky shoreline, past the hens and chickens clustered together in the shadowy warmth of their enclosure. She scrambled past the prolific vegetable garden with its row of almond and peach trees, where two large dogs loped through the dense scrubby bush, and on to the deserted bank beyond the house, rising silent and still, like a stone sentinel. The house commanded a good view of the vast ocean, where ponderous waves rose over deep, oily depths and dipped over the horizon southwards to the bitter cold savagery of the Antarctic. A whiff of wood smoke from the kitchen chimney came to her nostrils mingled with the moisture from the air. Someone was rekindling the kitchen fire for supper.

Oblivious of the steely sky overhead, with swollen clouds scudding across it, and the off-shore north-westerly wind blowing a few drops of rain across her forehead, she raced to where she could get a better view

1

of the stranger, still a small dot that had detached itself from the rocks eastwards, and was slowly approaching across the pebbled sands.

Shielding her eyes with her free hand she gazed into the distance as a flock of gulls flew by like phantoms; with here and there a high-pitched cry, sounding seemingly at a great hollow distance in that lonely place. Below her, between the shore and the sea, the land looked lost and empty, the man's figure small in the loneliness of the strange toothlike rocks, invaded by black and white cormorants silhouetted against the opaque sea, and the pale sands. He was following the rough, twisting path that wound its way between white pebbles and patches of dark green scrubby bush. Though it was overcast across the shore, it was clear out to sea where the sails of a two-masted brig rose and fell on the small swells, out of danger from the treacherous underwater reefs.

Fascinated by the spectacle of the man approaching, she stood motionless on the grassy verge just before it descended steeply below to the rocks and sands then, for the first time, she was aware that the hill had already vanished in the clouds as the wind dragged a slanting curtain of gentle rain towards the house built of ship's timbers and local grey, white and red stone, and decorated with white pebbles on the promontory further back, surrounded by the vegetable garden, stables, the barn and men's huts. A yellow light showed between the cracks in the shutters of the front room, warm and mysterious against the lowering sky.

But the stranger had not turned around; he continued to move unsuspectingly towards the small, isolated settlement.

Rosina did not move. She gazed at him innocently limping towards danger, dragging one foot heavily behind him, as the first slithering tongues of cold water from the incoming tide lapped around the nearest rocks. He slipped once or twice, and dragged himself upwards until he was close enough for her to see he was a redcoat. With a quick intake of breath, she noted the red of his tunic, with its gold buttons and braid. He was bare-headed, his blond hair stark in the surroundings, as the grey shadow of soft rain came slanting towards him.

There was a short, awkward silence as he reached her on the bank. He was a tall man, but square-built and athletic. His uniform, though torn, sea-stained and covered with slime, was of excellent material and well-fitted, the buttons and braid distinguishing him as an officer. His face, what she could see of it beneath the dried blood and bruises, was a surprisingly young, handsome face with a firm jaw line and a nose that was straight and sharp over a wide, straight mouth. It was an almost classical Greek face, the eyes very blue, the brilliance of the whites under the thick head of blond hair giving them a wide-eyed, almost innocent look. There was a deep cut across his cheek and the beginnings of a golden beard, and his one hand clutched a blood-stained cloth tied about his chest under the tunic. His blood-stained knee also indicated a further wound.

"What a mercy to find someone in this God-forsaken place, ma'am . . ." he said, breathing hard. "I've walked for miles along this damned coast, with not a soul in sight." He took a deep, rasping breath. "Lieutenant Andrew Buckleigh at your service, ma'am. Can you help me? I'm just about done in. I haven't eaten for some days, and am in need of some medical assistance."

The colour drained from Rosina's young face, and before she could stop herself, she said, "No! You cannot stay here. The Cap'n'll never agree, and nor'll the men."

The soldier's face darkened abruptly. "I can go no

3

further, ma'am. As you see I am in no condition to travel any distance. Who is this Captain? Is he your father? Can I talk to him? What is his name? And who may you be?"

"I be Rosina Webb, sir." Rosina stiffened, her heart racing thunderously. The thin rain was soaking her thick hair as she stood there, wetting her face, and running in trickles down her neck, but still she stood there, staring at him. "The Cap'n – Cap'n Skewthorn – he be my guardian, yes, that's what he be." She spoke slowly as the painfully shy do, very much aware that the young man was one of the upper class folk from his well-spoken voice and the cut of his clothes. "He be the head of the settlement – all the men – we all listen t' him. That's the way it be, sir. He don't like strangers hereabouts – never has, and he won't like you here." She looked at him for an instant, then shyly lowered her head.

There was a silence. His eyes confronted her as she lifted her head, and she was painfully aware of his sudden interest, as he studied the face that disappeared in a soft pointed chin, so that attention was drawn to the large dark brown eyes, and the slender, shapely body proudly carried in the old-fashioned graceless clothes. She was without a hat or bonnet, but with her apron filled with herbs held before her, and her thick curtain of blue-black hair loose, she looked strikingly bewitching – passionate and yet innocent, a combination unwittingly irresistible.

"I was ship-wrecked back there, ma'am. Three hundred and fifty of King George's soldiers drowned, beyond that point." Briefly he indicated the direction in which he had come, as the soft rain beat in flurries about his head. "We were on our way from India to fight Bonaparte in Europe. Now there is no-one left, except me, and I need your help. Who is this Captain, anyway – is he army or navy, and what is he doing here?"

4

Rosina pushed back her mop of wet hair, suddenly looking tired. Under the flush on her cheeks was a hint of pallor. "He be a sea captain, sir – he was ship-wrecked, same as yourself sixteen years back, on the same ship as myself and my mother. He built this settlement with the survivors and the slaves."

He nodded. "Why doesn't he like strangers here? It's not very hospitable for him not to help those in need."

The colour drained completely from Rosina's cheeks. "He just doesn't, sir – it's always been like that."

He stared at her, and there was something about his eyes . . . but then he turned away and stared thoughtfully at the white foam-flecked edges of the sea. "Well, we are getting drenched out here." He smiled a sudden engaging, friendly smile. "All I ask is some food and a bed for the night, then I'll be on my way. Is that too much to ask, ma'am?"

He was not looking at her now, his eyes were on the bandage tied around his chest, his hands holding it tightly. They were fine, long-fingered, very capable hands, which disconcertingly stirred her imagination. "I have no where else to go." For a second his eyes raked her and brought a deep blush to her cheeks.

There was a flash of fear in her eyes, then it was gone, as a twinge of conscience invaded the moment. "You'll catch your death of cold out here, sir – you'd better come on up to the house. On reflection, the Cap'n can hardly mind a man in your condition."

The drizzling rain fell against the wood and stone of the house as they started to walk up the promontory.

"Where exactly are we, ma'am – I seem to have completely lost my bearings," the soldier said, breathing painfully.

Tempering her swift stride to his laboured steps to

5

bring him up the weathered, wooden steps of the stoep made from the poop deck of a ship, she said, "L'Agulhas, sir – the southernmost point of Africa, where the Indian and Atlantic Oceans are said to meet."

He steadied himself with one hand on the wooden rails of the stoep, and stared at the large brass bell hanging on the wall above the rails. "You said something about slaves – what slaves – where do they come from?"

She paused, her grip tightening on the rails, as her attention was suddenly distracted to a point out to sea, where two moving smudges heaved and dipped, coming out of the drizzle quite close to the coast. His eyes followed hers, but before he could speak, she said quickly, "They be the slaves that were on the ship when we went down, sir."

He frowned, and pushed the wet hair off his forehead. "A slaver, you mean? The Captain was taking a slave ship to some port? You must know by now that what William Wilberforce fought for so long in England became law five years ago – the Slave Trade from African coasts for British subjects and in British ships, was abolished."

Another flash of fear raced through her, as the smudges grew swiftly nearer and darker, revealing the blurred size and shape of longboats. "They don't do that any more, sir – not that I know of – two ran away and some ten were sold at the auction in Cape Town, but I don't remember it, seeing as I was but a small child."

"And what are those longboats doing here, Miss Webb?" the soldier asked, his eyes frowning curiously towards the water's edge. "They seem to be coming in."

Above the surface of the sea, now a steely grey, the longboats sidled in towards the sands, the crewmen inside them rowing them inshore with easy, light touches. There were other men, black and white at the edge of the promontory, where suddenly storm lanterns winked here and there like glow-worms. Below them, on the beach, was another cluster of lanterns gleaming where some more men waited to help the boats ashore.

Rosina tore her gaze from the boats to glance at him. "It be the Cap'n and his men returnin' – please now sir, please come inside."

As she held open the thick wooden door, and he staggered across the threshold of the entrance and into one of the dimly-lit, wood-scented front rooms, he gasped, "From where do they return? What do they do out here in these outlandish parts?"

Water began to trickle at once to the floor from their soaking garments. As the yellow light from two candles pushed the gloom back and upwards towards the high raftered ceiling, the furnishings of the room began to take shape. It consisted of several teak chairs, a table, and small, long wooden-framed sash windows – without glass and shuttered. There was an oak table under one window, and on it, neatly laid out, were several leatherbound first editions. A walnut clock hung above the open fireplace where a fire glowed, casting wavering shadows across the rough wooden beams supporting the ceiling, throwing the room into warm, golden-red relief, and catching the ivory butts of pistols on a sidetable.

The man stopped at the sidetable, to look at a superb silver ewer. "This is splendid workmanship, ma'am," he exclaimed.

"It – it belongs to the Cap'n, sir," replied Rosina, flushing at his close scrutiny.

"Where did you come by these beautiful things?" He whistled under his breath. "How could it be that you live in such splendour – out here – away from everywhere? What does the Captain do, Miss Webb?"

She did not answer. After depositing the herbs in a

container, she knelt down over a basket in one shadowy corner. Beside it was a bowl of water, some rags and a saucer of milk with a spoon. In the basket lay a cat, breathing in short, laboured gasps.

Quickly she wiped its mouth with a rag, and dipping her fingers in the milk, let the cat lick a few drops, which it did with eagerness. She looked up to find the soldier gazing down at her with enquiring eyes.

"Is she ill?" he asked, frowning as he contemplated the scene before him.

She nodded, then rose, wiping her hands down the front of her pinafore. "She be bitten by a honey badger and I rescued her. We have many such small animals here for which I care."

"Those books – very fine editions they are too – does the Captain read them?" he asked.

"Sometimes, sir. Though none of the men can read well – except the Doctor – Doctor Hargreaves that is – was – he passed on more 'an a year ago. Sit down here, sir, by the fire – Achmat will bring you a blanket and a towel – there be some fresh clothes too. I will tend your wound, and fetch some food and drink." Her slender, work-roughened hand indicated a chair. Her voice was now calmer, melodious and low, and if he noticed it, he gave no sign.

"Can you read those books, Miss Webb?"

Confused by the gentle warmth of his gaze and the directness of his words, she could find no tongue to reply. He was not like any man she had ever met in all her eighteen years. At last she found her voice, which came out low and husky in the silence. "I can read a little, sir, and write, and do some figuring – I – I – old Doctor Hargreaves – he taught me."

He was shivering uncontrollably in his dripping clothes

8

so she silently sped off to change her wet clothes, and then on to the kitchen towards the back of the house. It was a large, low-ceilinged room filled with warmth and culinary smells, where kitchen utensils winked and glittered, and the sea-stained ship's oak table was being set with a clatter of heavy cutlery and dishes. A kettle of soup and a pot of boiling fish were on the fire over the open fireplace, simmering gently and throwing off the odd golden spark amid the roasting spit and cauldrons.

She went back into the sitting-room with a pewter bowl of water and some rags and bandages, where a large, malay slave with iron grey hair had already piled fresh billets of wood upon the fire and set to work with bellows to work up a blaze, and another had brought the soldier clothes and a blanket. The slave had towelled the soldier dry and he was sitting heavily in one chair, in a warm woollen shirt and breeches.

Kneeling down beside him, Rosina dipped a rag in the water, and carefully wiped away the dried blood. In the golden glow of the fire, her skin gleamed like rich, warm satin, her hair shimmering about her head.

The soldier lay a little back in the chair, his eyes closed painfully, and allowed her to move aside the fresh borrowed shirt. As she worked she could not help but admire the strength of his body, the hard, muscular chest, warm through the cloth of his shirt, the wide shoulders, the trim waist. She was aware of the heavy thudding of his heart, and with an unnerving sense of shock she became aware of his masculinity. He looked what he was, self-confident, easy in manner like one who had never struggled without wealth, position or rank.

With trembling effort she kept her head bent to her task as a bewildering temptation came over her; for a few moments she felt the urge to throw her arms around his neck, draw his face towards her, and kiss him. With the sudden realization of what she felt, her eyes flew upward to find his gaze warmly upon her.

Utterly shocked by her unexpected feelings, she quickly tied the bandage around his chest, then tended the wound on his leg. As the shutters at the windows rattled with the wind, she picked up the bowl and hurried away to the kitchen, without speaking.

For a few moments she stood there, with a trembling hand to her mouth, surrounded by the savoury smell of pie, the aroma from the herbs she grew in the kitchen garden, and the winking and glittering of copper pots and pans salvaged from wrecks along the coast. There was the hiss of the kettle over the fire, and she turned to busy herself with it, trying to forget the feelings the stranger had aroused in her; trying not to think at all . . . Never in all her life had she felt such feelings, never had she felt so vulnerable . . .

She brought him a large bowl of soup, bread, tenderly boiled white fish, vegetables, cheese and ale. He watched her put a tallow candle into a large green bottle and set it down on the table before him. Then he sat for a moment after he had finished the supper, eyes closed, with an almost blissful expression on his face, savouring the feeling of repleteness after his long, exhausting walk.

After a while he opened his eyes, and surveyed her from under long blond lashes. "Where did you learn to cook like that, Rosina Webb?" His voice was hushed but sounded hollow in the room. "That was the best meal I've tasted in many a month."

She hesitated. In an effort to still the inexplicable trembling that possessed her, she pressed her slender hands deep into the pockets of her pinafore, clenching

10

them tightly together. But under his warming gaze, her creamy skin flushed slightly, and she could not hide the sudden confusion in her brown eyes, fringed with jet-black lashes, matching the long hair that was now taken up unfashionably into the two braids around her head, shining like new coal. Her soft pink lips were unconsciously tantalizing and gracefully curved; now, obviously anxious.

"Old Mistress Lacey taught me – she's been gone these four years, sir – she be cook to Lord and Lady Hattingham, before she came with us on the ship all of sixteen years gone. She was saved with me – by the Cap'n." She hesitated again, then cleared her throat. "Would you like some more, sir?"

Shyly she stood there, all unconscious vitality and vividness, in the way of a damsel from a fairy story, without the wiles and knowing ways of city women, a princess who had been caught in the past, someone from a faraway and distant dream.

And as Rosina saw the soldier's expression change, though she could hardly know the intense thoughts and feelings rushing through his brain, she blushed furiously and quickly stooped down to clear away the empty dishes from the table before him.

All at once there was the tramp of booted feet and they heard the low tones of men's voices from outside, which continued to grow steadily louder and nearer. The soldier heard the quick inhaling of Rosina's breath as her face paled. She rose, with the tray of dishes in her hands, and stared at the heavy wooden front door.

11

Chapter Two

The soldier's eyes followed her stare as the door crashed open and a number of lanterns flared the room into full light. A knot of wet, sweating men entered with pistols and cutlasses and loud voices. The rain was now falling steadily outside, and a gust of cold air rushed inside. The men started to walk further into the room, then stopped, surprised in the light of the small tallow lanterns. They were a motley crowd, several with handkerchiefs bound round their heads and earrings in their ears, their faces burned by the wind and pickled by the salt. Many wore blue jumpers with black neckcloths.

The soldier turned his head, his eyes meeting Rosina's. His brows gathered in concern as the men stood in a semi-circle, staring at the newcomer, then stood aside for a big, heavy, middle-aged man with a wooden leg in a dark coat of unfashionable cut and old three-cornered black hat as the door banged closed behind them. He had a full, heavy, grey-bearded face and dark eyes whose glance betrayed the habitual suspicion and resentment of his thoughts. He moved with surprising agility and speed in spite of his handicap, obviously considering himself a man of importance, expecting others to recognise him as such on sight. He pulled off his three-cornered hat, revealing grey hair worn in the old style, and caught with a black ribbon at the nape of his neck.

Rosina watched, with a tightening of her stomach, as he stared at her with mouth agape, his large bulk filling the middle space of the half-circle of men, as if she had conjured up for him some awful image.

"And by God, who do we have here?" he said in a harsh gravelly voice. "You sir, by what means did you gain entry into this house? Not by your own initiative, I'll be bound."

The soldier slowly and painfully rose from his chair, an almost apologetic smile on his handsome face. "Lieutenant Andrew Buckleigh at your service, sir. I have the doubtful fortune of being the only survivor of the Cornwallis wrecked to the east of this place. Miss Rosina Webb kindly bandaged my wounds and gave me food and drink, for which I am deeply grateful."

"Did she now?" The Captain searched the younger man's face and then sidled over to the borrowed shirt and breeches for a long moment. "Rosina, by whose orders did you bring Captain Buckleigh in here?" The hard lines in his face set harder still.

Rosina stared at the black eyes peering from the spider web of crags and folds on the weathered face, as a horrible feeling rose in her stomach. "He be – wounded sir, and could not walk any further. There be no one to ask, sir."

A strange light seemed to flash for an instant across the Captain's face, then it was gone, as he narrowed his sharply-calculating eyes on the soldier. "From the Cornwallis, you say? Grounded off Northumberland Point to the east?"

There was a low, discordant rumble from the men, which died almost as soon as it had started.

The soldier smiled, his honest blue eyes meeting the Captain's without a sign of flinching. "If that's what you call it, sir. A dangerous reef out there, close to the shore. I hate to inconvenience you, but your hospitality would be most welcome at this low point in my life. The only living souls I met from that place to this, were a few yellow-skinned little men and women."

The Captain fixed his eyes inscrutably on the young man's face. "Hottentots, they be. You say you saw no one else – nothing at all?"

The soldier's eyebrows went upward in a tiny shrug. "Why no, sir, nothing out of the ordinary – why do you ask?"

The Captain stiffened for a second, and there was a spark in his black eyes, like sudden fire, then he shrugged, pulling a small knife from his belt. He ran his finger delicately along its glittering edge. Then he looked at the soldier. "No matter – tis of no importance. I just wouldn't want there to be any trouble in these parts, sir – we run a very peaceful settlement here."

The soldier's eyes fell on the knife and he stiffened for a second, then he lifted his blue eyes to the Captain's face. "I wouldn't want to be any trouble, sir, but I need shelter for the night."

There was a long silence as the men talked in low voices among themselves, then stared first at the Captain, and then at Rosina. The realization that she was facing a sea of disapproval made her close her eyes in a silent plea for help.

Then the Captain replaced his knife. "So be it – but only for the night, mind," he said curtly, while behind his back his hands clasped and unclasped in secret strangulation. "Rosina, heat up a poker for my ale, and be quick about it, girl."

He turned a broad, hunched back, with disdainful

14

effect, and stumped through the room, motioning his men to leave for their quarters.

A while later, Rosina carried the kettle of periwinkle soup to the oak table in the dining room, and poured its contents into the dishes of the men gathered around it. Tallow candles stuck in empty wine bottles dripped grease and cast fitful shadows on her young face as the clamour of angry voices rose, and out of it sounded, above all others, the voice of Robert Blaine, who doubled as coxswain and mate, at the far end of the table, as he flung down his empty white clay pipe, and demanded a hearing.

White-faced, Rosina began to cut the bread, her face cast downwards so that her expression was hidden from the company.

The Captain called for attention, and banged thunderously on the table. There was a sudden silence, and all eyes turned towards Blaine's long thin face, with its cheekbones standing out like sharp shelves under slanting, glittering eyes, and beaklike nose which gave him a savage look, as did the two fingers missing from his left hand.

"'Tis not safe to have that redcoat 'ere, Cap'n and that's the end o' it! Even though 'e says 'e saw nothin – and 'e couldn't 'ave seen the brig – from where he was," he said agressively. "'E can be all manner o' trouble – what wi' the law and suchlike. I don't like it, I tell ye – I don't like it at all. I say 'e must be gone on the morrow before 'e pokes his toffee-nosed face into our affairs." And with a gesture of impatience, he sat down.

Rosina moved close to stand before the Captain. Her eyes wide and appealing, she stared into his and spoke almost in a whisper. "Hear me, sir – I know – I know nothin' of the ways of men and such – but – I do know

15

that Lieutenant Buckleigh be not ready to leave yet. His wound be not healed." She paused uncomfortably, waiting for his reaction.

There was an outburst of astonishment from the men and the Captain's brows lifted. He also could not hide his amazement, for though Rosina had spirit and intelligence she was rarely able to show it. When she was with him and the men, she scarcely said a word and always did her tasks without complaint or comment.

"By God!" he burst out in disbelief. "What on earth makes you plead for this stranger, Rosina?"

Abraham Dance, the ship's cook, a deeply tanned old sailor, with a tarry pigtail, earrings and a squint, leaned forward to rest his arms on the table. He shook his head and laughed derisively, "Don't go sweet on the likes o' 'im, Miss Rosina – 'ell betray you in the end – they all do. 'E's no good – 'e's the King's man, 'e's not wi' us, and that's that." He seized a tin mug and raising it high, gave a sneering toast. "To your good sense, Rosina – and death to the redcoat!"

Rosina covered a swift gush of fear which swept through her, but her eyes flared with suppressed anger. She turned and fetched the large steak and kidney pie from the sideboard, which was golden-brown and cooked to a turn as she told herself to gain control. Dance leaned his head back and laughed at her embarrassment, as the others eyed her maliciously, and whispered among themselves.

She lowered her eyes, dimly aware of the trap that closed slowly around her. He was daring her to face him and declare herself, something she had never done in all her life.

She placed the pie before the Captain, who took up a sharp knife with a silver blade to cut through the crust.

Then she lifted her head. "He be a redcoat, sir, in the service of his King and country, with nowhere to go," she whispered, her voice hardly audible to the others. "We all of us know that it took one party of survivors of the wrecked ship Penzance all of twenty-four days to reach Cape Town on foot. The Lieutenant be wounded – he'll never make it."

At the Captain's silence, she turned towards him and tried to see his features in the gloom, but he was sitting well back in his chair and it was she who was presented full to the candlelight. She watched as he slowly swished the wine in the glass before him from side to side. Then seeing that the company expected him to speak, he nodded and spoke forcefully into the waiting expectancy of the room. Rosina held her breath in fear of what he was about to say.

"My good sense tells me not to trust the redcoat officer now sleeping upstairs, but, all said and done, he's young, untried, probably his first commission – doubtless a commission bought for him by a doting, rich father."

His sneering words echoed through Rosina's brain.

"A second son, I'll be bound," the captain continued. "Of some great house back home. A family, I might add, with influence as they all have, with the Powers That Be – Powers that could get us all into a mighty lot o' trouble, and don't any of you forget it. But the lad seems honest enough, and he is wounded. He never saw the brig coming back to harbour at Struisbaai, that's for sure. A wounded man can do no trouble. I say we keep our counsel to ourselves and guard our privacy; but that we grant him a few days of rest, then send him on his way, before we return from Cape Town. That way there's no harm done."

17

Rosina's jaw dropped for barely an instant. She had not expected it. Suddenly she was elated. It was almost worth facing the sneers of the men.

As they busily handed around generous helpings of the pie with lashings of gravy and vegetables, she gazed down into the Captain's impassive face. Staring into those enigmatic, curiously hostile black eyes, she could find no reply. Taking up a platter of freshly baked bread, she numbly began to hand out thick slices around the table. Robert Blaine and the boatswain, Israel Wilkins, sitting side by side, were eating sullenly, pushing bits of pie into their mouths with a vicious air. Only the mute and deformed Henry Mostyn sat, gazing with quiet melancholy at the pewter plate before him, seeming to have forgotten where he was. The others ignored him, and leaned across him at intervals to fill their tin mugs from the cask of wine at his elbow.

Israel Wilkins, his mouth full, regarded the Captain thoughtfully. He was a tall, strong, fleshy man with a deeply tanned face. He wore a soiled skin jerkin that hung open to reveal a dingy and patched jumper; his hands were ragged and scarred, with black, broken nails, and there was a sabre cut across one cheek. His face possessed a stubborn and cruel expression, the mouth that of a ruthless man who had relentlessly fought his way through life. Yet, for all this, he had a subtle and a crafty look, which was difficult to define. After a few moments, he said, "'Tis the Cap'n's decision, men – what harm can be done by a wounded man, I ask ye? 'E's too poorly to notice much— " He quickly stopped, looking in Rosina's direction, then he dropped his eyes, and continued, clearing his throat noisily. "'Tis all right by me if 'e stays awhile."

Tom Harding, a small, shrivelled man with a long

nose and a persistent sniff snorted sharply. "There'll be trouble from that redcoat yet, you mark me words. Don't say you wasn't warned. Wot'll 'appen if he finds the stores, eh? And the rest o' the cargo from 'is own ship, I ask you that!"

Both the Captain and Israel Wilkins looked at him and at Blaine silently, their faces splashed with vivid orange light.

"'Tis no easy thing to decide with a stranger come to these parts, of a certainty," Makepeace Trelawney, the ship's doctor growled, eyeing each man in turn with his bluff face, roughened and reddened and lined, a savage frown bitten between his thick black brows. "We've kept safe all these years – there's no saying what a stranger will do, or how he will react."

"It's a chance we must take, Trelawney – there's no other way at present," the Captain said, eating a piece of pie. He turned to Rosina, who was standing at the fireplace, his black eyes like cocked pistols. "There's just one thing, Rosina," his harsh, gravelly voice announced sharply, "Just you keep silent, girl, d'you hear? You play your part and all will be well. You get the redcoat well enough to leave this place for good and all. We leave for Cape Town on the morrow, and he'd better be gone by the time we return."

The bitter tone of his voice spoke of much Rosina did not understand. While she digested this statement she stood awkwardly looking at him with a strange relief.

Then he was speaking again, in a more conspiratorial tone as the men leaned forward to hear him. "The Navy bought the French prize corvette L'Alliance in Simonstown, men; news which should delight one and all. Two-thirds of the prize money goes, as you know, to me – making it exactly two thousand, six hundred

19

pounds. A thousand and four hundred goes to you lot. But, for good measure I intend to divide one thousand between you for good service, and by my reckoning that is a substantial bit of money."

There was a low, excited murmuring among the men as they began to work out their share, and at last, ready to leave as the meal ended, Rosina looked up and saw the Captain sitting there, his eyes on her, caught unawares, unfamiliarly soft and yearning.

In rising surprise, she gazed into his face, with its harsh, craggy furrows which instantly became expressionless, and she wondered if she had imagined it. "Goodnight, sir," she said, bracing up her courage. "Will you be wantin' breakfast before you leave?"

"That we do, girl – and a hearty one at that – but when I depart I leave Maarten, the Dutchman in charge – and I want no trouble." His dark eyes pierced her so that she froze, but dropping a respectful curtsey, and with hard-won poise she turned and left. At that moment she could have laughed with joy. Not even the Captain's threats and the opposition of most of the men could have dampened her happiness as she fed the animals. Across the yard, in the slave quarters Rosina could see tall and wiry, grey-haired Abdoul mending a tool-handle in the inadequate light of a tallow candle, soaking a strip of rawhide in water and then sewing it round the crack with rawhide thongs, which she knew would hold fast as a clamp of iron when dry. The fowl, the cow and the horses had settled down and there was a deep silence as she returned to the kitchen where the table had been cleared and the wicks made from old stockings and linen were arranged in rows for the winter store of tallow candles.

The pot of hot water with a deep layer of melted

mutton suet on it was keeping warm over the fire, as she, the buxom female slave, Clara and her young son Abel proceeded to roll each wick in the melted fat, hang them from a stick to cool and harden, dip again and re-hang until the desired thickness was reached. It was a long process, and not unfitting for a cold winter night, though tonight Rosina's thoughts were far away – with the redcoat in the room upstairs.

"Remember, Missy – how the tallow dips went all over to one side last winter?" Clara laughed with the memory, her great body shaking with mirth as she rolled a wick in the fat. "Aai, but my Abel did laugh!"

Rosina looked up, little dark curls peeking from under her housecap, her eyes brimming with mischief as they fell on Abel's gleaming dark head bent industriously in the candlelight. "I promised Abel a prize, Clara, if he gets the straightest dips."

Abel looked up, grinning. "Yes, Mama – Missy Rosina – she promise a big soup-plate of raisins and almonds and spicy sweets!"

At last the wicks were done, and Abel, clapping his hands and giggling with delight went off with his prize. Rosina looked into the dining room and found Captain Skewthorn alone, lolling in his chair, his one booted foot on the table, his wooden leg hanging on a hook against the wall. There was a bottle on the floor, and an empty goblet in his hand. Quietly she withdrew, holding her breath.

She passed the door of the room the redcoat slept in, on the way to her own. On impulse, with swiftly beating heart, she quietly opened it.

She looked at the bed in the far corner, and could just make out the recumbent figure on it, in the borrowed nightshirt. A candle had been left burning at his bedside and he was already asleep, on his back, careless of appearance, snoring faintly at the base of his throat. He seemed to have suffered no ill effects from his ordeal and exposure – his strong frame must have grown used to hardship in the army. He never felt the touch of the blanket with which she returned, minutes later, tiptoeing up to the bed to spread over him. Silently she blew out the candle, then softly closed the door.

A small animal rubbed itself against her leg, and she looked down to see her small black cat, its green eyes glowing in the darkness. Smiling, she bent down to pat it, then rose and walked purposefully to her own room, as something soft and furry jumped on top of her and tickled under her chin. It was her pet golden mongoose. Laughing softly she watched the little animal rub his nose and scratch himself, then fluff up his bushy tail, peering at her inquisitively. She allowed him to snuffle at her ear, and finally climb down to the floor, running away under the table where he would stay all night.

Closing her bedroom door behind her, she listened to the silence of the house, then began to close the shutters and draw the curtains over the glassless window. The small room was simple and plain but almost painfully neat and orderly. A narrow bed with a straw-filled mattress filled one corner covered by a light patchwork quilt which was frayed and much mended but neatly folded back, the worn sheets white with sun-bleached cleanliness. There was a single, once-broken chair repaired with small rope, a little table bearing a small pile of books pushed to one side, and a wooden trunk beneath the one small, long window with a bible on it.

Shaking out her two braids, and letting the thick silken mane of hair fall in disarray about her shoulders and down her back, she undressed modestly, and put on her nightgown. Then she knelt by the side of the truckle bed, mumbled her evening prayer and, showing the whiteness of shapely calves as she raised her gown, climbed into bed.

The moment she settled down, the small black cat jumped onto the bed and settled at her feet. She was pleasantly conscious of the warmth of the little animal the Dutch pedlar Jan la Motte had brought her from Cape Town, and the fragrance of a pomandered orange hanging over the bed – a gift from Roosje, Jan's wife, before she died in childbirth, as drowsiness crept over her. She listened to the muffled noises of the night outside, the surf pounding against the rocks, and felt secure in her dry little shelter of warmth and light.

Finally she wetted her fingers and reached out to snuff the candle flame, then stretch her legs luxuriously under the blanket. She heard the little animal sigh and settle herself down too. She lay there, in the darkness, thinking of the redcoat, as she fell asleep.

Dawn was not fully come, the room only faintly illuminated by grey light when Rosina awoke. She lay staring at the shaft of gentle light, full of dancing dust, falling through one of the shutters that had blown open. For a few moments she savoured the warmth of her bed, then, with a racing heart, she jumped out of bed and pulled open the other shutter from where she could see the grey glitter of the sea rolling against the strange toothlike rocks. One of the longboats was creeping over the water. A seagull was wheeling overhead, dazzling white against the grey sky. For a long moment she stared out across the unbroken expanse of sea to the horizon where the outside world lay.

Chapter Three

As dawn was breaking, the loaves, brown and hot to the touch, were being drawn from the depths of the oven, with the help of a long-handled wooden implement, a rake without prongs. Young Abel appeared at the kitchen door, calling his mother with a shrill lift of the last syllable. The brass bell on the stoep was clanging and Clara put down the bread-rake and bustled to the door where Abel stood, shivering in his cotton garments.

"Now you go away Abel – go and polish the knives before the Cap'n finds you here," she commanded, clapping her hands at him. "I must help Miss Rosina with the coffee and you stand there ready to get under my feet. Out! Out!"

Abel snatched a piece of bread and slipped away from her grasp. He turned to look at her, grinned briefly, and ran.

Rosina quickly and quietly placed out the daily supply of sugar, unlocked the coffee-canister and spooned out the coffee for the coffee-urn, and cut and buttered the many slices of dark brown bread. As Clara and Abdoul, now in charge of the kitchen garden, good-naturedly dawdled over their duties, she broke eggs into the skillet. As they hissed and spluttered, her mind was happily busy with the day ahead.

It was cold outside, but dry; the drizzle had ceased,

and bright shafts of sunlight pierced the broken clouds, setting the sea a glitter with shifting shards of colour. Thin smoke crinkled into the sky from the tops of the chimneys as faint mist hung like a floating veil over the hill. A horse whinnied in the stable and a group of seagulls were winging their way slowly out to sea.

Rosina was an excellent housekeeper, in a settlement composed, except for Clara, entirely of men. She cooked and baked, washed and cleaned and tended the animals for which she had a deep attachment. She worked well with the slaves, of which only six remained from a cargo of two hundred and sixty, and now in their middle years. Her days were long and tiring but never once had anyone heard her complain.

Outside, in sheltered enclosures, the wounded animals were kept. As she had discovered a talent for helping hurt wild creatures, most of them birds and small bush animals, life had burst open for Rosina. These creatures needed her, and soon they were tended with more love than she had ever shown to anyone. But now there was the soldier who needed her attention. To her, he was like the wild, wounded animals and birds, handsome and strong on the outside, but hurting inside and needing great care.

She picked up a breakfast tray, and made her way to his room. She was vividly aware of the calls and cries of men, of the stamp and click of hooves from the stables as the animals gathered for their daily work in the slowly awakening world and her heart rose in an excitement for which she had no words. With faint colour tinting her creamy cheeks, and a sparkle in her dark, liquid eyes, she stood shyly in the doorway. There was a table with a white cloth already spread beside the truckle bed.

He opened his eyes, and yawned before he was aware

of her presence. She walked slowly towards the bed with the tray in her hands, and halted before him. Scarcely breathing, she waited, feeling his nearness yet not daring to move.

"Miss Webb? I didn't realize it was morning yet," he said, and his voice, though soft, seemed to fill every corner of the room.

"I brought your breakfast, sir," she said, her voice low and husky.

He gazed at her as she stood above him, innocently admiring him. The long woollen shawl she wore was old-fashioned, loosely woven, and warm. It made her look older than her years, but the face above it was quite enchanting.

Lieutenant Buckleigh drew a ragged breath and by an extreme effort of will replied casually. "Thank you Rosina – may I call you that?"

She nodded, shyly.

He sat up, painfully propping himself against the pillows, as she carefully placed the loaded tray across his knees, then moved away. He slowly picked up a thick slice of bread. Rosina braced herself in a corner as he raised his head and studied her in his open, boyish way. "Will you stay while I eat?" he asked.

"I shouldn't really, sir – if the Cap'n— "

"Damn, girl! Do you have to do everything he says? I shall not eat another bite unless you stay." Decorously he put the bread back on the pewter dish, his eyes easily embracing and flattering her.

The seconds slipped past, flying on silent wings as she stood there, confused and unprepared. All her senses were completely involved with this strangely compelling man. His tousled golden hair beckoned her, his handsomeness quickened her very soul. There was a need in her to help him back to full health, to feel the warmth of his arms about her . . . But she was painfully aware of her own poor, graceless clothes and manners; of her painful shyness with the few strangers she had met.

She could bear it no longer, and she said, "I will stay but a little time, sir – to see you start your breakfast." She sat down demurely on the only chair, across the room from him, her tense body relaxing only when he smiled and started to eat what she had cooked.

His face was so handsome, she thought, folding her slender, rough hands in her lap. Then her eyes met his, and, if a flicker of wariness remained, it was immediately dispelled as she looked beyond the thick, blond lashes into deep blue honest eyes.

"Tell me, Rosina." The words burst from him as he helped himself to scrambled egg. "What is it like beyond that hill outside?"

"I don't know, sir, I've never been beyond it."

The man stopped eating and frowned into the exquisite face across the room. "Never been beyond it? Good God, you mean to say you don't know what the outside world is like?"

"I've climbed the hill, sir, many times – but I have never ventured to the other side. This be my world. Cap'n Skewthorn don't like me to wander too far." She glanced towards the shuttered window and experienced a new anxiety: outside was the sound of men's voices and footsteps. "I often watch the men go off about their adventures, sir, but I – I must stay at home and provide for their comfort."

"And what do they *do*, Rosina – the Captain and his men? You seem to live very well in this isolated place."

Her face was expressionless, but something flickered

in her eyes. She rose quickly. Her words stumbled out awkwardly: "I must go now, sir – the men are about. They'll be wantin' their breakfast before they sail to Cape Town."

He raised an eyebrow, watching her curiously. "Do you know how cruel it is, to keep slaves, Rosina? To take innocent people from their homes by force and sell them in foreign lands? Do you know what their lives are like? They are prisoners under a cruel and vicious system. Do you know anything about the dreadful conditions on the slave ships? Is that what the Captain and his men are doing? Is it?"

"Lieutenant Buckleigh, sir!" she gasped, then picked up the empty dishes on the tray and made to flee to the door. But a hand on her arm halted her. The touch was gentle but as unrelenting as an iron band.

"Look at me," Andrew Buckleigh murmured when she refused to acknowledge him. Hesitatingly she lifted dark questioning eyes to his and found an easy, slow smile that seemed to search her. "I know there's something going on here, Rosina – something the Captain doesn't want the authorities to know. I can smell it. He has a ship hidden somewhere, hasn't he – a ship in which he smuggles slaves into the colony against the law?"

She tried to wrench away as her heart fluttered in her breast, but he held her fast. "Good sir— "

He looked up at her, his brows lifted. "You are far too beautiful to stay locked up in this desolate place. You must go away – to Cape Town or England where the world is bigger, wider. You are like the slaves here – a prisoner to the Captain and his men. You must learn to dance and wear beautiful clothes in the latest fashions, to widen your experience. There

28

is an exciting world out there, Rosina – beyond that hill."

Rosina jumped as if she had been stung. The prickling of fear became strong. Something warned her to leave at once. "Please, sir – let me go – I hear the men!" she whispered hoarsely. Her eyes dared him to refuse as she jerked hard at his elbow.

"You are wasted in this place, Rosina." The blue flame in his gaze kindled brighter, burning her with its intensity. The muscles in his arm tightened as he held her arm, and the stiffness of her body was like that of one waiting for doom.

"You must learn to trust me," he admonished, as he let her go. "If anything is going on here, believe me, I will soon enough find out."

She stood holding the tray and looked down at him. Suddenly she spoke with surprising conviction. "I be unlessoned in the ways of the world as men talk of it, sir. But I live in this place and must do my duty. Cap'n Skewthorn he saved my life, and he's saved many a life along this coast, he has."

There was a quiet alertness in the soldier's manner as he stared up at her: like that of a cat, its strength ready to explode but, for the moment, docile. She was reminded of the animals she had tamed, which had that same waiting quality. She could not help but admire the fine figure he made, even in his present condition. Then she coloured hotly and turned away in sudden confusion, leaving him to stare after her with a thoughtful frown.

Chapter Four

Rosina stepped out into the mild winter sunlight which revealed the house on its rocky promontory in hard outlines, and stood looking out at the sea, the little mongoose, with its tail like a cat and its head like a weasel, riding on her shoulder. She could see eleven-year-old Abel roaming the beach to find driftwood and bits of wreckage, fuel being the everlasting problem.

"Rosina! I forbid you to go into the redcoat's room alone, d'you hear me?" a harsh, peremptory voice said behind her. "'Tis scandalous!"

She whirled around to see the Captain stumping along on his wooden leg, his black eyes peering sternly at her from the craggy folds of skin in his weathered, fleshy face. He was unaware of the relentless ferocity of his glance, being only conscious of a momentary anger at anyone crossing his will.

"But, sir, he's poorly – he needs attention so's he can leave."

"You'll tend his wounds only and always with Abdoul – the sooner that soldier leaves, the better!"

She demurred for a moment, full of fine words regarding the English soldier, but at the sight of Captain Skewthorn's expression she was reduced to instant submission. Then he turned around and marched towards the edge of the promontory, spyglass under his arm, the old tri-cornered hat cocked to shade his eyes from the morning sun. He was a clever, forceful man whom life had turned into a morose and bitter one. Rosina, in her almost timid vulnerability and her deep gratefulness to him for being her saviour served his every whim in silence and a certain fear.

She walked quickly away down to the rocks, with one of the dogs, a large stiff-haired stray at her heels, as the mongoose bounded away and disappeared. She listened to the echo of the dog barking at the waves as she sat at the water's edge, thinking of the redcoat.

Idly she watched the lazy antics of a dark brown Cape Clawless Otter, the top of its head a silvery sheen in the light as it dived through the breakers as they gathered and plunged to shore tossing lace-fringed ruffles to the breeze, the odour of salt pungent in the air. Today the deep blue of the open sea gave way in the shallows to a brilliant iridescent green where one longboat crouched on a small strand of beach below the bushes. It had brought some of the men back last night and would return them to the brig anchored at Struisbaai filled with cargo from the Cornwallis. Rosina knew that the goods and tackle were to be auctioned to brisk bidding at the Commercial Coffee House in the Keyzersgracht in Cape Town, but the whole process had never interested her before Lieutenant Buckleigh had arrived. Now she was aware of it with a new sense of apprehension, wondering what would happen if he ever found out.

There had been other cargoes too, during the years – rice, sugar-candy, sago, turmeric, chintzes, rolls of Brazil tobacco, some of it damaged by sea water; Rhenish wine, bar and plate lead. And slaves.

She had, in earlier days, been greatly excited about the cargoes coming back to the settlement, for on rare

31

occasions, the Captain would pick out some woollens or cloth from a consignment to give her, or something new for the kitchen: some spices or utensils. But now that the redcoat had arrived, something had changed.

Her days, up until now, had been nearly always monotonously the same, with nothing much to plan or look forward to. Having Lieutenant Buckleigh as an albeit unwelcome house-guest had injected something unexpectedly exciting into her life, and, despite the captain's warning, she looked forward to the hours ahead when she would spend more time in his company.

The Captain was a harsh, hard-working, bitter-minded man, who had reduced Rosina from her earliest years to complete submission to his will. But through all his blundering cruelty, which she was only now dimly beginning to understand, there ran the memory of a certain unspoken affection, and the yearning for his love. She had come, under his harsh rule, to a quiet acceptance of her lot . . . until now.

She thought about the slaves and what the redcoat had said. And especially she thought of big, generous Clara, who had nursed her as an infant and had been almost like a mother to her. Rosina had not thought about Clara's past life before, or about Clara's suffering; of Abdoul's and Achmat's too, on the slave ships. But something stirred in her now, and she pictured their torment at being forced away from their homes into the service of strangers; of the fear of a sudden and drastic change in their lives.

All Rosina knew about Clara was that she had been a young slave on Captain Skewthorn's ship, and that she had always worked hard and cheerfully. She remembered how astounded the Captain had been when, in Rosina's seventh year, Clara had produced a child, Abel, obviously fathered by one of the men. Abel was an attractive, unusual boy of mixed heritage, with a light skin and high cheekbones, who was quick and clever, but like most, totally ignorant of the identity of his father, as Clara had refused to discuss the matter with anyone.

She turned her head. Behind her a puff of smoke drifted from the chimneys of the house.

She could see broad, muscular Achmat and tall, wiry Abdoul squatting beside the stoep, twisting ropes and cords from an old anchor cable. Achmat, with his big shoulders which showed scars from continual carrying of yokes with pails. Rosina sighed.

Now and then, high above the hill, a lonely bird of prey cut the sky with curving wing, and sank out of sight. For a while longer she sat there before going back to her numerous household duties. Perplexed by a lifetime of conditioning. She did not know what to do. But there was one thing she was sure of: she was growing restless with wanting to be near Lieutenant Buckleigh. He drew her like a magnet. And, for the first time, ever since he had talked of the outside world, Rosina was beginning to have thoughts about wanting to see it.

When Rosina went to re-dress Andrew Buckleigh's wounds, in the company of Abdoul, who brought him a bowl and a knife to shave himself, there was a little colour in his cheeks and much more strength in his movements. At first she sat and gazed admiringly at him, so handsome, in the light filtering through the open shutters. She watched his deft movements as he washed and shaved, using the cold water in the washstand jug with washing glove and soap, wetting a few inches at a time. Then he sat back on the bed to allow her to remove the dressings from his wounds with her dexterous fingers.

He flinched for a second with pain as she removed the bandages from around his chest and knee. She peered at the wounds which appeared to be healing already, and examined the dressings she had removed. There had been a slight oozing from the chest wound, but it was only slightly tinged with blood, and the tissue around it seemed healthy. She had a saucer of cold vinegar beside her, in which lay a soaking lint, and clean bandages. She found her hands were trembling as she applied the lint to the scarred surfaces, but with an effort she steadied them as she re-bandaged the wounds then rose to her feet.

"Thank you, Rosina," he said, as she asked Abdoul to bring the midday tray. "Cold vinegar is used in the British Navy very effectively, did you know that?"

Abdoul came back, bearing a tray with slices of cold meat, bread, wine and cheese, which he set deftly and quickly on the bed, and withdrew to a corner, without looking up.

"Soup," said Lieutenant Buckleigh, peering into a bowl which steamed deliciously. "And what is the meat, may I ask?"

"'Tis venison, sir – some of the men went hunting further afield."

He placed a napkin under his chin and ate with increasing appetite. "Some more of the soup, if you will, Rosina," he said, and she relayed the order to Abdoul who nodded, and taking up the bowl, vanished to the kitchen.

"This venison is dashed good, especially to a man who fed only days ago on weevil-infested biscuit and over-salted meat on board ship."

Feeling oddly shy in the presence of Abdoul who had

returned with another bowl of soup, she looked at the Lieutenant surreptitiously. His open, warm gaze stirred something deep within her. A moment of silence passed as she struggled with her own emotions, and behind her back she tightly folded her hands.

"I see you are guarded against me now," he observed. "Well, that's a pity. Sit down and talk to me – I've been devilish lonely for hours."

After a few moments of silent embarrassment, Rosina took the chair across the room and desperately tried to speak while Abdoul clattered the crockery between them. The bowl of soup and the platter of meat were both empty; the bread had disappeared; there was only a small piece of cheese left, and the bottle of wine was only half-full.

"Come have some wine with me," he suggested, smiling into her anxious face. "I can't drink all this alone."

She shook her head, wishing there was something she could say. He shrugged his shoulders, and held up the glass in his hand, as Abdoul left with the tray.

"I see I shall have to battle on alone then," he said, amusement creeping into his eyes. "Can you dance, Rosina? I thought not. I thought not. I must teach you, it really is an excellent pastime, and dashed energetic too."

Rosina shifted and glanced at him uneasily then she rose from the chair, and smoothed her skirt. "There be much to do about the house, sir."

His eyes suddenly gleamed with wicked humour, and his lips drew back into a wide, boyish grin. "That's right, leave me alone. What do you care of my feelings!"

"That be not true!" she gasped, as anxiety whirled through her words.

His grin disappeared and he held up a forestalling hand. "I was only jesting, my dear girl – don't upset yourself so. I can see that you have been moulded into a creature that is not supposed to have feelings. Forgive me if I am blunt, but it's all to obvious to me that your feelings have been controlled and imprisoned from the time you were two years old and saved from the wreck. Even your body is not your own. Nothing is your own, Rosina – when will you see it? Are you going to waste your whole life, miserably existing here, under the Captain's orders?"

Angrily he tossed the wine down as a moment of silence passed.

Rosina fumbled for a reply, shaken by his abrupt words. "It be that way, sir – ever since I can remember. Old Mistress Lacey used to say that most of the things men did be forbidden us women. She used to say that most women feel the pain of their existence until they can feel no pain anymore, sir, for that be expected of us."

She felt strange having spoken about a matter she had never mentioned to anyone, but his eyes turned in silent question to her. Unable to meet them, she averted her face. Tears came, and she did not know why.

"How do you remain so innocent, Rosina – so child-like?" His voice was hoarse and low in the room as the sun spilled through the windows. The day was cool and cold with a clear blue sky. A fresh breeze had risen and swept away the low clouds, leaving the air clean with a hint of salt in it.

Slowly it dawned on her that there were sounds outside, and without a word she hastily left the room.

Out to sea, the sails of the heavily armed brig flapped and bellied as she slowly crept westwards past the settlement, rolling in the swell, and Rosina watched through a spyglass with veiled eyes. She could see the sturdy beauty of the ship, the two full, square-rigged sails, the flag fluttering, the hands on deck – all familiar sights of the life in which she had grown up, but which no longer moved her as it had done in the past.

With most of the men gone, except the landlubbers and Israel Wilkins who had woken with a fever and had to remain behind in his hut, and the slaves moving quietly about their labours, she felt strangely alone. Wistfully she gazed towards the redcoat's room, almost imagining him beside her. Warm phantom arms crept about her, and she closed her eyes with the deep pleasure of it. Then it was gone, and she felt pensive and lonely again, as if the day had lost its savour, and she could only wonder what it would be like to share a life with him.

That night she climbed into bed with the small black cat, and blew out the candle, listening to the waves lashing against the rocks. It was late, nearly midnight and a small breeze had come whispering over the misty surface of the sea. It was the beginning of one of those wakeful nights which she recognised from the moment she had blown out the candle and settled her head on the pillow. It was like a dream – only two days ago she had never known of Lieutenan Buckleigh's existence; she had never questioned anything the Captain and his men did. Now as she lay surrounded by the misty darkness outside, she was full of doubts and torments, no longer sure of her narrow existence, of the strict parameters of her life, no longer sure of what was normal.

She lay grimly rigid as memories of her childhood years came flooding back with a rush. She could well remember the many ships devoured by the sea that rolled in from the seething wilderness of the southern

37

oceans, ensnared by the vicious reefs beyond stretching dangerous and unseen out to sea. Some of these had yielded treasures of gold bullion, silver and jewels and priceless pottery and on much of this plunder the Captain and his motley collection of men lived, most of them pressed-ganged into the British Navy, some captured from foreign vessels and pressed into service, though not reluctantly when they discovered the good life the Captain promised them. But what she now remembered so vividly was the English vessel that had sunk within minutes near Cape Agulhas, only one year ago, with a cargo of jute, sinking almost immediately. There had been no chance to use the boats and the three survivors had reached the shore clinging to wood. She could still hear the distant cries from the wreck in the night above the thunder of the waves. She knew what the Captain and the men did out there on the sea in the brig armed with guns, and she hated herself for it.

She groaned miserably for a second, and turned over restlessly as she thought about the Cornwallis and the redcoats drowned off Northumberland Point. She knew the cargo the men had salvaged from it . . . and she knew a little about the cargoes of slaves. Not much, but enough. The Captain thought she was unaware of that side of his work, but she had heard scraps of conversation between the men from time to time. She had always thought it was legal, and so it had been, until the British law abolishing the trade, a fact of which she had been ignorant until the arrival of the redcoat. Outside in the dark, the horses stamped in the stable, and late she heard some of the men returning late from their work.

Somehow, she thought wretchedly, she must stop Lieutenant Buckleigh from ever finding out . . .

Chapter Five

The next day had grown heavier and greyer, and there was once more a freckle of rain in the air. But somehow it did not affect Rosina as she flew about the house seeing that the midday meal was brought to Lieutenant Buckleigh on time and the larger evening meal was ready when the men came wearily back from their labours. She saw in Andrew Buckleigh a beloved shining knight, who had been wounded, and felt an overwhelming compassion drawing her towards him. A subtle change had overcome her as she baked almond tartlets for him, spending time shaping the small pastry cases into a perfection, which gave her a strange, almost physical pleasure. It gave her the same pleasure to wash out his cup and saucer and plate, and he would never know the exquisite joy it brought her to bake and cook his favourite foods, or fill a big pottery jug with bunches of wild heather or an exquisite protea or two and place it on the table in his room. To please him, she began to read once more the books in the front room, and to improve her grammar under his guidance. She was a very quick learner and as the days passed, he was amazed at her rapid improvement.

The only thing that vaguely troubled Rosina was her feeling that Haas Maarten, the strange, silent seaman from a wrecked Dutch barque, now watched her with unusual intensity. He had always shown her a certain consideration, but she always felt inwardly that his attitude had all the appearance of being forced, and as she grew to know him, she could not rid herself of the feeling that his care of her was the result, not so much of his natural liking for her, as the determination to do his duty to the Captain, to whom he owed his life.

But this did not stop her brushing and combing her hair until it glistened beneath the new homemade white muslin bonnet set well back on her shapely head, as her heart cried out to Andrew Buckleigh as it had never done before.

As he healed, she built up the courage to read to him. In the absence of the Captain, she expanded rapidly in mind and curiosity. Quickly, her way of life was changing. The English soldier, with his easy laugh and his charming manners, broke down, in his determination to reach her, the barriers between her and himself, between her and the outside world of which she knew so little.

Under the assault of his carefree friendship, she found herself borne into a new world of adventure and beauty. With the simplicity and assurance of a child accepting the inevitable she turned towards his company. She was in some ways, still a child, a child whom circumstances had all her life cut off from friendship with others her age. And it was not so surprising that she drew now so close to the English soldier.

Andrew began to visit old Samuel Leach, an able seaman who had sailed for years with the British East India Company before joining Captain Skewthorn, in the barn where the great brandy casks, the ploughs and spades, the whips and harness and fishing tackle were stored. Surrounded by the smell of tobacco and brandy and hides, the two would talk for hours about the First British Occupation, which old Leach remembered, a year after the settlement was established, and the second, of 1806. They would talk about Napoleon, the continuing war in Europe and the possible outcome for Britain. And all the time, they were watched silently by Maarten and the few men left behind during Captain Skewthorn's absence.

It was one afternoon towards the end of winter, that Rosina pushed the bolt across her bedroom door for complete privacy and sat down on the bed, her eyes moving round the small room which she knew intimately. Through the long sash window she now looked with the changed eyes of a young woman, knowing that here in her own room, where no one ever came, she could give way to her suppressed emotions. As she sat in the quiet room, hearing the cluck of the fowl in their pen, and the whinnying of the horses, she knew that for her, now her eyes had been opened to Andrew Buckleigh there would always be the unchanging ache of loneliness and loss for the world she would never know; that with her busy hands and efficient housekeeping ability, she would forever be at the beck and call of the Captain and his men. Her life in the settlement had been unusually sheltered in a long succession of busy days. She had never looked far ahead or reasoned deeply; it had never been expected of her, and she had been kept so busy that she had scarcely had time to think. She had never found her duties irksome in the past, but now she suddenly felt faint and sick with despair, desperately tired of living this way.

The sudden appearance of Lieutenant Andrew Buckleigh had at first scared, and then thrilled her.

But, of late, she had felt the restlessness in him to leave, to return to the world he knew. He spoke of fighting Napoleon Bonaparte with patriotism and pride, of the blockade that was strangling the Empire of the French, of fighting all of Europe to free the Continent and England from the menace of the ambitious Corsican. As her hands clenched together in the lap of her pinafore, she knew that she had to do something before the Captain returned. Either she must do it or accept the idea of Andrew returning to the outside world. She knew he had his own life to live, his own way to go; but she could not bear the thought of his departure.

She thought of what it would be like with him gone, and she was forced to admit that she did not want to live without him. And she realized too, that underneath the turmoil of her mind, was an gnawing hunger for him which was growing into an unrelenting ache.

Chapter Six

The door of the Lieutenant's room was opened slowly one quiet night soon afterwards. It was Rosina, bringing the last coffee of the evening. She went towards him and placed the tray on the stool beside his bed. She stood close, looking into his eyes as he sat staring at her from the bed, where he had been reading by candlelight.

"I've brought your coffee, sir."

"Come, Rosina," he said, a charming smile breaking the line of his lips. "Come sit on the bed beside me."

Her breath caught in her throat, and for a moment the world seemed to stand on end as he put the book down, and giving her his full attention, drew her down beside him.

"I want to free you, Rosina," he said softly, holding her two hands in the strength of his own. "I want to teach you everything I know. I want you to experience it all."

Gently he tilted her head back and kissed her face. "You are so very beautiful, my dear," he whispered, "like a strange and exotic bird that has been caught in a cage, but longs to be free.

Her heart thumped in her throat, as she found his blue eyes smiling at her, in the flickering, smoky light of the candle at his bedside. The blush on her cheeks mounted high as she experienced that sensation of being stripped naked by his gaze. She gazed down at her tightly clenched hands, and when she lifted her head, there was a kindling of blue flame in his eyes. Short heavy wisps of blond hair curled slightly about his face, accentuating the square handsome features, and there was now health and vitality about him that was mesmerizing. Her young body burned with the yearning she had experienced often recently.

"You are right, Lieutenant Buckleigh." Her voice was low and husky, a little above a whisper, carefully using the correct grammar she had been practising so diligently. "I am trapped: from the day I was born; I be – am trapped now." She blushed. In the flickering candlelight, which gave her beauty a softer radiance, she raised her eyes to his.

"But I am going to show you, my darling, something wild and beautiful in life." He had been speaking quickly and with unusual fierceness, using the words and phrases her secret love had forged in the solitude of her bedroom for so many days.

The candle fluttered in the draught from under the door as silently he raised his arms and pulled her towards him. He kissed her mouth, and brushed away the luxuriant dark hair from her shining eyes. His warm breath stirred shivers along her flesh, and a curious excitement tingled in her breast. With a burst of fear, she struggled for a moment, then tenderness awoke passion and under his caresses her last reserve broke down. Fear, isolation, loneliness and childhood were all swept away as she sank with him onto his bed in the candlelight, in a rustling tangle of skirts and petticoats.

She put her arms round his strong, firm body as he took her with a passion that enabled her to express what she was unable to put into words, and, after

44

fleeting pain, she gave herself to him in wild, insane abandon.

Outside a barn owl swooped from a cluster of shrubs, and winged away, low to the ground, to the loud "kie-kie-kie" of a large grey mongoose in the underbrush.

And later, as Rosina stole back to her bed, it seemed as if during those few stolen hours she had blossomed into a different person, the woman of her daydreams.

The next morning, she lived only partially in reality. Although she resumed her household duties with cutomary quiet efficiency, inwardly she continued to savour the raptures of this unexpected and dear love. She seemed to float through her routine with slow sensuous movements, filled with a sense of utter wellbeing. It was for this, she reasoned, that she had been born, and she gave thanks for it.

And the fullness of love stayed with her all day. When evening came, she saw that Andrew had left his door ajar. She tried to centre herself; but instead she continued to plane in the sensuous contentment in which she had lived all day, reliving the glorious experience, savouring every moment of it.

She blossomed into exquisite beauty as the hours slipped by in secret joy. Her eyes were keen, her way was sure, her entire personality soared. Despite the dangerous road she was travelling, she knew that she was experiencing what might become the only richness and fulfilment she might ever know.

It was on a cold night soon afterwards as Rosina retired to her bedroom that she saw Haas Maarten's thin, tall figure standing in the front room, with his back to the dying fire. He was swarthy with long black hair like a gypsy and looked every inch a crewman of a

45

smuggling craft. When he saw her, he quickly turned, with his lips pressed together, and left the room. He had never once expressed a dislike of her, but it was obvious enough at the moment. A sharp little tremor of dread struck her, and she wondered if he had found out about her and Andrew Buckleigh. For all the weeks of the Captain's absence Maarten had appeared only at meal times. He had answered all her remarks with sufficient politeness, but gave her never a word more than necessary. When she was alone again, she looked around the room uneasily. Perhaps she should not go to Andrew this night – yet, she hated the thought of not being with him, of not feeling that wonderful joy and comfort in his presence.

She retired to her bedroom undecided, put the candle-stick on the chest, closed the shutters, and undressed. It could not have been more than a few seconds when the door of her room opened, and Andrew, his face pale and tense, limped into the room with the aid of a crude wooden crutch.

"Rosina – Rosina – the most dreadful thing has happened!" he said in an urgent, low whisper. "Old Seaman Leach – I went down to see him in the barn – he's – he's dead, and I suspect it has something to do with me."

Tongue-tied and terrified Rosina stared at him, hardly able to speak. "He – he can't be dead! I saw him sometime after dinner!"

Andrew Buckleigh cleared his throat and when he spoke again his tone was low, soft, gaining control. "The old man is dead, Rosina – he's been stabbed with a knife – he's lying in the barn where I left him only a half-hour before."

She stood facing him, quivering with sudden fear yet

daring neither to move or to speak. It seemed to her as if an age had passed as she was driven, by her desperation, to speak again. "I cannot believe it – who would have done such a wicked thing?"

Andrew Buckleigh drew in a rasping breath. "That is what I want to know! Who would do such a senseless thing to an old man? But come – we can't leave him like that!"

Rosina turned and lifted the candle and the tinderbox beside it, then throwing her heavy woollen shawl about her shoulders, followed him outside. At the top of the stairs she stumbled, splashing hot candle wax on to her hand, and held back a gasp of pain. Working their way through the kitchen, it took them some time to reach the outer door, and the candle, as it encountered gusts from changing directions, flickered, seeming to people every dim corner as they went. They turned in the direction of the barn, going slowly in the enveloping darkness, and saw two shadowy figures looming under a lantern outside it. One of the dogs barked suddenly and rushed forward. Andrew pulled Rosina roughly into the dark shadows of the house, his hand descending on the candle and extinguishing it. Hardly daring to breathe Rosina saw the heads of the two men draw together, in deep conversation. The lantern was knocked over, its light dying so it was too dark to see who they were, but suddenly one of the men made a grab for the other's throat, and the two rolled together, kicking and struggling on the ground. Then the dog was off, faster than they had ever seen him move. As he reached the men, there was a low cry, and a cutlass fell from one of the men's hands, but he was too quick for the dog, and darted away, leaving the other, sitting up slowly on the ground. The dog stood beside him, barking madly, but standing back as the other dog joined him and excited voices rose from the men's huts further away, and the slave quarters nearer by.

Not for a second could Rosina relax as she watched in horror, with a strange cold feeling of terrible apprehension at her back. "'Tis too dangerous to be seen here – who knows what they will do if we're discovered?"

"You're right by God! But I've got to see old Leach again, Rosina," Andrew murmured, as the faint moonlight made his face just visible in the darkness. "It's no good getting mixed up in this gory business – but I've got to get proof about the body."

The few men left behind joined the wounded man, and helped him away. Two of the men then entered the barn. When they left soon afterwards in the direction of the stables, Rosina stood there, quivering with fear, forgetting that she wore only a nightdress and shawl, and that the cold sea breeze was coming in upon her. Then, seeing Andrew limp awkwardly towards the barn, she followed.

She stumbled and blundered her way after him, past the piled-up stores inside the barn, while further away she could still hear the men's urgent voices. Andrew weaved his way around the stores, and crouching nearly double, his hands fell upon three big hogsheads of gunpowder.

"I knew it!" he whispered some way ahead of her. "Gunpowder! That's what old Sam said – used for illegal slave running!"

The men's voices were much nearer now, and Rosina's heart began to pound with terror. "Come, Andrew – we'd best leave here – tis too dangerous to stay— "

"You're right," Andrew whispered, "they're coming this way. Let's go." His shadow rose, and pushing her before him, they quickly made their way out of the barn and keeping in the shadows, back to the house.

Once inside, she stopped, and striking the tinder in her hand, she brought it to the candle. A moment later she was holding the trembling light before her, its small illumination shed upon the pots and pans in the kitchen.

Andrew turned to her in the flickering light, and she could feel his hot breath like fire, near her face.

"It's better for you to go to bed, Rosina – safer that way," he said hoarsely. He came a pace nearer. "You know it was only today that Old Leach, in his cups, admitted that the Captain has the letter of marque – the necessary privateer's licence, and under the pretext of being a legitimate trader he calls at Table Bay and is sold supplies." The next moment she felt her wrist seized in a grip of iron. "But he has other cargoes that are far more lucrative and they are not the lawful prizes of a privateer – they are slaves from Mozambique or seized from Portuguese ships plying these coasts. Did you know this, Rosina?"

His words were so fierce that she cried out in fear. "I suspected – but nothing was told me – as I told you, he has saved many lives— "

He flung her arm aside. "As well as causing the deaths of many more in his ship carefully built to take his special cargoes, so that not a square inch of the hold's space is wasted." His tone grew suddenly sharp and unfamiliar. "His so-called ship-rigged privateer has tens guns a side, and with all that gunpowder in the barn and more besides, with its crew of seasoned seamen, is able to put up a good fight even against some of our fastest ships. They are the wolves of the sea, Rosina. Since his cargoes sometimes get desperate and try to

49

jump overboard, shackles and bolts are part of the ship's furniture. Air and sanitation are not considered because it would cut into profits. Did you know this?"

"No!" she suddenly cried in a cold fury. "It cannot be true!"

"Yes," he answered, peering furiously into her face. "It is all true – and that is why old Leach died tonight. Someone discovered that I knew!"

She waited for his next move, not daring to anger him further.

And now she shook with a new fear that reinforced all her dreads. He had discovered something extremely dangerous, and she feared for him if the Captain ever found out. Even more devastating was the fact that he did not want to spend any more time with her that night. She could see it in his withdrawn, angry expression as she watched him limp back to his room. Biting back a swift surge of sharp hurt, and still shaking with terror, she crept away to her own bed.

She lay there, on her back, asking herself questions and fearing the answers. Was it true that the Captain's ship was so terrible? Was he really as cruel and ruthless as Andrew said he was? What would happen when he returned and found Leach dead? Who had killed Leach? Which of the men was a murderer? What would happen to Andrew? Did Andrew not love her anymore?

She opened her eyes and heard the ship's clock, far away, strike one. She could hear the familiar stamping and snorting of the horses outside in the stables, and the ghostly cry of a barn owl. Nothing moved inside the room, and the little mongoose still slept perched on a large wooden peg, with its side pressed against the wall. The small cat nestled warmly at her feet. Suddenly, another sound reached her and she sat up at once, in a strange, cold, expectant terror. It was the sound of a cart being driven over rough stones. It came past her window, and as she listened, it seemed that the animal pulling it was being urged; for it moved with sudden jerks, as if the burden was too much for it. She waited to hear this uneasy transport roll past the house, before slowly lying down again.

While she lay, listening to its departure, a certain conviction overwhelmed her. She knew with a horrible revelation, that the cart carried the body of old Leach. She lay quivering in her bed, and as she thought of what had happened, she shuddered, sunk in terror.

She did not sleep that night, or attempt to sleep. She kept the candle burning, renewing it when it burnt to its socket. And not until the morning light poured through the chinks in the shutters did she draw a free breath.

Chapter Seven

When she entered the kitchen the following morning, everything appeared to be as usual. No one, who did not know that Samuel Leach had been murdered, would have known. Andrew, she found to her relief, appeared to be his usual self again and Maarten announced in his laconic fashion that old Leach had been found, drowned in a drunken stupor. Wilkins was feeling better and had risen from his sick bed to join the men for breakfast, and after the first mutterings of excitement, nothing more was said, as the men settled down to discuss the news of the day.

Rosina sought in vain for any sign of the two men who had fought outside the barn, but there was nothing. Her eyes surreptitiously searched each one to discover the culprits, and failed miserably. She busied herself in the kitchen, rolling out spiced dough and cutting it into small round biscuit shapes, and twisting ropes of the sweetstuff into sweets flavoured with cinnamon, peppermint and ginger.

She welcomed, with unconscious relief the lively presence of young Abel, who was always hungry, and she gave him the pots in which her sugary mixtures had been boiled, along with the wooden spoons with which to scrape out the last fragrant crumbs.

As she worked, she was acutely aware that Haas

Maarten had scarcely said a word during breakfast. She knew he was a refugee from a Holland seized and controlled by Napoleon; one of those stateless individuals with whom she had been told by Andrew all Europe seemed to be peopled nowadays. He certainly did not have much in common with the background of most of the men, though he was as able and efficient a seaman as they, and as effective a part of the group. But she instinctively knew that this was not the reason he remained silent. She noticed that as the day wore on, he grew more silent and more moody, and the apprehension she had felt the night before deepened.

It was in the warm sunshine of an early spring afternoon, that Jan la Motte paid his annual visit. He visited the settlement once a year on his way to the outlying districts of the Cape Colony. This time he had brought among the goods in his wagon, a copy of a three months old Government Gazette, precious ambergris from Mauritius for cooking, a copper skillet smuggled from Europe, a pair of new fancy black shoes with silver buckles and a new dress in the latest Cape Town fashion for Rosina. She knew she would never wear them, but it had always delighted her that he always arrived with some of the new fashions. She loved the delicate, feminine things he brought her. But this year it was different: for the first time she longed to be able to wear the lovely gown and the fancy shoes . . .

Jan now stood in his skin breeches and blue jacket, exposing the leather belt with pockets for powder and shot, and leaned against one wall of the front room, his great frame diminishing everything around him. At thirty-four, he was a man who looked as though he had seen a lot of life, with his strong featured,

53

genial face, brown beard, eyes deeply wrinkled at the corners and premature lines across his forehead. A pewter mug of steaming coffee was held firmly in his large strong hands, as he looked speculatively at the young Lieutenant standing in the doorway, leaning on the rough crutch Henry Mostyn had made for him in the winter days now gone. After a while, he turned away. Out of the window he could see a solitary black water mongoose forking a crab out of a hole on the beach, not far from a great sun-bleached whalebone washed up in a storm. The sea was very quiet under the warm sun. Languid currents of air moved across from time to time, brushing soft dark shadows over it. And where the water was shallow, its surface was a shifting pattern of turquoise and dark green wrinkles, and the row of peach and almond trees near the house were bright under their load of pink and white blossom.

Rosina was busy at the spinning wheel, her fingers deftly crafting the last blanket for next winter, which she had neglected since the arrival of Andrew. Already the weeks with his presence seemed like a dream, a dream from which she never wanted to awaken. But now, since the arrival of Jan la Motte with his news from the outside world, she had noticed a change in the Englishman. It had started after Leach's death, but was now even more marked. Her slender feet in the soft veldschoen boots never stopped at the wheel, as la Motte's voice rolled through the room, the English roundly accented with Dutch.

"*Ach, ja* – I have a shop now – in the Town where I sell everything I can lay my hands on from the cargo of French prize ships. The stuff is knocked down to the highest bidder – so cheap it is unbelievable. *Ja*, Lieutenant Buckleigh, there is much activity at the harbour these days, in spite of the storms and wreckage. The Town's whole livelihood depends on the ships, it always has."

"Are there many English ships in port, sir?" Buckleigh swung round on his crutch, his back to the door. "What news is there, of Europe and the war?" His hands shook a little with the sudden passion that consumed him, and Rosina was conscious of the hot flush on his cheeks as he met the eyes of Jan la Motte.

"There are English ships, *ja* – even neutral Americans who take advantage of their neutrality to trade with everyone."

Buckleigh waved aside the rest of what Jan la Motte was endeavouring to phrase, saying, "That dishonourable Corsican rogue! How I wish I could join our forces under Wellesley in Spain soon and get to grips with those despicable Frenchies! And those American ships – what is the earthly use of England blockading the European coast and enduring all the hardships and perils of that service if neutral vessels sail where they please – and England is at this very moment fighting for her life against a tyrant who dominates all Europe?"

"But there is already talk, Lieutenant Buckleigh, that many of Napoleon's friends are deserting him in Europe as well as in France – that the English blockade has put his country into great trouble because it has lost British and Baltic trade – that many of the French ports are dying of slow strangulation," Jan answered, his robust energy infusing the atmosphere with its good-natured warmth. "Already they say that Count Bernadotte of Sweden has joined the English against France and that Napoleon may attack Russia." He chuckled suddenly, taking a sip of coffee. "Last January there was a cartoon in one of your English newspapers of Bonaparte as the frog who tried to blow himself up as big as an ox."

Buckleigh reeled a little, as though he had been struck. "Russia?" How can Boney take the tremendous step of waging war on Russia? He would be better to finish the war with Spain and try to strike down England before trying to conquer the East."

Jan meditated for a second before replying. "Bonaparte has conquered so often – he has struck down every nation in Europe, except England – that it seems that Russia will not be able to stand up against his massed forces, or so it is said in some quarters. But nobody knows whether he will fight the Russians or not."

"With Russia beaten he would have no enemies left to oppose him in Europe – only England to fight him, single-handed. But what of Wellesley in Spain? How has it gone with him there?"

Jan finished his coffee and put down the mug on the nearby table, glancing quickly at Rosina who was still busily spinning away. "Ach, from what your newspapers say, and from the news on the ships, Wellesley has been helped by the fierce Spanish guerrilla fighters, and he has beaten some of the best French armies, *ja* – they say that the attempt to conquer Portugal has failed and the affairs of Spain are in a mess. But, of course everyone is asking – how long will Bonaparte remain in power? You must know that here in the Cape not everyone is on your side." Jan hesitated, his bearded, mobile face suddenly impassive, but in a moment he had twisted it into his usual wry smile. "There are many French in the colony, sir, from a stranded Frigate and a privateer who of course favour the Corsican. But then, there are local Orangists who hate the way Napoleon took the throne of Holland to give to his brother, Louis. And then there are those who want to return to the rule of Holland."

Buckleigh listened to the explanation with attention,

56

and there was a faint play of expression in his face. "Those against British rule are insane – if they hate British rule here, it will be far worse under Napoleon's iron hand, I tell you. And you, Mr la Motte, what do you want?"

Jan shrugged broad shoulders. "My father, Lieutenant Buckleigh, was the landdrost of Graaff Reinet in '95 – a kind of magistrate in English, when the burghers rose in revolt against him, setting up a republic based on the French model. It was short-lived, but my father never forgot it. I myself am not interested in politics – I watch with much interest from the sidelines," he said, in a mild tone contrasting strangely with the intense emotions of the other man.

Andrew pulled in perplexity at his chin, deep parentheses of tension at the corners of his mouth. "God, I would give anything to help the English Army in Spain!" he burst out in feverish impatience. "I feel so useless here!"

The young Lieutenant's angry and impatient words threw Rosina into a sudden panic, and suddenly her body grew chilled. Her mind was tortured by the frustration of his mood, and she shuddered under the touch of a terrifying unseen enemy who had returned to plague her. No longer could she find satisfaction in the simple pleasures she had loved – the breath of the sea, the caring and cooking for him – not any more, with all these bitter thoughts thronging her mind.

A silent tear fell unnoticed from her eye as she smoothed a thread. Recently she had become aware of his restless unhappiness as she had been aware of his desire for her body, which she had given him so entirely. She had come to love him, but she was slowly realizing that it was not, as she had thought, love that had kept him

57

in her arms. She had found a small, cracked miniature amongst his clothes only yesterday, of a beautiful blond young woman, of whom he never spoke, and which she, in her innocence had never dreamt. Never before had she suffered the anguish of jealousy, and she wondered if this was what she now suffered? What was this sadness that the love he had for this other woman had never been hers? But it was strangely not the thought of her which brought tears to her eyes; it was the growing knowledge that she was not a part of his real life, that his stay here was as unreal to him as a dream, something to be enjoyed until he could go away to Europe, into that mad world of war where he belonged. And she despaired as she thought of the long period of solitary hell she was doomed to in the future. All she knew was what she felt at the knowledge that the man she loved wanted to go away forever. And she knew that the moment he left, her heart would break and an awful sickness would begin: the agony, the hopeless yearning with every fibre of her body, every nerve, for his presence, his touch; her every waking thought, her every dream would be centred on him in unbearable, self-inflicted torture.

Jan la Motte lifted his head and read the tragedy in her eyes, and for an imperceptible moment their eyes met, then she lowered hers in confusion, her cheeks stained the colour of blood.

Jan tied his big black kettle and the three-legged pot back under his wagon with its old sail cloth top. Though he moved with slow and easy movements, his voice was quick and brisk when he spoke to the little yellow-skinned Hottentots dressed in leather trousers and loose mantles of sheepskin who had accompanied him, and were inspanning the oxen. He filled a small water-cask from the well, tied it below the wagon, and slung his huge gun into the tilt. That done, he tied some new bundles of forage behind the wagon, as Rosina silently went forward to give him a small bag of coffee, the cinnamon biscuits and the big lumpy sweets that he especially liked, along with a kidskin full of shark biltong, salted ribs and a large custard pie tied up in a spotted cloth.

Seeing him off had eased for a while her pain, and her smooth, vulnerable face was once more alight with a faint smile as he packed the food away in the painted wagon-box he used for a seat in front of the wagon.

There was silence for a moment as he faced her. Then he said, with an odd, searching look in his dark eyes: "Be careful, Rosina – the world is a dangerous place for those with innocent feelings and generous hearts."

The words coiled about her head, her hands, folded before her, went white at the knuckles. Then, hiding her deep unhappiness, she cleared her throat. "I – I – thank you for your concern, *Meneer la Motte*."

He smiled slowly and thoughtfully, stroking his neat brown beard. "Thank you kindly for your hospitality and the food for the journey, Rosina – and for the jerkin you made for my young son, Jacques. His grandmother will be very pleased, her eyesight is not what it used to be to make him clothes."

He smiled down at her, but there was a shadow in his eyes, hinting at emotions he kept hidden deep within himself, and she remembered the death of his beloved young wife Roosje, the mother of his little son. "I go now to Swellendam and then on to Graaff Reinet. Only three months ago, His Excellency, Governor Cradock and a large force of troops and burghers fought the Ndhlambi and Gunukebe people in the Zuurveld and

59

swept them beyond the Fish River. I hear they are building a double line of block-houses there to hold the frontier, garrisoned with troops. I won't have time to go that far this year – but I hear there is constant friction between the black tribes and the Dutch farmers on the frontier. I now have Titus, an excellent free-slave working for me who looks after my shop while I'm gone, but I mustn't be away too long."

He climbed robustly up on to the wagon-box and took the reins in his large callused hands. For a long moment he stared down at her, knowing with regret that he could never warn her directly about the English redcoat, who, in his weakened condition had obviously found it easy to seek emotional shelter with this beautiful, innocent young girl. She looked so lovely and so vulnerable, standing there in the sunlight, so different from the women he had known . . . so different even from Roosje, whom he had loved with deep devotion. He thought of the young redcoat with sudden hostility. It seemed to Jan that the handsome young man wanted no responsibility for Rosina or her feelings, that he had not hesitated to take his pleasure where he found it, and now he was bored with her and the isolated life which had at first charmed and intrigued him. He had regarded it only as a temporary adventure, but she had given him her whole heart.

He could see the redcoat moving restlessly about the stoep, and as he touched his low-brimmed felt hat and flicked his long, bamboo-handled whip over the backs of the massive oxen, he felt a sharp stab of unexpected jealousy knife through his body. Embarrassed by this sudden rush of feeling, he quickly turned his head away.

Young Abel laughed and clapped his hands as

he ran alongside the small Hottentots shouting and gesticulating at the oxen as the wagon laden with goods jerked forward. Part of Rosina cried out to Jan, a desperate cry for help, but the other part, the part she trusted, had withdrawn, as the wagon lurched and bounced down the track. Dust swirled around it in clouds, obscuring the view; only as the oxen disappeared around the bend did the dust subside. Rosina stood there for some time, but there was no order in her thoughts; her mind was muddled. There was now an undercurrent of sadness, a hurt feeling indistinguishable from physical pain, but fatigue and lack of sleep deprived her of any ability to think clearly. Finally with a desperate effort she pulled herself together, and turned back with a heavy heart to the house.

Chapter Eight

Captain Skewthorn returned a week later with the rest of the crew. On discovering that Andrew Buckleigh was still in the settlement, he called Rosina to his study. As she walked into the room – cluttered with sea charts, spyglasses, all manner of pipes, pistols, cutlasses, and smelling strongly of leather and tobacco, he quickly pushed to one side a packet wrapped in oilskin, and stood facing her, fingering his grey beard. Rosina glanced at the package, stained and worn as it was, and wondered if it was money paid for illegal slaves.

"Well, girl, what have you to say for yourself? The redcoat was to leave weeks ago!" His voice was slow and ponderous, as he rocked back and forth to emphasize his words. "Why is he still here?"

Rosina was almost caught off guard until she realized that his eyes were hooded, and his tone had been strangely flat, a sure sign of anger simmering in him. Her mind flew to all the weeks he had been away, and her breath almost stopped as she knew she had no answer.

"He – it took much longer for his wounds to heal— "

"Don't give me that!" He slammed a ledger closed on the desk, and tossing a quill aside, stared at her, irate sparks flaring brightly in his black eyes. "Have you sinned with that man? Well, have you?" His voice was flat, hard and biting

Angry tears stung Rosina's eyes, her pride raw beneath this savage attack. "Nothing we did was a sin, sir – he is an honourable gentleman."

"Honourable be damned! No man is honourable when he wants to bed a piece of female flesh! This is MY house, and he has stayed long enough as MY guest. But, he has abused that privilege!" His face, crossed with its innumerable lines, was fierce and unrelenting.

The colour drained from her cheeks. "He has done nothing to deserve your wrath, sir!" she burst out with frustrated rage.

Her eyes found his face and were suddenly trapped there as his eyes raked her like dark talons while he started to shout in harsh, abrupt sentences, which at first did not make much sense. Then his face began to change in a way she had never seen before, as his eyes glowed and with a furious roar he hurled out the most dreadful abuse she had ever heard. For a moment she went rigid with the fury his words stirred in her, and she wanted to rake both hands across his cruel, outraged face. But she resisted answering him back.

Finally he dismissed her harshly, and retreating from the torture, she fled to the yard, seeking out her animals, not able to face Andrew.

When supper was ready, she waited on table to serve the men in a state of extraordinary tension. At eight o'clock, the Captain turned to her, as a sudden silence fell about the table.

"Go to bed, Rosina – at once. Your duties are over for tonight."

Startled, she looked at him, unable to believe her ears. "But, sir, there is still much to be done— "

63

The Captain paused, lifting a forkful of custard pie to his mouth, in the midst of suppressed mutters from the men.

"Do you have the temerity to argue with me, girl?" His eyes pierced her viciously, and she took a deep breath, steadying her racing nerves.

"No, sir – I – no, sir." Dropping a shallow curtsey, she turned away to leave the room, when he called her back.

"Rosina," he said, his voice hoarse and mocking, "It were, perhaps, well if you said a God-speed to Lieutenant Buckleigh. He is leaving in the morning."

He said the words slowly; and looking at him with sudden despair, Rosina saw that his eyes rested, with a strange expression, upon the English redcoat. She stood motionless, staring at the back of the golden head, which remained averted from her. Then, mastering her shock, she bade Andrew goodbye, and went to her room.

As she sat in the darkness, thought of his departure sent a sharp pain sweeping through her, a pain so sharp that her anguish became a panic. What was she to do?

A little later she heard a low murmur of talk on the stairs, which Andrew seemed to have joined in. Finally she caught the sound of doors being opened, then of a hurried word of farewell, and she realised anew, with black despair that Andrew would be gone in a few hours.

A moth came flying through the open window, and fluttered past the candle, brushing her nightgown before pattering against the door. After a prayer for the man she loved, she got into bed. But, disturbed by thoughts of him, she could not sleep.

Then, after hours of sleeplessness she climbed out of bed, flung on her shawl, and quietly made her way downstairs to the kitchen where, by the light of the flickering candle, she packed a kidskin bag with all the delicacies she knew he liked, then, as she quietly left the kitchen and passed the study door, she suddenly remembered the oilskin packet Captain Skewthorn had pushed out of sight before her confrontation with him. Curiosity overcame her in that moment and her fingers itched to discover what was in it. Hardly daring to breathe, she fumbled at the door knob, and slipped inside the dark room. One of the shutters was open, and the candle, catching a breeze, cast an unsteady light on the desk which was littered with papers and charts. And then, as she moved some of them aside, she saw the packet, hidden underneath a chart covered with writing the colour of rust. Carefully, she put the candlestick on the desk, picked up the package, and pulled away the soiled wrapping. Inside she gasped as she saw a thick, stiff wad of grubby papers, and a small oilskin bag filled to the brim with gold and silver coins. For a short while, she stood there and gazed at the papers and accompanying fortune. She knew now, that all Andrew had said, was true, and that without doubt this money was payment for illegal slaves. She thought of the pain and suffering caused because of this money, and felt like hurling it out of the window.

Then, with a deep, frustrated sigh, she put things back as they were, closed the door and hurried upstairs to Andrew's room. But when she reached his door, she hesitated. It was more than possible that he would not want to see her. But, having come this far, she set her teeth and turned the handle.

"What are you doing outside the room of the redcoat in the dead of night? Well, answer me, girl! And you'll tell the truth this time, I'll see to that!"

She spun round hearing the unmistakable thump of Captain Skewthorn's wooden leg in the dimness of the passage, and she blanched at the cold ferocity gathering in his face in the flickering light. Then, before she could gather her wits, he had sprung across the space between them, his black eyes flashing, and seized her by the throat, the candlestick crashing to the floor. Miraculously, the candle still continued to burn.

"You've been sinning with that God-damned redcoat, haven't you? I'll get the truth out of you if I have to shake it out!"

She gasped out in terror as he shook her and then flung her from him. She had never seen him like this, not even during her terrible confrontation with him earlier. Before she could escape, he seized her again, though he held her now in a less severe grip.

His teeth showing in a savage snarl, he cursed her violently. "Damn you to hell's flames, you useless strumpet, just like your mother before you! How dare you sin with that man under my very roof!"

She felt outraged and at the same time helpless, as must those who faced him from the deck. "I'm sorry, sir – but I love him – I didn't mean any harm . . ." Suddenly, in spite of herself, she was pleading, desperate, tormented.

"You! You're the devil's child!"

She cowered against the wall, her hands clutching the kidskin bag of food as he vented his wrath in searing words. Then he shook her so savagely that she dropped the bag so that the contents spilled all over the floor. As he stared incredulously at the contents on the floor in the wavering light of the candle, which had remained upright, she covered her eyes in fright, for his face had grown instantly strange and more terrifying.

66

A sudden weakness in her chest made her clench her fists and she could not speak any further. She turned, fled back to her room, and closed the door. For a long moment she stood with her back to it, covering her face with her shaking hands, and it was only much later that she realized that Andrew had not come to her aid, even although the commotion had taken place outside his door.

Chapter Nine

Rosina lit another candle and looked at her haggard face in the small mirror over the bed thinking of Andrew gone forever from this place in the morning. She found herself in the throes of an anguish that struck her almost as a physical pain.

Never before had she been faced with a dilemma of such magnitude in such utter loneliness. She had known that life without him would be bleak; but she had not realized it would hit her this hard. His mere presence had sharpened her senses, enhanced her enjoyment of life. Never had the days seemed richer, the colours around her so vivid.

But now all that was soon to be gone . . . Andrew was taking all her life, all her vitality with him. She was overwhelmed by a terrible, heartbreaking grief. No! It was not true!

She went over to the window and looked out at the sky, where the disjointed Southern Cross was embedded like jewels in the gold dust of the distant stars glittering coldly in infinity. She felt like praying, but her words would be lost in the immensity of the night; all she could sense, for the first time in her life, was something awesome, the impersonal indifference of enormous vastness for her unimaginable smallness.

Recalling the harshness and cruelty of the Captain's

bitter tongue, her thoughts turned to flight from the settlement. She could go with Andrew, her dear Andrew. For surely he wouldn't turn her away – leave her in this misery – even if he did not love her as she loved him. She would go with him and she would cook and wash for him and comfort him, and they would be together, for he could never be as cruel to her as the Captain.

It was morning when she again crept towards Andrew's room. Smiling, but holding herself in tight control, she advanced towards the bed where he lay still sleeping under a sheet. But what she saw, however, as she approached nearer and stood beside the bed so filled her with horror that she could hardly breathe.

Great stains of blood splashed the sheet and the pillow and a large pool lay on the floor. Blood had soaked into the clothes that had become stuck to his body. Trembling violently, she leaned forward and as she lifted away the sheet, she found herself staring into Andrew's sightless eyes and ashen face. She stood gazing helplessly before her, at the deep slit across his throat, and the many, vicious stab wounds all over his body, and then, in utter horror, at her long-handled sewing scissors projecting from his heart – the scissors that Henry Mostyn had specially made for her in the forge a long time ago!

Her mind was in a turmoil; all she could feel was outraged shock, fury. He was dead, he was never coming back . . . he had been brutally, ruthlessly murdered, with her scissors! So irrefutable was that knowledge, that she could not bear it.

"So – I knew it! You haf killed the English soldier! You will pay for this terrible crime, Miss Rosina!"

She whirled around to face Haas Maarten, the Dutchman, who had silently entered the room and now stood beside her, his swarthy face gloating eerily in the ghostly early light.

"I did not do it!" she gasped with impotent fury. "I could never have done such a dreadful thing! And never to Andrew!"

"No one will believe you – they are your scissors in his heart, are they not? And I haf caught you red-handed as they say." His eyes shone with a malignant gleam as the light played grotesquely on the shadowing of a moustache on his long upper lip.

Then, unable to bear any more, she turned around with a desperate cry, and ran from the room, through the house, out of the door, and wildly, into the dawn.

She ran down to the beach where the foam of the breakers glistened in the pink and spectral light and there she stopped, looking out towards the distant horizon where the sky and sea met. Soon the noise of the waves beating against the rocks was louder to her than the thoughts running madly through her head, tumbling over one another in blinding confusion.

It seemed so much later that she stood for a long time staring at the body, noticing with vague relief that the scissors had been removed. A patch of sunlight lay across the bed, making the sheet and the arms resting on them whiter. Who could have committed this hideous crime? It had to be one of the men who had found out Andrew knew about the smuggling.

A buzzing fly, flashing in the sunlight, bounced against the wall. The stillness in the room was so intense that the buzzing seemed accentuated a hundred times, as memories of kisses and intimate words engulfed her and she heard his voice again.

Looking at the body that had once been so warm and

alive, trembling with passion, tender and comforting, she was overcome then, by a black sorrow. She had known that body better than her own.

As she made her way towards the door, she heard the murmur of voices coming from behind it.

"Maarten has gone – disappeared, I tell you! Wot a damned pickle we're in now!" She knew that voice of Robert Blaine well enough, and shrank back into the room.

"'E did it, as true as bob! Why else should 'e slink off like this, I ask you? As if we've not had enough trouble already since that stinkin' redcoat arrived."

That she knew was Isaac Wilkins, as she cautiously opened the door and peered out. There was a knot of men about the Captain farther away down the passage. He was standing with his back to Rosina, swathed in a familiar blue boxcoat with its triple row of capes.

"We're not giving way under this, men – we've faced worse, and well you know it!" Captain Skewthorn's voice suddenly roared. "We must find Maarten, he's the danger now. If he harms us in any way, he'll pay for it. Blaine – I want you and Trelawney to ride off and find him at once and bring him back here. Wilkins, you'll take the others to the brig and start working on her. She must be careened and caulked at once for the journey to Madagascar, then we'll be on our way."

Blaine replied in a loud, harsh voice, "'Tis my belief it's the wench, Cap'n – Rosina did it – she killed 'im when 'e lost interest in 'er! I tell you she did it!"

Rosina grew rigid with horror and disgust as an angry rumbling of voices followed.

"Silence!" Captain Skewthorn suddenly hissed viciously, as, transferring a brace of pistols from his pockets, he shrugged his arms out of his boxcoat. "Get on with the

71

job of finding that rogue Maarten, and bury the body –
we'll deal with *her* later!"

The loud voice of Abraham Dance, the ship's cook,
followed; "'Twas 'e that did it – why else should 'e 'ave
run off like that?"

Rosina stepped back into the room shaking, her
face as white as tallow as they followed the Captain
stumping forward in her direction, then, paralyzed
and bewildered, she looked from the naked enmity
that filled one face to another, her lips cold. Captain
Skewthorn's attention and fury veered sharply towards
her, as he took three surprisingly agile and purposeful
steps forward. His face was white and full-scale anger
blazed in his eyes.

"Why did you do it, Rosina – why?"

Rosina backed away, her young face withering, so that
it almost resembled a corpse. "No! No! 'Tis not true!"

Abraham Dance gave her a hot look of loathing, but
before he could speak, Blaine had intervened.

"Of a certainty, you're the only one with a strong
enough motive, who could'a done it," he said, his thin,
wiry body, alive, quivering with menace. Maliciousness
flooded through him, twisting his features with spite.
"You got us into this mess – and you'd better get
us out."

Rosina, numb with horror, began to speak in a
halting voice: "'Tis not true! I didn't kill Lieutenant
Buckleigh!"

Isaac Wilkins cast a belligerent eye at her, as they
faced each other in the confined space, the sabre
cut along his cheek deep and livid in his heavily
jowled face. "'Twas you or that devil Maarten as
sure as it's day!" A sudden speculative look came
distinctly into his eyes. "Mayhap you're in league

72

with that rogue and planned this together, and we been the fools!"

"'Tis an outright and terrible lie!" Rosina cried, her eyes full of tears. "I could never do such a thing! I could never touch another living soul, and well you know it!" She was visibly trembling, and struggling to control herself.

"That's enough!" Rosina saw the Captain's face looking strained. "You've done wrong, girl – like your mother before you – and you'll be damned to hell's flames! Now go and attend your duties!" he barked.

Rosina stood aghast, rigidly trembling, then finding her voice, she answered: "'Tis a lie, I tell you – a terrible lie."

Panic and fear clutched her, as an ominous silence developed. She felt that the weeks of wonderful pure joy had crumbled to cruel and bitter disillusionment, that no one believed her innocent of the hideous crime. The men followed the Captain downstairs, their voices loud and acrimonious. During the next few hours Rosina worked about the house in silence, avoiding the knot of men gathered around a sea chart on the dining room table, which they discussed in low, urgent voices.

She was aware of a terrible feeling of forboding about her; there seemed to be sinister shadows of the past and the future, the shadows of her new enemies, as Abdoul and Achmat carried the body outside, where a burial party was commanded to dig a grave below the hill beside the other graves of those who had died in the settlement. There was the sound of horses galloping away over the turf as Blaine and Trelawney sped on their way to find Maarten.

In the afternoon, Rosina was pacing restlessly about her room when she heard the sound of a child's wild shriek of pain, and running to her window, she peered out, just in time to catch sight of an oxhide whip flailing on the turf, and a pair of legs writhing on the ground. They were bare legs, those of a slave and she knew, with a feeling as if something was freezing inside her that it was young Abel. The wielder of the whip was stuttering with rage as he laid on his strokes with the force of hysteria and she knew it was the Captain. She had never seen him in such rages as those he had displayed since his return, and she knew that the situation held danger. No one could help the young boy – as far as she knew any slave lifting a hand against his master would get the death penalty. She had heard about the new Circuit Court that was now held in the outlying districts which allowed Hottentots to bring their masters to court for ill-treating them, but she had never heard that it was also for the benefit of slaves.

She turned from the window, her eyes and mouth hollows of terror, and stood pressed against the wall of her little room. The men and the other slaves had crowded round, but none dared check the master.

She crept to her bed, and for a long time, she lay there, with her head on her arms, and it was as if there was nothing left in her world but the sorrow that was so strong it must surely break her heart. Poor young Abel – he did not deserve such a thrashing. And poor Andrew – he had not deserved to lose his life.

She began to weep so hard that it was difficult to breathe. She had never known such pain and anguish could exist. As she pulled the patchwork quilt closer about her, her mind reeled, striving to discard the horror of Andrew's death.

Chapter Ten

Some days later, Rosina lay on her bed, watching through the open window of her room, the last of the sunset reflected down from the sky. Restlessly she closed the shutters and continued to lie there as it grew steadily darker, unable to sleep until after midnight. Suddenly, out of the dark stillness, immediately beyond the door, she heard a faint footstep. At first she panicked, rose, and fled to stand at the window which let in a finger-thread of light from the moon between the shutters. There she stood, listening.

As Captain Skewthorn and most of the men had left for Struisbaai in the brig which had been overhauled for the next expedition, she was alone in the house, except for old Tom Harding, who, careful, wily and experienced seaman that he was, was a great confidante of the Captain, who trusted him with almost anything. The few other men were in their huts, and the slaves in their quarters across the yard.

It seemed an eternity before the sound she dreaded came to her ears; a fumbling of hands at the door knob, which she had taken the precaution to bolt before climbing into bed. She swallowed hard, a feeling of wild hysteria rising in her.

The doorknob rattled three times; she remained silent. Then there was no more rattling, only subdued breathing. A coldness spread throughout her body as she forced herself to creep away from the wall, her heart thundering in her chest. She slowly sat down on the bed. There was no sound beyond the door now, and she sat there hunched on the bed, for more than an hour, horribly awake and full of foreboding. She was suddenly aware of her terrible danger in an isolated house, where a desperate murderer may have stayed behind to kill again. She shivered, her mind swarming with the frightening images of this new, sinister menace. It was in this house, all around her, and she was too isolated, too shunned by everyone except the slaves, to call for help should something happen.

Then reason took over and she willed herself to quietly rise from the bed and creep to the door to listen. There was no sound. Whoever it was, must have gone.

She drew a deep breath. Her first fear had been so great that she felt now almost calm in her relief. Feeling better, except that she was shuddering with shock, she went back to bed, and was able to sleep for a few hours, woken only by the sounds of slaves chasing away a wary and cunning black-backed jackal from the small livestock.

The barking of the dogs and the pounding of the massive hooves of oxen spattering stones in clouds of dust startled her the next day as she was mending a jerkin in the sitting room. She glanced through the open window, where the sea was a brilliant blue, glistening in the early afternoon light. A fresh sea breeze had risen with the sun and swept away low clouds leaving the air clean with just the hint of salt in it. A small ox-wagon came into view, and she nervously looked towards the dining room, where the men left behind were gathered. They were sitting about the dining room table where there was much talk and laughter and the chink of money. She knew old Tom Harding, and three or four others were playing a card game with thick greasy cards. There was the clatter of a wooden bucket outside, and she saw Clara walking towards the wagon, whistling some song between her teeth. She watched her stop, and put the bucket down, whereupon she nodded to the man clad in plain dark coat and breeches who was tethering his horse beside the wagon.

Pushing back tendrils of damp, dark hair, and running a tongue over dry lips, Rosina put down her mending and walked to the front door, her eyes widening in surprise to see that the man was a field-cornet, who had duties similar to an English Justice of the Peace, followed by six Hottentot soldiers.

As his short, stockily built figure stood before her, he politely touched the low, wide brim of his hat. "Good day *mejuffrou*. Are you mejuffrou Webb? Rosina Webb?" He spoke English with a strong Dutch accent.

"Yes," she heard herself say as his eyes quickly assessed her unfashionable clothes and simply-dressed black hair. The Hottentot soldiers stood behind him, and she was dimly aware of one of them – a younger man with inquisitive dark eyes.

The official nodded abruptly, his voice clipped with icy disapproval. "Field-Cornet van Reenen at your service, mejuffrou. You must come with me, to the drostdy at Swellendam, to be tried for the murder of one Lieutenant Andrew Buckleigh, late of His Majesty King George's troops."

The colour drained from Rosina's cheeks. She felt her whole body surge with momentary panic at his words, and stared at him as though he had struck her in the face. "But, sir – I didn't kill him – I had nothing to do with his death!"

Field-Cornet van Reenen's eyes glinted suddenly like hard green stone. "Landdrost Meurant in Swellendam has evidence, mejuffrou that you had a strong motive to kill the Lieutenant – and most damning of all, that you were found beside the body after you had stabbed him several times with your own scissors."

All in an instant, Rosina's vital youth seemed gone forever, and something terrible had taken its place. It was as if an indefinable evil had subtly crept back into her life, a sinister, malevolent overtone.

"But sir – I loved Lieutenant Buckleigh – I never took his life. Who could have told you such a terrible lie?"

Field-Cornet van Reenen drew himself to his full height, and cocked a glassy green eye at her. "A certain Dutch refugee, Mr Haas Maarten, mejuffrou. He told us to dig up the body and see for ourselves that Lieutenant Buckleigh was killed with the scissors, not once but many times. He gave the murder weapon to Landdrost Meurant for safe-keeping before it was hidden away by the guilty party for obvious reasons. He has given evidence that he caught you in the deceased's room just after you had stabbed him."

Rosina's legs would not move. Helpless, all she could do was to stand and stare at the man.

So! It had been Haas Maarten who had removed the scissors . . . Rosina tried to think, and after a moment's frightened hesitancy took the risk of trying her voice. "But – where be – where is Mr Maarten now? He has not returned to this place."

"He left for Cape Town, mejuffrou – there was nothing to keep him in Swellendam – and nothing for us to keep him for, if you understand me. He has given us all the evidence he had written down in a deposition by the Landdrost and signed by Meneer Haas Maarten personally."

Rosina was conscious of a feeling of nauseating sickness, as though she had been caught in some kind of deceitful, horrible treachery. Her whole being sagged, and she began to speak in a halting voice: "But I be – am innocent of such a terrible thing."

"As from last year, we now have a circuit court with proper judges from Cape Town. They sit twice a year. If you are innocent, mejuffrou, you can prove it when the judges arrive next month in Swellendam. Now if you will be so good as to pack a few belongings and food for yourself, I will take you to the wagon after the grave is dug up."

She knew with a heavy heart that further protest was pointless, that the official was doing his duty, and that any further effort to change his mind would be useless. He gave her a withering look then curtly said something to the Hottentots in Dutch, who were now joined by the men, grumbling and talking and crowding the doorway behind her. She moved away as if in an unreal nightmare as they shoved passed her to speak to the field-cornet, then she watched them shouting for the slaves and move off with the soldiers in the direction of the small cemetery below the hill.

Rosina's life had changed once more, as she turned back, trembling, into the house, closely followed by Field-Cornet van Reenen. Even though everything seemed to stand against her, something inside her, some instinct for self-preservation urged her to run away, to flee . . . she could not stand it! She must get away! She must!

While roaming the sunlit rocks, the sands, she had never realised until then, what real terror was. It seemed to her then, that the condition of all living things around her, appeared to be in a permanent state of terror. It was the state in which she now stood. Even hell was better than this, anything was . . . Yet, she knew that she could never escape from the silent, implacable field-cornet following her up to her room.

While he watched her from the open doorway, she walked to the wooden chest made from golden-brown fruitwood under the window. With her back to him, she could not stop the tears flowing down her cheeks as she bent down, opened the chest and methodically took out the few neatly-folded clothes which she laid out on the quilt on the bed. There was the beautiful peach-coloured muslin dress from Jan la Motte, the fancy shoes, the tortoiseshell combs from his late wife, Roosje. Then she picked up a fine gold chain set with blood garnets Henry Mostyn had given her off one of the ships years ago, which she had never had the occasion to wear. It winked and glittered in the light as she held it in her hands. Then, on impulse, she fastened it around her neck, hiding it beneath the high collar of her dress. For a moment she was filled with hope as she gazed at these lovely things, then the hope died and she bundled them up with her few other clothes in the quilt, fastening it securely at the neck. No one, not even Captain Skewthorn, to whom she had submitted so obediently all her life, could help her, if he wanted to. Never in her life had she been faced with such a situation. Suddenly, she found herself praying, "Father, help me find a way out."

There was no answer, either from within herself or from the silence around her, and she was left only with the growing fear in the pit of her stomach.

As she wordlessly left the room with a last glance around, she found herself staring at the floor just beyond the door. Something lay there, until now unseen, against the wall. She picked it up and examined it as the field-cornet hurried her forward. It was an unusual brass buckle which was strangely familiar to her. She turned it over. She knew this buckle, but she could not remember where she had seen it. She knew she had seen it, many times.

Her head suddenly throbbed as they walked towards the kitchen. She felt sick, exhausted as she remembered the incident on the night of Andrew's funeral . . . the person who had tried her doorknob. Who had it been? Had it been the owner of the buckle? What had he wanted with her? Was it the murderer? Had he wanted to kill her too?

She looked at the buckle again, and to her it became a sinister and repulsive warning of her danger in this house. The Field-Cornet left her in the charge of two Hottentot soldiers as he busied himself asking questions of everyone in the settlement, which he wrote down laboriously in a large book covered with skin. In the kitchen Rosina packed a canister of shark biltong, rusks and a little kidskin full of dried fruit. She passed the kitchen door where Clara was stamping mielies for the evening meal, and gazed outside for a brief moment at the chase of light and shadow on the low humped hill. From the stables came the restless whinnying of the horses; high over head, screeching thinly, a flock of seagulls wheeled in the sky. Scalding tears stung the back of her eyes. She felt worn down, and totally defeated.

By the side of the mielie-stamper she paused, and looked at Clara not able to speak. But as Clara paused in her work, her eyes filled with unaccustomed tears, and in spite of her effort at restraint, a cry was wrung from her: "Ach, Missy Rosina! What a sad day it is for me – what sorrow it is in my heart to see you go away with the soldiers when I, Clara, know you never kill that English soldier! And my poor Abel – he has run away – where I do not know. Ach, Missy – my heart it is breaking!"

"I'll be all right, Clara," Rosina said heavily. "But when did Abel go? 'Tis unsafe for a runaway slave, and well he knows it."

Clara slumped on her stool, and shook her head. "He was gone this morning. Missy Rosina – he go and now I do not know where. What am I going to do?"

Rosina was silent for a moment. "I'll see if there be a way to find Abel – for I go to Swellendam," she said, her dark eyes still shimmering with tears. "There may be news of him in that place." She patted Clara's buxom arm. "Now don't you fret yourself – I return very soon seeing as I be innocent of Lieutenant Buckleigh's murder."

"It will be well, mejuffrou, if you hurry yourself," she heard Field-Cornet van Reenen say, in his stern Dutch voice. "We have buried the body of the English Lieutenant again, and I have the evidence for the judges. We are now ready to leave."

The silence was again charged with tension as Rosina turned toward him. She was disconcerted by the intentness of the man's gaze, and opened her mouth to speak, but then, filled with a bewildering array of feelings from intense anger to deep terror, she closed it, incapable of saying a word. He believed her guilty and she knew that there was nothing she could do except go with him to prove her innocence. She realised more than ever that she was caught in a hideous web that had woven itself around her, from the moment she had seen Andrew Buckleigh on the beach.

The Field-Cornet turned and went to wait for her outside, saying, "Do not be long."

"But where be this place – this Swellendam, Missy? Is it far from here?"

Rosina turned back to Clara and instantly saw the misery in the older woman's eyes.

"I don't know, Clara – it be somewhere in the – somewhere to the north. Look after the animals while I be gone."

All at once panic seized her, but as she turned away her eyes alighted on the canister over the fireplace where there was always some money kept for necessaries, which no one dared to steal. Quickly she opened it and took out a small selection of coins – a few English shillings, Venetian sequins, some silver Spanish dollars, copper dubbeltjies, one golden guinea and one rixdollar on a stiff square of paper. She poured them into a large spotted handkerchief, the clinking of the coins making a liquid sound, then pushed the bundle down the front of her bodice.

Moments later, she stood outside, blinking in the warm sunlight, watching despairingly for a moment the scorpions and lizards creeping from the shelter of the stones, their sharp black shadows crawling with them. The restless little mongoose ensconced himself in her neck, pressing himself against her as she desperately scanned the world around her, storing memories for the dark days ahead. She drank in the sun throwing out deep black shadows from the rocks, the seagulls, the clouds, the rippling silver water, the strange, sharp sweetness from the fynbos stinging the air. Here, in this isolated place, was the world of uneasy security she had

83

shared with Captain Skewthorn, his men and the slaves. The men, now stood watching her, as if they were stone statues in the sunlight. Mahogany-faced Tom Harding stood at a distance, watching as she turned her head away, closing her eyes. As she did not respond to the small animal now riding on her shoulder, he ran down her arm, and leapt to the ground where he disappeared into the bush. And from the moment she climbed up into the wagon, with chains manacled to her wrists, she left her girlhood behind forever.

The sleek dun oxen, patient under the yoke, dragged the wagon away, the turf thudding, hard and dry under their massive feet. With little skirts of dust rising behind them, they left the sparkling sea sleeping in the heat, the waves hissing up the narrow shoreline and splashing the warm rocks, the flies feasting around the fynbos. Rosina, standing in the cramped stuffiness of the wagon, peered out at the world from the depths of her black calico sunbonnet, and saw for an instant, the little golden mongoose, standing on its hindlegs, and peering curiously out of the bushes at the departing wagon, and for one timeless moment he appeared so dear, so comforting, and so heartbreakingly remote from her. The stiff-haired dog broke into a long stride, barking, with the other dog at his heels. Rosina watched in a deep, brooding silence as the two animals bounded after the wagon through the waist high bushes and finally gave up the race, breathing heavily, their tongues lolling from their mouths. She felt like one who gazes at the precious earth for the last time before retreating into the darkness of a living death.

As the small troop of Hottentots rode alongside, the lead man urged the animals on with a long bamboo-handled whip, which reached the whole team of oxen with one blow. A bird rose with a shrill cry from some

84

tufts of grass, and floated over their heads. There was no one to comfort her. There would never be anyone to comfort her again, and still as silent tears fell down her cheeks, she was unable to believe what had happened.

Chapter Eleven

The journey to Swellendam, the nearest village with its drostdy where the circuit court judges sat twice a year on their rounds of the colony, was northwards, over the long, wide Breede River towards the Langeberg mountains. As they journeyed around the low-lying hill and turned north, they left the coastal region behind them. The country ahead was flat as a calm white sea, its *veld* carpeted with wild flowers and unbroken by *kopje* until the long line of the Overberg Mountains was reached.

For Rosina, sitting under the canvas tent roof inside the hard, uncomfortable wagon, it was a new experience in hopelessness and despair. Beyond the Hottentot driver, she could see a square of sky filled with dark grey masses that swung aside from time to time to let the sunlight slip down to the earth. She sat uncomfortably on the floor, her shoulders pressed for support against the side of the wagon. In the frightening vastness, the immense loneliness, with only a few solitary farmhouses appearing here and there, the feeling that only this small band of people and the stocky field-cornet, riding out in front on a bay gelding, were real, overwhelmed her. She was being carried forward, somewhere, anywhere, but wherever it was, it was an alarming prospect.

She wondered what this place Swellendam would be

like. the only facts she knew about it were from snatches of talk from the men and Jan la Motte. She had never seen a village or a town before; never been far from the settlement. Swellendam was the only village before the Hottentot Mountains, of which she had heard, nearer to Cape Town. There was a drostdy there, with a landdrost who administered some kind of justice over those in his district, but how or what kind, she had no idea. She wished she had listened more closely when the men had spoken, wished she had asked Jan more questions about it, for he seemed to know so much about the colony and its people.

So many thoughts flashed through her mind as they lumbered on through the wide flat plain bordered by its long broken chain of mountains in the distance, where there was a heavy barrage of clouds hanging. Every now and then they passed a farm with its long-legged, long-horned cattle and broad-tailed African sheep, with hair instead of wool, and sometimes one of the newer stocks of woolly merinos. Some of the deep and intense pain inside her was lifted slightly, as though the mighty struggle of Nature and its elements drew out her torment, and she seemed to lose the wretched agony of her own consciousness for awhile as she felt herself become a part of the enormous unseen space about her, losing the sharp edges of awareness.

As the time passed, she numbly pulled her woollen shawl tighter about her, even though the heat of the dying spring still poured down, the clinking of the chains about her wrists reminding her of her situation. Slowly and uncomfortably, bits and pieces of different panoramas formed and sank and disappeared before her eyes, her body lifting and falling with the rise of the wagon. She could see glimpses of the ranges of gigantic mountains rising on the horizon as they climbed an endless plateau, or the long forest of yellowwood trees moving upon them, or the walls of red-tinted and grey rock, sculptured by the wind and made tortuous with jagged boulders and sharp stones. Now and then, she was helped out of the wagon as they climbed particularly precipitous passes, then she climbed back as they descended into broad, fertile valleys strewn with wild flowers, and every so often they passed another isolated farmhouse.

Here and there, a river ran, shining like a cracked mirror, and at intervals a solitary Steppe buzzard or an eagle cut the sky with a graceful, curving wing, moving soundlessly, and then sank out of sight. At times, the wind rolled and swept over rock and hill and valley like a great ominous shadow, making progress difficult, and enhancing the isolating silence.

As they moved northwards, the ranges of mountains reared higher, sinking and rising and curving. At night she was allowed to join Field-Cornet van Reenen at one of the fires kindled to scare away wild animals. The oxen, for greater security, were fastened by their horns to the wheels of the wagon. Here she partook of a frugal meal, mostly dried biltong seasoned with a tot of Cape brandy from a huge horn slung in the wagon beside the powder-flask. The Hottentot soldiers congregated round another watch-fire, and made their simple meal without the brandy, but with more merriment than Field-Cornet van Reenen, who sat against the bole of a tree, smoking his huge pipe with easy though watchful calm.

Afterwards he would stick his pipe in the band of his broad-brimmed hat, wrap himself in his great coat, and, fearless of snakes or scorpions, stretch himself on the bare ground, as Rosina was chained back in the wagon. The Hottentots, while not guarding her, drew themselves under sheep-skin karosses and lay, coiled up, their feet to the fire and their faces to the ground. Rosina would lie on the floor of the wagon, gazing into the darkness which outside was lit with the glimmer of fireflies and clusters of stars, shimmering in the luminescent swathe of the Milky Way. Sometimes the echo of the high-pitched howl of a Cape fox or the long drawn-out call "nyaaa" followed by the stacatto "ya-ya-ya-ya" of the black-backed jackal, or the rasping cough of a leopard, would echo eerily in the deep silence.

But she felt no stillness, no peace beyond her turbulent thoughts. They were not really thoughts but flitting images, whisps of terror that became stronger as the night wore on. And when she finally slept, tumultuous dreams came to haunt her – dreams of Andrew, with which she struggled, sweating, knowing that his body was now cold; nightmares of death and imprisonment, of the strange, frightening people she was approaching with every passing day.

And then, one day, just as the sun was setting, and the wagon tossed and the oxen heaved and lumbered over the veld resembling blowing seas, nearly throwing her from her position on the floor, they came in sight of Swellendam, the sixty-four year old village against the impressive backdrop of Langeberg Mountains.

Chapter Twelve

Standing between two Hottentot soldiers, Rosina gazed bewildered up the wide, winding piece of wagon road crossing the mill-stream and disappearing over the rise on its long way to Mossel Bay and then to Cape Town. She gazed at the attractive avenue of tall oak trees, the hump-backed wooden footbridge over the shining Cornlands River, where dragonflies moved swiftly over the surface. And then at the houses, white-washed and thatched spreading out along the green foothills between the village and the mountains, where shadows to the west were falling quietly over the veld. It was a pretty village, scattered about a valley, and much larger than anything she had seen. The smoke of fires lighted to cook evening meals was curling in the serene evening air and she watched the faint smoke drifts, as a slave-girl from one of them, came out to throw a pailful of soapsuds into the river. She gazed at the deepening colours of the landscape, its many kinds of green intermingled with the red and gold of the sun lying on the hillocks and the mountains fading into the sky where the clouds piled up, ballooning, layer upon layer, their upper reaches burnished with gold. Towering above the rest of the mountains like some medieval pile was the dome-shaped Twelve O'Clock Peak, whose sheer rocky sides sparkled like gems in the dying sunlight – the jewel-studded crown of the Langeberg range.

She heard the lowing of cows returning to the fold and the ponderous clanging of the slave bell behind the oak trees where the white-washed, gabled, Cape-Dutch style Drostdy was set in green lands of oak and fruit trees, and the Union Jack fluttered from the tall flagpole near the roadside. Further away, was the simple church, a few trading stores where some wagons were outspanned, and opposite the drostdy stood the square whitewashed gaol.

All her life she had seen nothing but the small world of the settlement, and at first she was oblivious of the low murmur of voices standing close by, of the curious eyes fastened upon her, measuring her and assessing what they saw. There was now quite a crowd of people, jostling around her, talking and scrutinising her. From where she stood, she could just catch the mumble of their voices but she could not understand what they were saying. She knew that they were talking about her. Seeing the looks, she self-consciously turned away, only to catch sight of a girl about her own age, talking animatedly with a young man in topboots and breeches. She could not take her eyes off the girl. Her golden hair was curled up into ringlets under her exquisitely stitched white bonnet and everything about her was beautiful: her fine pale green dress and shawl, her smart black boots. And her laughter sounded like the tinkling of polished glass, as she looked up at the face of the young man, carelessly flirtatious, as if she had not a care in the world. It was not the harsh laughter of the men, or the crackled wariness of the slaves . . . it sounded more carefree than that, as if she was content, and felt friendly towards the world.

The crowd turned to one another, the women's skirts rustling menacingly, disturbingly. Rosina could sense that in their minds was one thought: "What if this young woman is a murderess?"

She was instantly conscious of this open suspicion and subversive feeling that flowed about her from one to the other. They stood whispering to one another and staring at her, and the emanation of their dark thoughts seemed to come back to her like a wave, a wide-spreading sky-reaching wave that hung above her, interminably threatening to break and engulf her.

She did not know how long she had stayed there, standing motionless . . . only when everything grew strangely misty did she discover that she was crying. She glanced round to see if anyone had noticed. Conversation had ceased behind her. Then she breathed again, and the sigh of her exhaling whispered along the crowd like the rustle of mice behind a wainscoting. The next moment Field-Cornet van Reenen was at her side, ordering her across the road between two of the Hottentot soldiers. She was in an agony of self-consciousness, the chains clanking at her wrists, but awkwardly she forced herself to walk forward towards the gaol. Her heart beat faster as she felt cruelly aware that she was alien, out of place in her old-fashioned, ugly clothes and her dusty, worn veldschoen boots and plain, unattractive shawl, knowing that her appearance and her awkwardness distinguished her from the others, and underlined her isolation. She then saw that they were about to enter the beamed front room of the gaol, and she was glad of the prospect of respite from the unpleasant tension outside.

"So! Is there not enough excitement in L'Agulhas, that you must cause it yourself, mejuffrou?"

Rosina looked up, startled at the stern, Dutch voice. The short, tallowy man who was the under-sheriff was darting looks of displeasure at her, as his words were quickly translated into English by the Field-Cornet.

Her tear-filled eyes were wide with confusion. "But I have done nothing! What – what will you do with me?" she burst out, wiping the moisture from her eyes with the ragged edge of her shawl.

The field-cornet again translated, this time for the under-sheriff who answered with a restless shrug of thin black coated shoulders, eyeing her curiously across a tray with its thick pottery cup and plate.

"Tell her we'll lock her up safely out of harm's way. She must be thankful to be here, for it would not be safe for her to walk the streets of Swellendam just now, not after committing such a terrible crime." He tapped his fingers on the desk impatiently, not looking at her.

While she stood there she studied the top of his bent head, where a pink scalp showed through thin, blond hair. Her shoulders and body suddenly stiffened with anger. How dare these suspicious strangers think she was guilty when nothing had been proved against her? They knew nothing at all about her. She would show them that she was innocent as soon as the circuit court judges arrived!

The under-sheriff fidgetted with his scrupulously neat black cravat, then smoothed the backs of his lean hands as his small eyes roved in their sockets like those of a predatory fish lurking in the weeds waiting for prey. "I have a problem – where am I to put her?" He continued, "Tell her that the judges of the Circuit will be here in a few weeks time – but until then, what must I do with her?"

He was an irritable, suspicious little man with an

93

almost fussy arrogance. Rosina realized that he looked upon her as an unneccessary nuisance in his busy schedule.

"She should go to Cape Town – the gaol here is overcrowded, and Landdrost Meurant is still on his farm." The under-sheriff glared at the field-cornet, who stood implacably at Rosina's side. "We have no place for a dangerous white woman, and English too."

"This is the nearest place which administers justice over the area she comes from so she must be kept here." Field-Cornet van Reenen's words jangled in the air for a few seconds and then died.

The under-sheriff coughed. He fixed his small sharp eyes on Rosina reprovingly, and said with weighty intonation, "Very well then, Field-Cornet van Reenen. Tell her she can have the smallest cell next to the larger cell for women." Having delivered this ultimatum he wiped the back of his hand across his mouth and watched her warily.

Rosina suddenly noticed how stiff and how dreadfully tired she felt. "But I be innocent, sir. Why won't you believe me? I have not been before the judges and yet everyone acts as if I AM guilty!" She jerked the words out and suddenly a tense, dramatic note was introduced into the situation.

As the field-cornet translated her words, the under-sheriff became fretful. "That's what they all say, mejuffrou. If you are innocent, you have nothing to fear. But if you are guilty, then you will suffer for what you have done."

The field-cornet shook his head and told her what the under-sheriff had said. "One of the guards – Johannes, he can speak English. If you want anything, ask him, mejuffrou."

He took his leave with obvious relief as the under-sheriff shouted an order to the Hottentot guards in the next office, who appeared immediately wearing cotton trousers, no shoes, worn blue tunics and tall hats upswept on one side, with white plumes. They each carried a walking stick, and their appearance seemed to enrich his self-confidence and lend him a sensation of new power and domination as he spoke to her in a peremptory tone, turning to one of the guards to translate: "Put your bundle on the desk, mejuffrou. It must be checked to see if you have anything harmful in there – knives and such like."

Rosina reluctantly set the bundle on the desk and he coughed and went through the contents carefully. With rising embarrassment, Rosina saw the muslin dress and shoes.

Then it was over, and he pushed the clothes away so that she could pack them up once more. Johannes, the English-speaking guard, said, "The Master says you must come now."

The under-sheriff rose, taking a large key from a ring hung on the wall behind him, and gave an order to one of the guards, who eyed her curiously as she drew back and stood apart.

"Tell her Johannes, she needn't be afraid," he said haughtily, "nothing will happen to her – if she behaves herself. Tell her to come with us."

Rosina was distractedly torn between anger and fear. "I'm not frightened," she said, in an almost normal voice. But there was now a firm twist to her mouth, and angry glint in her eyes, as she was imbued with a strange new courage. "I can walk by myself."

Her anger began to grow as they made their way out into the walled back quarters of the building. They might think she had murdered Andrew but that gave them no right to treat her as a criminal before it was proved to be so. Nobody should have that right, nobody. Something deep inside started to flicker, some unknown part of herself she was discovering.

The gaol was placed square to the roadway. At its entrance was the gaoler's office and that of the guards, and a corridor leading to the courtyard. This was enclosed on all sides by the building itself, a rectangle of rooms with doors giving onto the central space, and windows set high and small. At the back on the left were the cells for the women prisoners, and on the right, the men. The great Dutch oven in which bread was baked, adjoined the gaol offices, immediately to the right and there was a door in the wall at the back, between the men and women's cells, leading to the fields outside. The place had been planned for utility in a rough-and-ready age, yet it was built with Dutch sturdiness. Its rooms were dark and airless, the courtyard nothing more than a prison compound, where now rang the ravings and wailings of the inmates. Its walls were thick and the bars stout, and it only had two outer doors, which could be securely closed on the prisoners, so that the decent citizens of the village who passed the gaol did not need to concern themselves with what went on behind those doors.

There was a terrible din coming from the cells as the west became one arch of dying red-golden light. The air smelled of wood-smoke, of the fragrance of the fruit trees beyond the wall and of bodies long-gone without washing as the door of one of the three women's cells was opened, and a group of women were hustled out by guards, who pushed them into the next cell which was already densely packed. The din grew and Rosina felt deeply depressed as the stench from the rooms assailed her nostrils. The high-pitched voices from within rose to a crescendo as the extra prisoners were shoved roughly inside, and the door closed with a crash, on about thirty human beings of all ages, crowded inside.

The baker and his slave assistants stood at the door of the bakery, dusty with meal, their sleeves rolled up to the elbow. The air close by was fragrant with baking bread, though on the doorstep its warm breath had met and mingled with the revolting stench from the cells not far away.

It was even worse in the men's cells where the prisoners were ranged about the walls, squalid with neglect and misery, and sickly with confinement. There were runaway slaves, standing with shackled limbs, sullenly awaiting their awarded punishment and the arrival of their masters, Hottentots dressed in sheepskin karosses and leather trousers, one or two wild Bushmen seated, naked, on the clay floor, heavily ironed, confined in a recumbent position, all waiting the annual circuit court to stand their trial.

"Two of those, they say they been driven by hunger to steal a sheep," Johannes remarked casually to Rosina, as they followed the under-sheriff. "They say the master's son, a boy of fourteen years shot one of the Xhosa peoples. This Xhosa, he did murder the boy's mother who was running after them. Everyone – the white peoples there they did hunt them down like dogs and here they are to wait for the judges of the court."

Rosina looked shudderingly towards the cell, a place which seemed to her, one of visible terror. "There are Hottentots here too – like us – we are now allowed to speak up against our masters in the circuit court to the judges. That is the law now, from the Governor's own mouth," the guard told her triumphantly.

Suddenly, from one of the cells, came a suppressed cry, and turning, she heard her name.

"Missy Rosina! Missy! Tis me, Abel – help me Missy!"

She stepped slowly forward, her heart sinking even more for it seemed that everyone, innocent or guilty, hardened criminal and those falsely accused were crowded together into those small, stinking cells . . . all herded together like cattle. Then she saw Abel, his ankles fixed to a huge iron ring. He had undergone a great change: his clothes were almost threadbare, his face looked pinched and thin, and almost like an old man, but his eyes were bright and still alert.

"What happened, Abel? How did you get here?"

"I been brought to this terrible place, Missy, by the field-cornet after I run away from Cap'n. I struggle, Missy, but I can't runaway. Why Missy here?" He spoke, as he always did, with great curiosity, in his sing-song voice.

"I – they think I killed the English redcoat, Abel— "

"But, Missy – you never did kill that man – you never kill nobody— " he burst out, but not before the under-sheriff urged her away in the direction of the women's cells. She tried to look back to catch a glimpse of Abel, but she was hurried away so fast that she was unable to do anything but walk forward. She herself, innocent, submissive, felt suddenly so much more of a child than Abel, in whom she dimly discerned the rudiments of a strong will, as yet unspecific, but almost impressive in its force which she had never noticed before.

But for all that, how could he stand the noise and the filth? And there he was, locked up and chained with hardened criminals. What would happen to him, she dared not think.

"Here – here is for you, Missy!"

Johannes' voice fell like an explosion on her ears. It was impossible to get away, for she was chained and the two guards were both a bit bigger and definitely stronger than she was, and the under-sheriff was armed.

The room furthest from the gate leading into the fields had been quickly cleared for her. From it came an obscene smell of stale food and more alarming human odours. Indignation welled up in her. Why did she have to stay in this dreadful cell when she was innocent? Why was she allowed nothing better?

There was a plain chair and table, and the window of the plastered room was high up in the wall and barred. A narrow cot was hastily carried in, covered surprisingly with a neat, warm blanket.

"The Master of the gaol – he say you stay in chains." The guard's voice was sneering. "He say you can't kill nobody here."

Rosina regarded him with a sudden strange calm, now that the time had come for her to be left alone. "I have never killed anyone, ever. I do not want to kill you, if that be what you're thinkin'."

The guard looked astonished. "Why don't you fight then – to be free? You white – you not like us."

"Because the judges must say that I am innocent. Everyone will think I have no right to be free if they do not."

The guard nodded, but there was a look of uncertainty about him and his eyes shifted uneasily. "You mad woman," he said. "You not kill now."

The under-sheriff barked at him and the other guard in Dutch. They both nodded and stood aside for her to

99

enter. The scurrying and squeaking of rats disturbed by the light, intruded upon the silence of the dimly lit cell, as Rosina sat down on the hard cot almost gratefully, for her legs were actually trembling with fatigue. As the door was closed and locked, all remaining light was shut out and barred by the ruthless hands of the under-sheriff. Then she was sick, and everytime she thought about the recent events she felt like being sick again. She was almost sure now, that the reason Andrew was killed was that he had discovered about the smuggling of slaves, and had been considered a threat, just as old Sam Leach had been.

It was difficult to understand that even with so much natural beauty around, there could be so much violence, and so much misery . . . especially in the cells next door and across the way.

It was later that the gaoler's wife, a large, buxom woman with inquisitive brown eyes and an elaborately frilled kappie on her head, brought over a plate of stewed meat, well-cooked in the Dutch manner, with baked fruits, salad and a pewter mug of fresh milk. She could not speak English, but she showed by her manner that she was curious about the white murderess.

She watched Rosina at a distance as she hesitantly thanked her for the food then, frowning, she left the cell, ordering the guard who accompanied her, to lock the door.

Rosina forced herself to eat the food, but found it difficult with the high-pitched wailing from the next cell, and the noise from across the way. She felt almost guilty that she had good food when the other prisoners obviously did not. She had so little, but they had even less.

"God!" she said softly. "Oh, God!"

Now it was night, and still she sat alone in the small, stinking dark cell. It was as if a trap had been sprung – a trap that caught but did not kill. It was silent now, and she heard the guard close and bolt the door in the wall at the back, leading to the fields where there was a threshing floor and the watermill fed by a stream running down from the nearby mountains. The candle lantern in the courtyard glimmered palely, the odour of its tallow sickening and rancid as Rosina lay down and tried to sleep.

There was something more than fatigue about her wish to sleep, for then she would be able to forget this cell, its stench and noise and evils; she would be free of her shame and humiliation; she would not be plagued with the stares and the orders and the wailing from outside; she would no longer be tormented with the feeling that she was fighting a desperate and hopeless battle against the authorities. Sleep meant forgetfulness.

Outside in the darkness the bats wheeled and soft-winged owls floated up and down the veld searching for voles and mice. Here and there little pin-points of green phosphorescence marked the slow movements of glow-worms working through the tall grasses, and velvety moths steered erratic courses through the air channels, like blown leaves.

Chapter Thirteen

The following days were the longest Rosina had ever experienced. The cell became her whole world. Night became her best time because it was quiet then, and very dark. She was not afraid of the dark. She was used to it. What she was afraid of was strange people, and of the fate awaiting both her and Abel. She was not given as much food now, only bread and soup, yet her helpings were if anything, more generous than those of the other prisoners. She managed to bribe one of the guards with a precious Spanish dollar to give some of her portion to Abel, but was dismayed to learn that the other prisoners had knocked Abel aside and devoured the food.

It was not many nights later when one of the guards, an Asiatic convict banished years before from Batavia, having returned from a few hours of cock-fighting with the slaves of the Landdrost, suddenly went beserk, and turned on the under-sheriff. There rose into the hot summer air a volume of sound that filled the darkness with incessant noise. A moment later there were the sounds of running footsteps as the under-sheriff and the other guards ran from the gaol. The night outside was spangled with the light of lanterns as Rosina jumped from her cot. She had to feel her way along the wall in the pitch darkness, to the small barred window. Her legs felt hardly strong enough to carry her on to the chair beneath it. She had hardly slept for days, and she had eaten very little that day, so that her head was swimming with fatigue and hunger. Climbing on the chair beneath it, she looked out, but all she could see was a string of orange flames darting passed, and shadowy figures running in a wild, clamorous noise.

"My God! Watch out!" she heard the under-sheriff shout in Dutch, "Take care – Hendrik's amok!"

A raving figure ran past the cell, the gleam of a short thick-handled knife with a bent grip in his hand. Rosina, standing on the chair, remained looking through the window as though mesmerized. One of the female prisoners next door shrieked as she saw the guard thrust the knife into the under-sheriff, who fell, screaming to the ground. As he fell, another guard leaped forward to catch him, and Rosina saw the flash of the knife as that guard, too, was stabbed. It was finally one of the slaves, used to run errands, who snatched one of the guns dropped by the wounded Hottentots in one hand and, brandishing a sword in the other, chased him over the locked gate in the wall.

Rosina turned away with a sick terror, and felt around in the darkness, for she was forbidden a candle, to find her cot. Sitting down gratefully, chains clinking, she wrapped her shawl round her, she trembled with shock, as all night long they searched for the man who had gone beserk.

Rosina learned from Johannes who had been only slightly injured in the chaos, that the terrifying news was running through the village like a tongue of fire, and that a price was on his head, dead or alive. Men grasped their guns and watched from every corner, and at intervals along the wide, wagon road. Women thrust their children before them and locked their doors, for

103

no one knew which way the silent desperate feet had gone. Until one of the men found himself struggling with the madman, who seized and stabbed him with his own bayonet . . .

By the time they overpowered him when he came down from the mountainside and hurled a stone the size of his fist at one of the burghers, cracking his skull, he had killed at least a dozen men and boys. Amidst all the excitement, it was discovered that he had, before chasing and wounding the guards and the under-sheriff, unlocked the irons of several prisoners, who had escaped over the wall, including young Abel.

Rosina did not know what punishment would be meted out to Abel if he was caught, but she knew it would be drastic. She sat in her cell feeling weary and disconsolate, a dark shadow hanging over any elation she might feel regarding the young boy's escape. There was something depressing about the prospect of him hiding in the countryside while the field-cornet and his Hottentot helpers vigilantly searched for runaway slaves, and other offenders.

The following day, she learned that the demented man had been locked up to await trial before the circuit court judges, as no longer could the Landdrost hang him on Execution Hill. When Johannes brought her evening meal, he told her that the man had gone beserk because of the death of his fine cock-fighting bird in the local slaves cockpit.

But the very next Sunday, on the outskirts of the village, there was once more the noisy bustling and gesticulating of men staking everything they had on two prize birds circling one another in the dust in a depression in the ground, as if nothing untoward had happened.

Now every time Rosina closed her eyes a vision of Abel's small, high-cheeked face behind a barred window in irons tormented her, and her ears rang with his high-pitched sing-song voice, calling for her help. She could no longer bear the struggle. She knew she must free herself from this inner conflict – but how? It was then that she would, in the privacy of the cell, bury her head beneath the blanket and pound her fists against the cot in frustration.

Chapter Fourteen

Four weeks later, the coach of the two new circuit court judges arrived in clouds of dust, with their retinue of servants and a few officials from Cape Town. There was much bustle at the drostdy across the street where they were to stay. The village was crowded with those waiting to be called before the court, which was now being rudely called "the black circuit" by the farmers, because it was instructed to receive Hottentot complaints. Day by day, the judges were busy with the heavy tales of charges, true and false, against the farmers, many of whom were indignant at the suspicion and resented being hauled to court at the insistence of Hottentots and missionaries.

In the midst of all this, Rosina was summoned before the court in the newly arranged Courtroom of the Drostdy with its yellow wood beamed ceiling and stinkwood furniture. It was a former parlour, recently converted into a public office with windows giving on to the long stoep overlooking the river, where a small group of dark-clad men had gathered. The procedure was held in the Dutch-style of closed court, and outside, a large assortment of townsfolk stood, all eyes upon her as she entered between the guards.

The *landdrost*, Mr Meurant, who was responsible for the prosecution of all crimes in his district, gave a brief description of the case in Dutch and handed a list of witnesses to the court. Rosina, who, as the accused, was not entitled to be legally represented, was called upon to make her own defence. She answered the preliminary questions in a halting, unsure manner. Every word of English used was translated into Dutch by a young man standing not far from her, in a dark coat and grey breeches.

The shock of Abel's disappearance had left her numb, with the same incredulous despair she had felt when she had discovered Andrew's body. She had lost the power to think, much less to feel, and it surprised her that she could still walk erectly. Some of the men talked in low tones, while the rest regarded her with undisguised curiosity and made whispered comments among themselves. Flies buzzed maddeningly; one lighted in her hair and though she brushed it away again and again, it always returned.

Mr Meurant called the prosecution witnesses, to be told that they had not been able to make the journey, and that most of them were on the high seas in a privateer brig, the *Leviathan*. He nodded, and allowed that the written deposition taken by the witnesses be used in their place. Mr Meurant read out the written depositions. His voice went on, it seemed to Rosina for hours, saying the same things over and over again in different words. She felt faint now, but tried to hide it. The voice still went on, welling sometimes in her ears, sometimes growing far away, describing, in English and Dutch, how Haas Maarten found her beside the body, with her scissors projecting from the heart, stating truths and half-truths, lies, until she felt she must scream. It was very hot in the room and she wished it was all over.

Then another official began to speak, but now she heard nothing of it. She had become aware of a strange

107

sound, from a room somewhere in the house, a haunting sound outside the crowded courtroom. What was it? It was a musical instrument . . . yes, and most wonderful music. When she had been in the settlement she had listened to Achmat playing on a fiddle made by Henry Mostyn, and Jan la Motte had once brought a flute to play to her, but she had never heard this instrument before. The delicate, tinkling sound filled the air hauntingly, which made her heart beat faster and flooded her being, drawing her upwards.

She was so absorbed in trying to make out the tune that she hardly realised she was being addressed in Dutch-accented English.

"Mejuffrou Webb? Mejuffrou – you haven't heard a word Meneer Meurant has said to you." Mr Olaf Bergh cleared his throat and stared at her with cold grey eyes. He was a stout, burly man with bushy brows under a high-domed forehead crowned by thinning, iron grey hair.

She hesitated, aware of the subdued murmuring among the landdrost and his Collegie of Justice consisting of four heemraden.

"What be – is that music, sir? It be so strangely beautiful." She blushed at the incredulity in his eyes.

As this was translated for the rest of the court, the occupants of the room leaned forward in their places, and she felt the slight rustle of excitement that followed.

"Good heavens, mejuffrou – this is a murder trial and here you are thinking about music! You really are the most unwordly young woman I've ever had occasion to meet." He sighed deeply, and, taking a pinch from his gold-plated snuff-box, turned to the landdrost, Mr Meurant whom he addressed in Dutch.

108

"It is indeed most inconvenient, Meneer Meurant that the government have not agreed to give you the money to alter these premises. There are so many disturbances one cannot get on with the matter in hand."

Mr Meurant, the last of the farmer landdrosts leaned forward. He was an elegant, fair-haired gentleman of French and Muscovite Russian descent, who spoke excellent English, only one of the languages in which he was fluent. "His Excellency, Governor Cradock has only agreed to a very small portion for alterations, Meneer Bergh. As you are aware, we have started alterations at our own expense which we hope to improve – but since we have had to change certain residential quarters into offices, while we hold court here, the deliberations prevent the work of my secretary in the adjoining room, so that only one room is available when the court sits." He sighed, and shrugged elegant shoulders. "Perhaps you gentlemen will be able to lean on His Excellency with a word about our considerable inconveniences."

Rosina did not really listen to their discussion carried out in low tones in a language she did not understand. Most of the facts of the case passed over her head in a sickly haze. Only some time later she was conscious that Mr Meurant had turned his quick, clever eyes to her. "The sound you hear mejuffrou Webb, is a French harpsichord, played by my daughter Helena, a girl of approximately your own age."

She became aware of his penetrating stare, and pieced herself back into the young woman who was standing trial for murder, like someone fitting together a jigsaw puzzle. She understood now. The sound had made her forget her fear and her unhappiness for a few precious moments. Then it had stopped and she felt an unwitting sense of loss, as if something infinitely special had been snatched away. And she knew instinctively that this Helena Meurant, was the beautiful golden-haired girl she had seen outside the gaol on her arrival. How she envied that beautiful, carefree girl, who was free and happy, surrounded by those she loved.

Outside, the noon sun stood high over the mountains; over the metallic glitter of the Cornlands River. Inside the hot, crowded room the air was close, heavy and sweaty, and a merciless glare filled the open windows, through which drifted the whiff of horseflesh, hay and leather, and the creaking timbers of wagons. There was a restless stirring from those outside the courtroom, but no one moved to leave, and those pressing close to the doors were unable to enter, while Mr Meurant continued to read out the written depositions of each one of the witnesses the field-cornet had been able to question, including his own findings.

A full minute passed while the other judge, Mr Jacques de Beer studied Rosina. He was a man of about fifty-two, lean, leathery of face, with deep furrows across his brows and down his sunken cheeks that gave him a sullen, sour look.

Then, at last, Mr Meurant opened his straight thin mouth and spoke directly to her: "You have told us that you did not murder the deceased, Lieutenant Andrew Buckleigh, *Mejuffrou*, even though we have read the evidence that you were found beside the body, with your scissors in his heart. Will you explain to this court exactly what happened on the night of his death?"

Rosina, pale and apprehensive, stood there trying to speak, and failed.

Mr Bergh studied her closely, putting up a quizzing glass to his sceptical eye, as Mr Meurant persevered, "Did you hear any scream, or any sound of a struggle

110

in the next room, Mejuffrou Webb – anything unusual at all?"

Rosina shook her head, trying to shut out that first terrible sight of Andrew's lifeless body in the bed, covered with blood.

Mr Bergh crossed one grey breeched knee over the other, and put down his quizzing glass with illconcealed impatience.

"But you must have heard something, Mejuffrou," Mr Meurant persisted. "In the quiet of night when no one else was supposedly around! Where was your guardian, Captain Skewthorn? The other men?"

He and Mr de Beer exchanged glances as Rosina shook her head desperately, confused beyond words. "There was nothing, sir. The Cap'n, he – he slept in his own room, sir, dead to the world."

Mr Meurant looked at her sternly. "You mean he had been drinking, don't you?" He paused, eyeing her with faint distaste, as, taking a deep, unsteady breath, she nodded. "It is hard to believe, mejuffrou, that something of such a dreadful nature could take place and not be heard. Where were these other men you speak of?"

"There be – was – only Mr Harding, sir. But he couldn't hear a thing above his own snores." As this was translated, there there was a titter of amusement from the *heemraden*, who were immediately quelled by Mr de Beer's frowning face turned in their direction.

"Go on, *mejuffrou*. Was there anyone else in the house?"

"No, sir." Rosina swallowed hard, aware of a deep pounding in her head. She thought of Old Sam Leach's death, of the illegal smuggling of slaves. She had been wrestling with her conscience ever since she had arrived at the gaol, and she knew she had to be careful. There

111

would be no peace until she admitted her knowledge, but she realised there was no escape that way, that it would place her in even graver danger if she did. "The others be – were in their own huts, sir. They never came to the house after dark, not that is – only— "

Mr Meurant eyed her speculatively. "Not until what? What did they come to the house for, Mejuffrou Webb?"

Rosina felt suddenly in despair. She could not tell them about the Captain and what he and the men did. Andrew had said it was illegal, that it was one of the worst of crimes against humanity. And she dreaded to think what the Captain would do to her if he ever found out that she had revealed his secret life. She could never escape his wrath, whatever happened.

She took a deep breath. "To talk about – things, sir – with Cap'n Skewthorn."

Mr de Beer leaned forward and spoke to Mr Meurant, who turned to Rosina. "What kind of things, mejuffrou? What would be of such importance that they would come to the house to talk about it?"

Rosina was silent for a moment, then she said: "Matters, sir – to do with the ship and such."

At that Mr Bergh spread thick sausage fingers across his paper. His highly-coloured face was not encouraging. Mr Meurant glanced quickly at him, then continued, "The ship – what is it that Captain Skewthorn and his men do, mejuffrou," he persevered, "What is their line of business?"

She stared at him directly though her heart was thudding painfully in her chest. "They – he be a privateer, sir. He – Andrew Buckleigh said he has the *lettres de Marque*, sir, to prove it."

Mr Meurant took a pinch of snuff and consulted the

papers before him on the table as there was another interruption at the door, and an ominous rustling from the crowd outside. Then there was silence. Everyone was listening intently now. "Where were he and his men when Field-Cornet van Reenen fetched you?"

She hesitated. "He – he went sailing – on his business, sir."

"Where to, mejuffrou? Where to?" Mr Meurant's voice was peremptory.

"I – I don't know, sir," Rosina replied, with a glance at Meneer Meurant, who stood with his elegant arms folded, his eyes never leaving her pale and drawn face. She watched his expression. It did not change.

"You say you loved this man Buckleigh, mejuffrou. Forgive me for asking this delicate matter, but did you sin with him, as Meneer Maarten and Meneer Thomas Harding swear you did?"

Mr Meurant's pale eyes bore into hers, as there was an audible gasp from the collegie members, and Rosina found her breath coming in quick, jerky gasps.

Rosina, though taken aback, looked empty of guile. "No sir. I loved him. What was between us was not a sin."

The flicker of surprise in his eyes looked genuine. "Your answer then, to all intents and purposes, is yes, mejuffrou. In the eyes of God, it was a sin. Our witness, Meneer Haas Maarten and Meneer Harding and one of the other men have sworn that you changed when you found out that Lieutenant Buckleigh no longer loved you, if he ever had. Is that so?"

She shook her head, her voice very faint with tension. "I – my feelings for Lieutenant Buckleigh never changed, sir. I just – I just felt very sad."

Mr Meurant tapped his snuffbox with impatient

113

fingers. "So sad that you took his life! In fact not so much sad as angry, furiously angry – a woman scorned, is that not so?" His bright eyes pierced her through his quizzing glass. "We have read the written depositions here from Meneer Haas Maarten, and the others from Field-Cornet van Reenen given to him verbally by the slaves and some of the men at L'Agulhas. You have heard that they all admit that it was easy for you to cut the throat of the Lieutenant, and then stab him several times, in the dead of night, with no one about, because he was asleep. All you had to do was to leave your own room which was next to his, and commit the deed before he or anyone else knew what was happening. If he had woken, he would not have been surprised to see you, and bending over him, you could easily have cut his throat." He paused, warming to his theme, and there was hardly a sound in the room.

"Then, the most damning evidence of all, was when Meneer Maarten found you beside the body, with your scissors stabbed into his heart. Now tell us the truth, Mejuffrou Webb. That was how you felt, was it not?" he suddenly roared. "You could not bear the thought of living without him. You knew he planned to leave, to return to his regiment as soon as he could, and you took his life on the eve of his departure, using your own sewing scissors – scissors only used by yourself?"

"No, sir! No!" There was a shocked silence. "It be not – it was not like that at all, sir! I – I've never killed anyone in my whole life!"

Mr Meurant's voice coldly penetrated the room. "But you lived such a lonely life, mejuffrou – never meeting handsome young men, especially not of Lieutenant Buckleigh's kind." He coughed. "And when he arrived at your doorstep so to speak, we have heard in the

114

depositions that you could not take your eyes off him; that you spent all your spare time with him – even in his bedchamber."

He turned his attention to the court. "What defence has the accused to offer us? We have all the evidence we need. Meneer Maarten, and the others have supplied it: this young woman had the strongest motive, the best chance to do it and she was found in the room with her scissors still in the body of the deceased."

The court was very silent now. Rosina's heart was growing colder and colder, then he turned his light eyes back to her, and barked, "Do you deny this, mejuffrou?"

A loud buzz of shocked excitement rose in the stifling hot room. Rosina's knees were shaking; her hands were clasping and unclasping themselves. Somehow she must make them understand that she was innocent. She must try to explain about it.

"No, sirs. Please listen to me. I could never do this terrible thing. I – I be only guilty of loving him too much. I – I was afraid to – I was afraid that my life – I could not bear to think he was going, yes. But there be nothing I did, please believe me – to – to – keep him back."

Mr Meurant's voice cut through her explanation, cool and crisp, and rounded with his Dutch accent: "It seems hardly possible, mejuffrou, that with such a display of feelings, such passion concerning the Lieutenant, you would have just let him walk away out of your life – your lonely, monotonous life – not after he had brought such new interest, such new amusement during those lonely weeks."

Rosina caught her breath sharply. "Can you not understand me? Sirs, I could not kill what I love! He be – was like my animals – my wounded animals. I could

115

never have harmed one hair on his head. I be – am telling you the truth, sirs. You must, you must believe me!"

Mr Meurant then opened a skin bag and brought something out which he placed on the table in front of her.

"These are your scissors are they not, Mejuffrou Webb? The scissors you always used for sewing? They were brought to us by Meneer Maarten, still soaked in the blood of the deceased."

Rosina's heart sank as she looked down at the scissors, now a rusty red with dried blood. They were the scissors Henry Mostyn had made for her, the ones she always used. She remembered now that they had not been in the body the second time she had gone back into Andrew's room, but in her deep distress at the time, she had been relieved not to see them again.

Mr Meurant stroked his bristling sidewhiskers and nodded as he took charge of the blood-stained scissors once more.

"Now, it is time, Mejuffrou, for you to make your defence."

Rosina did not know what she said. Nothing made sense to her anymore. She was completely bewildered as she described as well as she could, what had happened that night. When she had stammered to a halt, the judges declared the examination closed.

Mr Meurant and both the judges, Mr de Beer and Mr Bergh then put their heads together, consulting each other self-consciously, aware of everyone's eyes upon them. It was horrible to see the faint play of expression in their faces, as they discussed her as if she was not present. Then the clerk of the court rapped with the hammer and Mr Meurant and the judges rose, bowed and went out. They had decided to retire.

116

The air crackled with excited tension as the people outside restlessly tried to move about, rustling skirts and baskets of food. Inside the hot room, Rosina thought she was going to faint, but somehow she gained greater control of herself as the time passed. It was as if the worst had already happened and now she was reacting against the blow.

It was only twenty minutes, but to her it seemed like a year when Mr Meurant and the judges returned, and silence settled on the courtroom as they sat down. Then Mr Meurant stood up and addressed the court in Dutch, which was translated for her into English.

"We believe that the prisoner, Mejuffrou Webb was demented at the time of the crime. It seems clear from the evidence that it was she who murdered the Lieutenant in a moment of passionate madness, for she was present at the scene of the crime, with the murder weapon," he commented dryly, staring for a moment up at the massive yellow-wood roof beams.

Rosina stood quite still, not quite knowing how to hold herself before his verdict. After a moment her dark brown eyes met his, and she heard him say, "Just as she committed carnal sin with the Lieutenant in the secrecy of his bedchamber."

To Rosina's fevered imagination it seemed that everyone glanced towards her as he spoke. As he paused to collect his thoughts, someone sniggered loudly in the back of the room. She realised then, all of a sudden, with the greatest dread, that the pure love she had thought she had borne for Andrew and the relationship they had shared was, contrary to her own innocent ideas, dangerous to her case, that it had already prejudiced everyone against her. She was beginning to understand, with humiliation, that no one looked upon her love as

117

innocent and selfless, but as something sordid and ugly – and shameful. It was with deep and agonising shock that she realised that they looked at her as a wanton woman.

"We're not saying she is insane. We are saying that, in our opinion she was temporarily not herself, through grief and bitter disappointment. But, that she was only too aware of what she was doing at the time. It is our honest opinion that she is guilty of murdering Lieutenant Andrew Buckleigh, but as we have no power to pass the death sentence, the case is reserved for the full bench of the High Court of Justice in Cape Town, to be tried and where final sentence will be passed."

A sharp, desperate protest rose to her lips, but the clerk of the court rapped with his hammer and the trial was over. For now the landdrost and the judges were done with her. Silence hung like a wave for a moment, and then broke, and in the general buzz that rose throughout the room, she saw the judges glance at the clock. It was getting late and there were several other cases from an already overloaded schedule to hear. A court clerk was already beginning to copy down the notes he had made of the questions and her answers.

Even though she could say no more, there were still protests trembling on her lips. She had not understood everything that was said, but she knew they wanted her to hang for Andrew Buckleigh's death, and she was too unschooled in the ways of the world to defend herself. She could feel that everyone in the room thought she was guilty, and no matter what she said, she believed they would keep that opinion. Her mouth dry, her heart beating, she was hurried through the doorway, stumbling now, her hope destroyed, on and on, somehow, until they reached her cell and she fell onto the cot.

118

Chapter Fifteen

That was not the end of it. Ever since she had been taken back to the gaol, there had been shouts of abuse outside, in front of the gaoler's office. In the temporary lulls that followed, some disconnected words in Dutch were caught. "Whore . . . Woman of the devil . . . unclean . . . against God's word . . ."

The village was crowded with litigants and witnesses to go before the circuit judges, the gaol filled with prisoners, and the space left for traffic in the dusty road was only wide enough for one wagon at a time. The road was now crammed with people, milling about in front of the gaol.

Then someone threw a stone at the gaoler's office, and another followed, and another. A horseman came down the road, picking a slow way among the people, trying to quiet his horse which was nervous and restless, and at times almost unable to go forward. Inside the gaoler's office, the under-sheriff tried not be alarmed as the guards scurried backwards and forwards in an attempt to quieten the inmates, as outside the noise grew worse.

It went on intermittently for another day, and then, on the third night, Rosina was startled to hear the door of her cell unlocked, to reveal the under-sheriff, followed by Johannes and another guard. The under-sheriff was still recovering from the wound inflicted by the guard who had gone beserk, and limped across the threshold with a sour and agitated look. Johannes told her that she must collect her things for she was going under the cover of darkness to Cape Town with other prisoners to be tried by the High Court of Justice, it being too dangerous for her to stay in the village any longer. Word had been sent to Cape Town and Field-Cornet van Reenen would escort them as far as he could until they were met by the officer and troops sent by the Governor.

Rosina needed no urging, and after the initial surprise, quickly fastened up her quilt, and followed them out of the door. They were joined by a line of other shackled prisoners, and the ends of the heavy chains fastened to her wrists were handed to the under-sheriff, who grasped them in his vice like grip. With a gesture to follow, he led the procession of prisoners through the gaol and halted only when they reached the street outside. There was no moon that night, but here and there yellow flickers of light gleamed in the houses. A farmer stood ready with a wagon and twelve fine, beautiful oxen, with horns that spread from pole to pole, ready to be put to the wagon. The tent-flap was down at the back as she was lifted with her chains inside. In the dark, barren interior, she slumped into a corner on the hard, unyielding floor, to seek what comfort could be found with the other prisoners, of both sexes and mixed race. She fell into a light, uneasy doze as the inspanning began, and throughout it remained silent and hidden. Nor did she speak as with a lurch, the heavy wagon jolted on its secret way, escorted by the field-cornet and his six Hottentot soldiers. The hour was close to midnight, but Rosina could not guess how long the journey would be, or what it would be like. Glimpses of dark sky flitted across the

120

open square beyond the driver. They travelled up the winding wagon road beyond the outskirts of the village and as the oxen were urged into a faster pace, Rosina managed to brace herself against the jostling. Her tensed body relaxed only when the wagon slowed down a bit as it came to a stream, and there, far beyond the village, they outspanned and waited for the dawn.

After making a tolerable breakfast from a tea-chest in the wagon, they started again. The journey was far longer this time, on roads that were only tracks, barely discernible across the veld, made by travellers, hunters and a few farmers with laden wagons. Every so often, the tracks were little more than a space cleared of shrubs and plants by the passing and re-passing of wagons. The oxen were depastured along the way, and Rosina was hauled out by the chains with the other prisoners, giving her no opportunity to object or resist. For a brief moment she was crushed between two of the prisoners and gasped with pain as their elbows found her slender ribs. Gathering her chains into a long loop, she recognised that one of the prisoners was the former guard at the gaol – the one who had gone beserk and was now on his way to be tried for murder.

After getting over her initial shock, her eyes flickered away in the direction of the wide, open space around them, and for the first time in weeks she saw carpets of wild yellow daisies growing in profusion in the damp marshy places. A swift film of moisture filled her eyes at the beauty and freshness of the sight, and she turned away in deep embarrassment.

Through the hot, cloudless days, they crossed the Breede River valley, and with a fresh team of oxen from a nearby farm, jolted on to the precipitous Fransch Hoek Pass. Over the line of mountains, or above the

121

long stretches of plains, greyish brown Steppe buzzards soared, and the motionless specks of reddish-brown Rock Kestrels hovered looking for small mammals, lizards, insects or birds. After what seemed like years to her, they penetrated the formidable mountain barrier enclosing the Cape settlement at Eland's Kloof, in the Hottentots Holland range. On the steep, precipitous ascent, she dismounted with the others, ready for the long climb upwards. Here, where the road was very bad and the clay surface no more than seven feet wide in width, they were met by Sergeant Hannah, a ruddy faced Englishman with a strong West Country burr, and his troop of Hottentot soldiers descending the perpendicular, jutting rocks on horseback.

With their help, the wagon was pulled upwards. Rosina was horrified to see how the poor animals suffered, their sides streaming with blood from the knives their driver had brought. She learned to her dismay, that the whip was not thought enough on such occasions, so sharp knives cut the massive creatures, until bellowing and kicking, they pulled their almost impossible load. Finally they reached the summit.

Rosina, tired out from the long climb upwards, gazed about her at hill upon hill, mountain behind mountain as far as the eye could see, with here and there, a scarcely perceptible thin thread of a stream, like a silver eel, winding through the valleys. To her, who all her life had lived in the secluded settlement at Agulhas, shut in between the hill and the sea, there was something overpowering and intimidating in this vast expanse of earth and sky, this ruthless extravagance and breathtaking beauty of nature. She found in it a sense of her own insignificance, which daunted her.

Field-Cornet van Reenen and his soldiers bade them

farewell, and as they turned their horses around for the descent the way they had come, she felt a strange regret, for she had become used to the field-cornet's taciturn, yet solid presence, for all his suspicion of her.

The prisoners slowly followed the arduous path of the wagon down the mountainside. The track over the pass was so narrow and so steep that it seemed as if the wheels of the wagon and the oxen's hooves would plunge over the edge of the precipice if they took one false step and they would be hurled to their deaths. To reach the bottom of the descent took the prisoners about half an hour, where they found the wagon waiting, with the oxen ready. Hours later with a new team of oxen, and after shooting some partridges for supper, they left the small, stone toll-house on the mountainside of one of the passes and, rounding a gigantic shoulder of rock, outspanned for the night.

The shallow bowl of earth was filled with purple streaks of fiery yellow splintered the west, as Rosina warmed her manacled hands at the dung fire beside the wagon. The Dutch wagon driver from Swellendam filled a battered iron kettle from the nearby stream as the sergeant paced to and fro beside the oxen, the noisy Hottentots and the sullen, silent prisoners.

"How – how much longer is it – to – to Cape Town?" Rosina ventured as the man turned to face her. His eyes flickered down her worn and grimy clothes and curiously came to rest on her dusty face. An expression of disgust was all too evident on his face, which sent a spark of anger through her. She gave him a level stare, as he plucked at his lip, and looked across the clearing which stirred and quickened with the movements and voices of his small troop, then back at her.

"We're nearly there: over the next lot o' mountains

– not that it's goin' to help you none, ma'am. 'Tis but nearer to the moment of truth, is it not?" His ruddy face was suddenly smooth and without expression as he patted his musket, then turned to give an order to the Hottentots and the driver returning with the kettle.

Early the next morning it was on again, and on and on, until painfully bruised and physically drained by the continuous jolting along the deeply-rutted and stone-filled track, Rosina thought it would never end. The fresh load of cattle were so strong that they pulled the wagon with ease up ascents which she could not believe they could achieve. She was once more obliged to get out and climb the rest of the way with the other shackled prisoners, marvelling at the brilliant everlasting flowers, pink with black hearts that grew amongst the heath. The descent was a little easier, though still precipitous, and she was amazed at the way the oxen picked their way down the steep rocky inclines, managing to avoid hurting each other with their horns.

Wearily she climbed up into the wagon again, and soon they were plunging into a pathless sandy world, but covered high with evergreens, with every so often a buck skipping out of a corner, many of which they had already seen running over the mountains. After what seemed like years, the sergeant, riding alongside the wagon, suddenly called a halt.

"Eh, ma'am – you can come on out for a while and see Table Mountain!" he sternly rasped as he peered into the wagon.

"Me? Be you talkin' to me?"

"Yes, ma'am – now hurry up there, or you'll miss it." His scowl darkened as she pushed her way forward through the stinking, grimy mass of humanity packed into the wagon.

Rubbing her chafed wrists, she was pulled out of the wagon none too gently, not knowing what to expect. Once outside she leaned forward to gaze intently about her. Among the ramparts and chasms of a huge distant range, the sergeant pointed out a flat, high mountain rising above the rest. Its profile, against the brilliant blue sky, was that of an enormous table, whose top was covered with a heavy cloth of white cloud.

She stared ahead. There was something terrible in that fixed and ageless giant, dominating the place where she was going to be tried once more, and her fear increased.

They passed through a few turnpikes, following a spoor towards Salt River where the track became the main road into the Town. From Muizenberg on the coast, there were signposts and occasional roadside inns, which she was able to glimpse if she leaned well forward. They jolted through the small village of Wynberg with its military camp, running between high hedges, and skirted the dangerous shifting sands of the Cape flats, where in the treacherous swampy area the tracks of hippos in the black mire were hard baked by the sun. Then forking left they travelled along the base of the gigantic buttresses of Devil's Peak. It was here that Sergeant Hannah allowed her to climb out again and see the Town, spread out below them, before entering main street, the Heerengracht, whereupon he grudgingly lent her his spyglass.

Whatever she had expected, it had not been anything like what lay before her. Bone-weary and pain-wracked, she stared up at the great flat-topped grey, granite peaks of Table Mountain. The billowing white tablecloth was gone and the bare and rocky sides were visible towering over the wide streets of low, flat-roofed houses and

125

buildings. At one hundred and sixty-seven years old, the former Dutch refreshment station on the way to the East was by no means a collection of peasants' huts, but the largest place she had ever seen. Even in that lowest point of her life, the neatly laid out cluster of gabled, white-washed houses and buildings, the squares along dusty tree-lined streets with farms spreading up the slopes of the mountains where there was the shine of a river, were astonishingly beautiful.

Two broad roads, yellow with thick dust, ran before the brooding walls of the castle near the bay, dominating the right-hand flank of the town, which housed the garrison, with its cannons bristling at every corner, and the Union Jack flying proudly above the ramparts. Other narrower, winding streets ran along the bay and up towards Signal Hill on the Lion's Rump. The horizon to the sharp right was serrated with the Tygerberg mountains, undulating in the sun's heat. The sunlight danced on the crowded British men-o'-war and Indiamen and smaller craft at anchor in the bay, not Dutch boats as of old, nor most foreigners, since they were unwelcome for fear of the French.

"They be whale-fishin' down 'ere in the bay, ma'am," the sergeant said, pointing to a crowded spot in the bay, where the spout of a whale could be seen, surrounded by what seemed like hundreds of fishing smacks.

The Heerengracht, with its brick-walled canal chanelling the water from a stream running down the mountain and spanned by several attractive bridges, was thronged with people. The tops of the houses suddenly blazed as if a shower of gold-leaf had settled on the town, and the sea danced and glittered, the polished brasswork of the ships in the bay glowing like balls of fire, while the cotton sails of the fishing smacks and smaller craft glanced brightly in

126

the sun. It was all so alive and so vivid. Suddenly she was gripped by a powerful loneliness, feeling small and lost in this strange, bustling world, a feeling which sapped much of her dearly-needed confidence.

Then it was down into the Heerengracht where the air was filled with the smell of the sea, and a peculiar odour which came from the grease the Malay slave vendors used on their hair, as they walked passed with laden trays of fruit and vegetables suspended from bamboo poles carried across their shoulders. Slaves were everywhere and every colour from ebony to yellow, in their short jackets, red neckerchiefs and bare feet, as were the Mulatto freedwomen in bright cottons, gold pins in their hair, gold earrings, and wooden clogs called caparangs. Rosina could hear their chatter, not knowing that those who had belonged to the Dutch East India Company had been taken over by the British Government as a prize of war. She saw Green Market Square where the local farmers brought their vegetables and fruit, ostrich feathers and butter protected with large umbrellas. And she saw the British redcoats and bluecoats, bearded Dutch burghers in blue jackets and broad-brimmed hats, Germans, pigtailed Chinese and a few Americans from the neutral ships with close-cropped hair.

But despite these distractions she was horribly aware of her impending destination and ordeal. Her hands, still manacled at the wrists, grew cold in her lap. Her face became like stone, and she was lost in her tormenting fears as wagons of wood moved by, driven by Hottentots, eight or ten horses moving to the crack of whips, enveloping everyone with clouds of dust. The sound of flocks of noisy gulls sailed overhead, reminding her sharply and painfully of the gulls at Cape Agulhas. But as always, then came the image of Andrew

Buckleigh's lifeless face with the cruelly-slashed throat and mutilated body. It was scored into her brain, and nothing could force the image to flee.

The wagon threaded its way down towards the beach where there was only one jetty constructed of teak piles driven vertically into the sand in close proximity to the castle where redcoats exercised their horses on the parade ground opposite, and where a chattering crowd of slaves waited their turn at the pump near the large fountain, finally hoisting a yoke with its two full pails of water to their shoulders to take back to the household where they lived and worked. The place was still jammed-packed with wagons and people all greatly excited by the whale catching.

Just above the beach there was a fish market, a large rectangular square filled with people where the fish and the dead carcasses of slaughtered animals gave off a stench of putrefaction that made Rosina put the edge of her shawl to her face. Endlessly crying gulls circled over the butchers at their work in the Shambles, severing joint from joint so deftly, their sharp knives flashing in the sunlight beside the carcasses of slaughtered animals. They were passing close to the beach where the slime and refuse from the Town rotted, adding another foulness to the air.

Here, at the lower end of the Heerengracht were storehouses for timber, for casks, masts and other naval tackle, for wines and spirits, and in a low and damp position, stood the square two-storey gaol, one of the worst in the colony, its long, rectangular-windowed cells flagged with slate, its flat roof tiled.

The wagon drew to a shuddering halt, and moments later Sergeant Hannah was at the driver's seat, rapping his riding whip against the wooden sides.

128

"Out, you lot! Out!"

Rosina cringed as the driver dismounted. Everything in her rebelled. She had been pushed, shoved, goaded, and betrayed, and the only thing she wanted to do was to escape, flee, anywhere . . . anywhere away from this terrible place. But as two constables in high black top hats and cutaway blue coats, armed with muskets started hauling out the prisoners, she knew with a chilling feeling of doom that struck her to the bone, that she was caught, trapped; that there was no way out.

She dismounted awkwardly and stared about her, trying to collect her thoughts. Far off, well outside the bay, she could just see the masts of a British squadron, where it swung at anchor. Tiny specks of ships, minute in their present surroundings, and yet of such importance in the history of the world. A tall ship was making her stately entrance into the harbour, her sails catching the sunlight and enriching the ripples that reflected her, possibly the loveliest thing ever made by man.

For a transient moment, the sight of its majestic, graceful passage, and the rigid line of British ships caught her imagination, and briefly she thought of the brave warships blockading the coasts of Europe, and the thought of Britain and the people the squadrons guarded and fought for seemed for a frivolous moment, glamorous and romantic. Then she thought of Andrew Buckleigh as she had first seen him, dashing and wounded – one of the hundreds of redcoats defending the country where she was born.

She could still smell the butchers' shambles from where she stood, the bones and offal thrown out for the dogs who were scrambling and bickering over them, and the stench from the refuse from the outlet of the town's canals nearby, not far from the skeletons of many wrecks lying half-buried in the sand. Then, more from instinct than conscious will, she allowed herself to be hurried through the curious crowd of onlookers that had collected around the wagon, and passed a grotesquely fat turnkey struggling to his feet at the entrance, with wheezing breath.

There was a long wait in the dim, gloomy waiting room before each prisoner was called into the small, cramped office of the sheriff, where, even though it was day, two candles burned softly. For some reason, Sergeant Hannah hurried her through before the others. She held back a shiver of revulsion at the fetid stench that hung like an unseen cloud about the room.

At a table covered with papers, quills and ink, sat a corpulent red-faced man slowly and laboriously writing a letter. He lifted his eyes from the paper before him, and gazed at her with sudden sharpness. Very slowly, he motioned her forward. He was a giant of a man, broad-shouldered, with a full wide weather-beaten red face to match his size though his eyes were small and alert, like a bird's. There was a black coat covering his huge shoulders, and a quill in his restless fingers. But more than all these, she saw in the man the veiled accusation, already in his eyes, and instinctively knew, with deep dread in her heart, that his cold abruptness would not make life pleasant for her.

Chapter Sixteen

The day dragged out interminably and within the confines of the cell on the ground floor, one of those used for criminal prisoners of all ages, races and both sexes, Rosina could do nothing but await her trial. Outside she could hear the resounding salute of muskets as a British fleet left Table Bay. The remains of her morning meal of the monotonous rice and meat, was supplemented with vegetables from the fast-diminishing coins in her handkerchief dried on a trencher. She had been shocked to discover that every penny the prisoners had was extorted from them for small privileges. Those who could not pay were starved and neglected and in many cases, forgotten. She was also alarmed to learn that since the British had taken over from the Dutch, most prices of everything in the town had doubled, that her paper rixdollar was not worth its face value, that everyone preferred hard coin of any denomination, of which she now had very few left.

The shadow of the noose darkened the days that slipped by, and doubt and fear tortured her mind. It did not help to be told by one of the prisoners that sometimes instead of hanging, those who were found guilty were banished to Robben Island in the middle of the bay, and left to rot, forgotten.

She had no way of knowing when her trial would

be held, and she yearned to see the outside world again. She rubbed her hand across her grimy, sweaty face and then winced as her shabby appearance was brought painfully to mind. Where had the young Rosina gone? That innocent, generous child, so full of hope and expectations; with such infinite capacity for love? She was still struggling to contain her emotions as the heavy door of the cell was unlocked and thrown open.

Two Asiatic convict guards with drawn pistols came in and motioned her out. Pleased for any break in the boredom, she hastened to obey. She followed them out and down the narrow dimly lit corridor, their footsteps echoing on the stone floor while the lantern held by one of the guards cast eerie, flickering shadows around them. They reached a broader corridor from which two dark passages led in opposite directions; then her blood froze. From the dark, gaping mouth of the passage they had passed, came such a bellowing, shrieking chorus of hatred, that she started back in swift revulsion. The rumble of the voices was amplified by echoes. Underneath a torch stood a Hottentot guard, armed with a musket, a key dangling from his belt. Without a word he pulled open a low, arched door on squealing hinges and they entered the darkness of a wider passage.

Suddenly she was struck by an overwhelming fear. She thought it was the stench surrounding them, but it was something else, an evil in the air. Perhaps, she thought, wildly, they are taking me to my trial before the High Court . . . what else could it be?

She heard voices ahead, and somewhat wary of who they belonged to, Rosina made her way between the guards more cautiously. Finally they emerged into the sheriff's office which she remembered from the day of

132

her arrival. Then, unexpectedly, Jan la Motte's voice came through the open door.

"Here she is. Rosina – it has been too long."

In a moment Jan's great bulk filled the doorway as he came to greet her. Rosina's breath caught in her throat, her eyes wide with amazement, and for a moment the world seemed to stand on end, as her mind screamed that it was all a dream, and she would wake to find him gone.

Taking her arm, he led her toward the candlelight. "Rosina – I came as soon as I heard," he said gruffly. After a perceptible hesitation, his mobile face lined with worry, he continued, "I want to help you – in any way I can."

An inward cry surfaced to consciousness. "Oh, Meneer la Motte – I be so glad to see you! They – I be found guilty of murder, sir, by the circuit court— " here her voice faltered, and he looked into her haggard face closely, devastated to see the change in her since they had last met at Cape Agulhas. She had lost a lot of weight, and there were unshed tears in her fine dark eyes.

Spontaneously he grabbed her chained hands and held them firm, and somehow the feel of his warm hands, the living companionable substance of him, was like a balm.

"I know of someone, Rosina – a lawyer, a good one, the best. He is here, in the colony from England, where he is exploring our wild animals. *Ach*, I know that in this colony you have to make your own defence – but that is a mistake – it cannot be right for innocent people such as yourself. What do you know of the law?" He placed a protective arm about her thin shoulders, his immense size looming comfortingly in the small confines of the office and dwarfing the guards behind him.

"We will cheat the hangman of his fee, Rosina. I will talk with this Meneer Gerard. He has won some difficult

133

cases far away in England. I will ask him to speak to the Governor on your behalf – to let him defend you."

Rosina took up a corner of her shawl and tried to stop the tears. "Oh, Meneer – he can't do anything against the law – it be too strong against such as myself. Besides I have not much money."

Deep concern marked Jan's prematurely-lined and genial face. "You must not give up. Rosina. You have to get help of the cleverest kind. Meneer Wellesley Gerard is the best-qualified man around here. No one else has such a knowledge of the law, and from what I've heard his cleverness is near genius. He has money – his family are rich Jews. I'll go and see him, first thing tomorrow morning."

She stood, staring ahead, her thoughts and feelings in a blur. She had never known herself so divorced from reality, so disorientated. It was so good to see Jan again, to know that someone cared what happened to her in this mad, bustling, frightening world. But what could he do against the decision of the court? Nobody could help her now – she was beyond help of a human kind, and even God seemed so faraway and uncaring.

She grew anxious in those moments, and in desperation she tested the name that Jan had mentioned which to him was so full of promise: "Gerard. Mr Wellesley Gerard." No one could deny such a fine distinguished name. But could he help her? Would he agree to help one as poor and bereft as herself? She doubted that one such as he would show the slightest interest in her predicament.

Depression weighed her down once again, and she could not bear the thought of the filth and mess of the crowded, stinking, dark, airless cell, damp with salt and mildew to which she was imprisoned, with so many other criminals, and their wailing children, most of whom had been conceived and born in the gaol. She dreaded going

134

back in the long, uncomfortable steaming hot days when she could feel streams of sweat running beneath her clothes, and forming two little pools at the backs of her knees. The stress of this steamy, uncomfortable heat had helped her to reconcile herself to the discarding of her chemise, which no woman from fourteen upwards ever went without, but which no one appeared to notice nor to take the slightest interest.

She dreaded the nights lying in a torment of heat, although she wore only her thin dress, on the stone-flagged floor on a straw pallet pushed up against one wall, surrounded by the clanking of chains, the snores, the groans, the wracking coughs, the grunts of feverish lovemakings and the ravings of the demented and delirious whose poundings at the barred door added to the daily and nightly clamour.

Her straw pallet, as with the others, was never taken up and put into the sun to rid it of fleas, nor was the floor ever swept. She found she could not think or plan surrounded by such conditions. They jangled her nerves unbearably. No matter if she was awaiting execution, she could not bear the thought of passing another hour in that dirt and noise.

Every night she waited to hear the castle bell striking the hour until its final peal from half-past nine to ten recalling all the garrison men from wherever they might be in town. Every night was filled with restless images and nightmares, and she always woke up in a terrible sweat from a recurring nightmare in which she saw a limp form dangling from the gallows at the foot of the Lion's Rump, and knew it to be her own . . .

She would be still awake when dawn came up over the Hottentot Holland mountains, to hear the Watch spring his rattle, call the last hour of the night and return to

135

the red stone Town House, the meeting place of the Burgher Senate alongside Greenmarket Square. Then she would listen, above the noise in the cell, for the sounds of the slaves outside as they carried water in pails, hauled firewood, peddled fruit and vegetables, fresh-caught fish, sweetmeats; ran errands, carried bales of merchandise, from sunrise to sunset . . . to disappear for the night, all but the occasional one on his master's business, carrying a lantern and a pass.

Jan was looking at her, his brown hair tousled in the candlelight, his dark eyes bright and anxious. He felt an overwhelming desire to take her in his arms. Her pale face beckoned him, the large dark eyes fringed with jet black lashes made him ache. Her haunted beauty quickened his very soul, and he knew that but for a strange quirk of fate, she would not be here.

"We will win, Rosina. We will not give up, do you understand me? It has all been a terrible mistake." He withdrew a small bundle from beneath his coat.

"This is for your hunger. You must put on some weight, get the colour back in your cheeks."

A shadow of a smile crept across her lips as he placed the large napkin on the rough-hewn desk, and opened it to display a small loaf of freshly baked brown bread, a generous share of tangy cheese, and a silvered flask of wine.

"Jan . . ." She looked astonished, as she bent to smell the delicious odours.

You are the most wonderful and kind man I know, she thought. You are everything that's healthy and whole and honest. I could love you with all my heart.

She said, "'Tis wonderful. I'd almost forgotten such food exists!" Then she looked up and saw him watching her. "How is your small son, Jacques – and his grandmother?"

He smiled broadly, exposing his big strong teeth. "*Ach*, but Jacques, he grows so quickly that his grandmother cannot sew fast enough to keep up with his legs and arms! He is a nice boy, Rosina. When you are free again, you must meet him."

The shadows were back in her eyes, and he quickly continued, "His grandmother – well, she is not young anymore— "

The gaoler was back to indicate that time was up, and Jan nodded. But he remained, standing stock still, sudden indecision etching the deep furrows of his brow.

"'Tis all right, Jan." Rosina tried to smile, clutching the bundle of food to her breast, and when he still made no move to leave, she nodded. "'Tis safe enough. Nothing will happen to me until the trial."

The big man spoke finally, but only in Dutch to the gaoler. "Take care that not the smallest harm comes to Mejuffrou Webb. If it should, you have my earnest word you shall regret it."

The gaoler's gaze weighed the other's broad frame, and respectfully he nodded his agreement. Still wearing a worried look, Jan patted Rosina's arm and strode out of the office, hat in hand. For a moment she stood without moving, then as the guards moved forward to escort her back to the cell, she walked slowly out of the office.

They proceeded back along the dim, stinking corridors where rats scuttled away into the deeper shadows. Seeing Jan again had caused a wave of longing to rise in her heart: a homesickness for L'Agulhas, for her animals, a memory of Clara's slow, sing-song voice, of the kitchen with its spices and herbs and cooking pans, and of the stables where she fed the horses.

137

She liked the good smell of the animals, the moth-wing softness of the horses muzzles, the brushing of the hides and fur to a satiny lustre, the whinny and sounds of recognition that greeted her step. When she was with animals she forgot that she was isolated from the world, a nobody who was forgotten and largely unloved.

Finally, they arrived at the cell, and as she was hustled back into its dark, soulless, and despairing atmosphere, she turned to gaze with sorrow back along the corridor and freedom.

With a burst of fear she realized she was lost without the help of the man of whom Jan had spoken – this Wellesley Gerard. And if he refused, if the Governor refused to allow him to help her, she would be more alone than ever.

As she stepped inside the cell once more, the dank, stinking, seething air enveloped her, and she began to tremble. She could do nothing about it, and stood shivering for a while like a leaf.

That night she lay on the pallet, listening to the noise all about her from the other prisoners, to the sinister rustling of a rat somewhere close by, knowing that her pallet was alive with vermin, that they were everywhere. Every muscle and tendon was drawn and tight, her neck ached, her heart beat painfully and heavily, her thoughts leaping on each other's backs, to turn and leap again in a vast confusion, as if searching for the answer that would magically resolve the chaos into order and make her life safe again.

What she must do, she told herself, was sleep to gather strength for the ordeal ahead, were it only to bridge the hours that separated her from the moment when . . . oh, my God!

Chapter Seventeen

"Miss Webb? Miss Rosina Webb?"

Rosina rubbed her eyes, and saw in the gloom the silhouette of a man she did not recognise.

For a moment, disorientated by an urgent but sleepy walk from the cell in the presence of a warder and a constable, she was at a loss, then she recognised the small, square room lit by a candle, the narrow, slotted window. She was in the sheriff's office.

Behind the candle on the desk, stood two men. One, a long, narrow Dutch warder with a beaked nose, shoved the candlestick towards the edge of the desk. The constable stood in the doorway, as the other man came round from behind the desk, his shining top boots glinting in the light.

After a brief bow, he attempted to make out Rosina's form with two penetrating unusual eyes of an amber hue flecked with golden lights. Failing that, he spoke to the shadows that shrouded her.

"Wellesley Gerard, barrister of the Inner Temple, London, at your service, Miss Webb. I've just returned from a trip exploring your wonderful country and its wild life. A certain Mr la Motte, a man of some learning and good reputation, with whom I believe you are acquainted, has entreated me to appeal to the Governor to defend your case." His voice came smooth and deep, pleasant to her ears. It was easy-flowing, with something else as well: an amused mockery that seemed to scorn everything about the gaol.

She held to the shadows for a moment longer as she carefully studied this Wellesley Gerard. Her breath caught in her throat, as she found herself gazing at a man who was perhaps a year or two short of thirty, as he stood with the negligent ease of one accustomed to being obeyed almost from birth. The body displayed beneath an immaculate cravat of starched muslin in a series of beautiful folds, and where the elegant black caped driving-coat with a double row of silver buttons was parted, was long and lissome and proud of its masculinity. The head that crowned it was bared to the light, and haloed in a feathered cap of dark hair. But it was his face that caught her full attention. It was, without being precisely handsome, remarkably attractive, with a strong, straight, finely-boned nose, a well-shaped mouth and firm chin. There was a good deal of humour about his mouth, and his lively, animated eyes were extraordinarily intelligent, and were set under a pair of the most expressive thick dark brows.

She stared at him for long moments, seeming not to believe what she saw, then she moved forward and saw only a flicker of surprise in his eyes. She had changed almost unrecognisably. Her long black hair was filthy and knotted. Her sojourn in the semi-darkness of prison had changed her rosy complexion into an unhealthy chalky colour. Her cheeks were hollow and her eyes sunken and through the holes in her filthy clothes could be seen the thinness of her body, with the bones almost protruding here and there.

"I – I have no money— " she heard herself say, in a husky, troubled tone.

140

His glance swept her face, then he smiled slightly.

"Well, sir— " her voice faltered and she could not go on. The candlelight now shone full on her face, further illuminating the thin cheeks and the pallid skin, the tousled black hair.

Wellesley Gerard gave the warder a piercing glance, then announced "I will be safe enough, I am sure, with the treacherous Miss Webb, Mr Voss – and I am no threat to the lady, I assure you."

"Very good, Meneer – but only a short time, mind." With a disgruntled scowl, the warder nodded, then gestured the constable outside. "We will wait just outside the door."

Wellesley turned his attention to Rosina, with a faint sardonic smile playing on his lips. He walked over to the mildewed wall and tapped it slightly with one superbly shiny top boot, then turned and faced her, his thumbs in the pockets of his waistcoat.

"Well, Miss Webb, I have heard all about you: there are placards all over the town calling you a malicious murderess. In England the influential family of Andrew Buckleigh are pushing hard for your execution, and most other people are of the opinion that you killed the late Lieutenant. Did you?"

"No, sir, I did not sir!" Rosina looked across at him, and for a second, the flash of anger touched her eyes.

He nodded, folding his arms, and leaned against the desk, with his shining top boots nonchalantly crossed at the ankles before him. "I would like you to tell me everything that happened on that dreadful night in question. Everything, d'you hear? Whether you think it important or not."

Her jaw dropped as overwhelming disbelief numbed her brain. "But, sir, I've already said all I know before the circuit court. And they didn't believe me!" she choked out.

The expressive dark brows rose in an expression of mild surprise as he considered her suddenly flushed cheeks and the soft, trembling mouth. Then he smiled and became more gentle. "Do you want to lose your life so easily, Miss Webb?"

Rosina summoned her sapped confidence and lifted her quivering chin. "No, sir."

"Then, Miss Webb, do as I say and there could well be the chance that I am prepared to appeal to the Governor to take your case before the High Court of Justice. It is highly irregular, I might add, in this colony, as the defendant usually carries the burden of his or her own defence."

His tone was low but challenging and her blush returned quickly as she noticed for the first time how the short, heavy wisps of hair curled slightly about his face, accentuating the strong features. Indeed, there was a health and vitality about him that was almost mesmerizing. She wondered if she should trust him.

Drawing a deep, painful breath she began as he remained against the desk with folded arms, listening quietly as she went back over the terrible events that had led her to this situation.

"Go on," he drawled leisurely. His eyes met hers as she finished. "Now I want you to tell me everything that led to that night, from the moment you met Lieutenant Buckleigh."

She blushed to the roots of her hair as she pondered his question. "It be too painful, sir—

"Miss Webb, there may be something – anything that could change the entire picture of what happened. I have to know, if I agree to help you, and I can only decide

142

on what you tell me, and know to be the honest truth."
His brilliant eyes watched her steadily as she nodded,
and began, trying to remember everything, every detail,
every nuance of her feelings for Andrew.

When she had finished, he stared at the door for a
long while, ignoring the warning voice of the warder
intimating that time was up, then he raised his head.
"I believe you are innocent, Miss Webb. But I also
believe that you are shielding someone – that there is
more to it than what you have told me. I need to know
it all. But that is enough for tonight. Think over what I
have said."

Rosina stared at him, hardly able to believe that this
man believed she was innocent, when everyone else was
against her. She realized he was clever, as keen-minded
as anyone she knew; that he was no stranger to the
bewildering, frightening world of the law. He had a way
of speaking without sympathy, while giving incredible
comfort, and she warmed to him before her suspicions
returned.

"I could never pay you, and I'm sure you get paid
for what you do," she managed to say as she clenched
her hands tightly before her, the narrow aperture of the
window throwing a pattern across her face.

The candlelight gleamed in his eyes as he lightly
measured her. She stared straight into the unusual
amber eyes which dipped momentarily to acknowledge
the truth in her words.

"We shall discuss that in due time, Miss Webb. For
now, I must find out all I can about your case. This
colony is in a stage of great change now that we British
have taken over. It is still governed by Dutch law, with a
modicum of English, and much weight is given to written
deposition and, as I have said, on the accused bearing

143

the full burden of proof. But I intend to request that I defend you before the full bench of the High Court. There are ways and means, which need not trouble you, if one knows one's way around the law and the people who wield it."

He smiled slowly, as he left the desk. His face was now in the shadows, but his eyes seemed to glow, challenging her. "It will be an unusual request, and not easy to attain, but it is well worth the effort, I assure you." His gaze swelled enigmatically on her. "The whole of this colony's legal system needs to be overhauled. It is inadequate and dangerously backward. There is no press, except for the *Government Gazette* printed from the Castle, so there is nothing to expose the weaknesses of the system. There is no impartial court with jurymen, and the judges of the High Court. Often part-time amateurs are exposed, like the landdrosts and heemraden, to all kinds of social pressure, as I suspect was the case in the verdict against you. The only good departure from the Dutch system we have brought is the abolition of torture, but that too, will take time to bring about. It needs a voice, Miss Webb. I shall be that voice, and I shall raise other voices before I am silenced." He smiled sardonically. "Good night, Miss Webb, I shall see you as soon as I have news for you about your trial."

Then, as the warder and the constable entered the office, he left, with a flourishing bow.

Chapter Eighteen

The door of the cell crashed open, to admit the bright glare of summer light. Rubbing her eyes from the assault of the brightness to her eyes, Rosina looked up from her pallet, her dark hair undressed and tousled, the curls tumbling down her shoulders. There was a crescendo of noise around her. One of the warders stood before her, with a constable, and abruptly beckoned her to follow him. Pulling her shawl around her shoulders, she rose, wondering what to expect.

In the sheriff's office, she stared at Wellesley Gerard, dressed in a silver-grey caped driving-coat, a single pearl set simply in the intricate folds of his cravat, slim grey breeches which displayed the long, muscular length of his thighs, and shining top boots. He carried a grey beaver-brimmed hat, and a riding whip.

"Good day, Miss Webb," he said, bowing from the waist. "I apologise for the delay, but I have finally succeeded in obtaining special permission from the Governor to defend you. After many days of negotiation, I have also obtained a promise from Mr van de Greef, the President of the Council of Justice that the case will go before the High Court as soon as all preparations are completed, otherwise you could languish here for God knows how long. I must, however, ask you to be patient as it could take a few months before we are ready to go to court." The light from the open door caught the planes of his strong, attractive face as he paced up and down before coming to stop before her.

For a moment his clever eyes assessed her, then, after disposing of the driving-coat, he threw his hat and whip on the desk, and pulled out a chair, urging her to sit down. It was musty and damp in the office, which showed signs of neglect: wild weather and salt air had already done its damage, and there were damp stains on the ceiling and a strong smell of mildew.

"Now let's get down to the business in hand. I sat up most of the week going through all the evidence against you. It seems to me, that the circuit court has failed you miserably. It would be quite possible for you to die, the victim of a legal system so backward and inadequate and so clogged with a backlog of cases to be cleared that the question of whether or not you murdered Lieutenant Buckleigh has become a secondary consideration. Under the present system, the Court seems more concerned with finality than fairness, they are so frustrated by the mounds of cases that the circuit court brings into being." His eyes sparkled and flamed suddenly with enthusiasm, as he set down on the table, the bundle of papers he had pulled from a leather folder.

"These are copies of the depositions, Miss Webb. The case is filled with the kinds of errors that make a review of the legal system vital. There is a suspicion that the trial may have been tainted by a biased court, bowing to social pressure of the townsfolk, that you made blunders through sheer ignorance, that someone else may have committed the crime. In a sense the most important clues may be the ones that are missing. I want you to help me fill them in."

He turned his head to look down at the papers for a second, and at the sight of his profile against the light from the window, an image rose unbidden in her mind of him commanding a battery of guns, her at his side. A red flush of colour brightened her cheeks, and she became acutely aware of her own unkempt appearance.

As he lifted his head, she wrung her hands in anguish and hurriedly said in a voice little above a whisper, "I will try, sir, though memories become false after so many months."

"That is true," he agreed, "But you must help me, if we are to win this case; there just isn't any way round it, painful as it will be." He paused, studying her, then drew a deep breath. "Do you understand just how easy it will be for them to hang you, Rosina?" His intense gaze seared her, as he used her name for the first time. "You were the only one there, with the murder weapon. They are clamouring for your death, dear girl: the Buckleigh family are pushing hard to punish the most likely culprit – which is unfortunately yourself, and they have powerful influence in the Government."

Rosina's face visibly paled, and she lowered her gaze as she struggled to maintain her composure, but her tone bore the pain his words inflicted. "Yes, sir, I be – I am aware of that. 'Tis just that – that – there's nothin' more for me to tell."

"I don't think that is strictly true. As I said before, I think you are shielding someone – or some others," he said quietly, his eyes searching her for some sign of guilt. "I think there was another reason why Lieutenant Buckleigh was killed, and it wasn't because he was leaving either you or the settlement. I think there was another far more dangerous reason, that the murderer was not a grief-stricken and jilted young woman."

147

Rosina's face flushed dark crimson, and her eyes snapped dark sparks. "Mister Gerard! That is not true! There was no one— " but Wellesley Gerard gave her no pause. Leaning against the desk, he said, "No one? Are you sure? What is it that you are afraid of? Or who, is more like it. Who is it that you fear so greatly that you will even go to the hangman to protect?"

Her hand trembled as she put it up to her face. "Sir – it is – there is no one." Her voice was ragged and tight – "all I know is I found Andrew there, dead. I had nothing to do with his murder, sir – and I don't know how my scissors got there— "

She could not finish, but he saw her tears as he looked at her in surprise.

"I do believe that you are not on trial because some witness claimed to see you murder Buckleigh, or because someone saw you take your scissors from the sewing box on that fateful night. The case against you is built solely on what we call circumstantial evidence: your presence at the scene, your scissors in the body, and on someone's notion that you had a plausible motive. The prosecution has offered no eye-witnesses, except this Mr Maarten, and there is little real proof to support his scenario because he arrived after the fact. And, most shocking of all is that there was evidence never presented by you because of your total ignorance of the legal system, which I went to great lengths to explain to His Excellency, Sir John Cradock. The case was inadequately prepared, and this we must remedy at once if we are to win."

He pursed his lips for a second, then smiled faintly into her eyes. "I suspect you know more about the circumstances surrounding the death than you are admitting, and which no one bothered to find out.

Was the Lieutenant a threat to anyone? Did he know something he shouldn't have known? Had he made any enemies at the settlement, among the men for some reason?"

Rosina had listened with mixed feelings. She was amazed, at once delighted that she should find so unexpectedly such a clever defence, and sorry that he should have discovered her inner fears so quickly. For a moment she was unable to speak as she struggled to control her shaking, as she saw again Andrew's angry and distraught face on the night of old Sam Leach's murder.

"Nothing will happen to you, Rosina, if you tell me the truth." He paused, no longer smiling. "Do not fear. On that you have my word."

Rosina stared at the paper-littered desk, considering for the first time the implications of what he had asked.

The warder returned, with the constable to take her back to her cell. She was suddenly aware of a sharp silence. She looked up and saw Wellesley regarding her. He frowned. "I have arranged for you to be moved to a cell on your own. Don't worry about how it was done. Suffice it to say, it has been taken care of. You will be taken there directly, where I shall visit you tomorrow. You and I will show up the dangerous weaknesses in the system here, Rosina. We will fight to bring about a more just one; one that is modelled more closely on that of Britain."

There was something infectious, something inspiring, about the notion of showing up an inadequate system, of fighting to save poor, defenceless souls from injustice. But after a moment's excitement, Rosina put the alluring vision aside. She was a victim of that system herself, a living, breathing victim, not a showpiece.

She raised her head conscious of some challenge – not only from this smart, debonair lawyer, but also from the circumstances of the case now rearing itself in other people's minds as well as her own. The thought welled up suddenly in her that this man was using her for all his fine talk of believing she was innocent. She suddenly pulled her shawl tighter about her shoulders, her eyes took on an unfamiliar chilling hue, and her lips stiffened slightly. "Mr Gerard, sir, ever since I can remember everyone – everyone has been giving me orders, telling me what to do. And now, there's you telling me I'm to be moved again, without one thought as to what I think. 'Tis as if I am not a person who matters – as if – as if I am a dumb animal with not one thought or feeling in my head – like the slaves – prisoners to their masters in mind and body!"

He raised his brows and, tapping the desk lightly with his riding whip, said crisply, "Do you want to stay in that rat-infested, lice-ridden cell, Miss Webb? No member of the High Court is going to believe the word of a skinny, unkempt, lice-ridden slip of a girl who cannot explain herself clearly and behaves as if she's guilty because she doesn't know any better."

He strolled forward until he stood immediately before her, where he stood looking down at her with a faintly sardonic smile. "Well – do you?"

She stood rigid and silent, staring doggedly up into his face, wanting to protest, to even beat him with her fists for the unflattering things he said about her, but she stayed inert, unmoving as he watched the quick flush of anger recede from her face, and saw the weary lines about the fine and changeful eyes, the damp, matted streaks of hair, and the frown between the brows in a face that though young, had recently lost its innocence and had acquired painful experience in its place.

For fully a minute she could not trust herself to speak. "You be – are only helping me 'cos you want to use me to show up the system!" she said sharply, drawing herself up to her full, slim height. "You, sir, be – are not one jot interested in me for myself! You care not if I hang if it don't – doesn't help your cause, and that's the truth of it."

Hunching up the high olive-green superfine collar of his coat, he regarded her intently, conscious of her new stance, and the unfamiliar conviction in her low, husky voice, then he shook his head. "You will have to listen to me, Rosina, in certain matters, and trust me. I have requested a delousing session for you this very day. And there'll be hell to pay if that is not attended to – whether you like it or not. I have ordered a cot and a table and a tutor to improve your speech and the understanding of what faces you, for at the end of this trial, you will have to speak in your own defence. Whatever you like to think of me, you have to impress the full bench of the High Court that you could never have stooped to such a low, heinous crime as murder. Your tutor, a Mr Thomas Berringer, will present himself at this prison every morning until my return to Cape Town."

Rosina lifted her chin defiantly. "Be you goin' away then, sir?"

"I am about to journey to Cape Agulhas," he remarked casually as he picked up his hat from the desk. "It will take several weeks, but I will see and question everyone while I am there. And I mean everyone, Rosina."

His meaning was obvious.

151

"'Tis better if you don't go there, sir. There won't be anything there to help you any— " she burst out, then checked herself. But it was too late. He had seen her haggard, terrified expression; as if she had seen a nightmare.

"Why, Rosina? Why mustn't I go there?"

She was so distressed that she stood there, trying to get back her breath, watching a spider crawling up its web in a corner of the windowpane. He waited, then she glanced furiously at him, and finally said stiffly: "I can see your mind is set on it, sir – so there's nothin for me t'say."

She was still distraught, but her face was calm now, almost serene, her eyes expressed no more distress, no emotion at all. His attempt to question her further met with no response. Then she looked at him with a hostile expression he had never seen before and said, "There be – is nothing more to be said, sir."

He bent her a cool, appraising gaze, and with a light bow, departed, as the warder and the constable came forward to escort her to her new cell.

Chapter Nineteen

Rosina was taken to a small cell on the second floor with a barred window high up in the wall. It was not long afterwards that the warder ushered in two constables with a plain table and chair, and a Malay slave woman who followed, carrying a large tray filled with covered dishes and a goblet from the George Hotel, known by the well-travelled for its renowned turtle soup.

She stared at the table, trembling with bewilderment as the tureen of hot turtle soup was revealed, the aroma filling the stale air with delicious scents and far off memories of another life. The warder motioned her to a seat, and gestured the woman to serve the soup, on the orders of Mr Wellesley Gerard, the esteemed barrister from London, who had left Cape Town for the Overberg.

Self-consciously Rosina sat down, and after the first few tentative mouthfuls under his watchful eye, she began to relax in the almost forgotten pleasure of well-cooked dishes: after the soup, mutton stew, a wooden platter with a brown loaf of bread and a mounded dish of butter. There was a slice of pigeon pie, vegetables cooked with spices, and late-summer fruits. She savoured every mouthful of as much as she could eat, not knowing when she would eat so well again, as in the silence the slave poured Madeira wine. The sound of the pouring was loud and musical in the quiet, as thin rays of sunlight pierced the falling column of liquid and lit it up so that it resembled bright blood . . .

The table was finally cleared away and the delousing session was carried out. Her hair was thoroughly washed and cropped as short as a boy, her clothes burned and a new set presented, again at the orders of Gerard. For all her resentment of the barrister, she found herself clean, for the first time since her departure from Cape Agulhas, and felt once more the thrill of putting on a fresh clean dress on a fresh clean body. Later, Thomas Berringer, a stout, rosy-faced man, presented himself for her first English lesson. At first, she was embarrassed and not a little angry by what she considered Wellesley's deception; by all the attention and fuss, but soon her natural curiosity and hunger for knowledge asserted itself and she found the lessons interesting, the books he brought her to read, a challenge and, with it experienced a small flare of hope.

From him she learned that Gerard was the second child of Jacob Gerard, a wealthy Jew of European extraction whose family was forced to flee their own country generations back. They had assumed the name Gerard on their arrival in England. Jacob, a quiet, scholarly man had a natural brilliance which led him into the literary field, one of his works becoming a classic. He had never taken his Judaism seriously and after a quarrel with the Elders of the synagogue in Wellesley's early youth, he had resigned, without becoming a Christian. Soon afterwards however, his four children were baptized into the Anglican Church, a change which had a profound effect on Wellesley's career, especially as he had his eye on politics, and Jews were not admitted into Parliament. She learned that the importance of the Gerard family had been established by Wellesley's great-grandfather, who had gained a fortune through the straw bonnet trade; that Wellesley had lived all his life in houses whose very stones were historic. He was a brilliant barrister, and an intense and forceful orator who had already won several difficult cases in England. He had travelled extensively in Europe and the Middle East, and was enjoying a long holiday researching the wildlife in the colony. Mr Berringer added, with a dry smile that Wellesley was very much admired by many of the society ladies back in England.

He carefully explained to her that it was an accepted procedure in the colony to accept written depositions, which Wellesley Gerard found to be inadequate, especially from those who could not read or write, and could possibly sign some falsehood. In criminal trials there was no jury as in England, and many of those involved with the law were not qualified to do so: a mere reading-up of the law was, at present the open door to working with it.

Rosina was silent for a moment, her eyes smouldering at the recollection of her last interview with Gerard. "But, with respect, sir, why must Mr Gerard use my case as – as some kind of example to show up the weaknesses of the system? Does he not care about my feelings at all? From what I can see, he's only interested in winning for his own glory. If he fails, well, then – it won't bother him over-much."

Mr Berringer poked the floor with his long malacca stick. "That is not altogether true, my dear young woman. Wellesley Gerard is well aware of the consequences of losing your case. He is not without deeper feelings, I assure you. But what can be wrong with wanting, at the same time, to show up the very weaknesses that have caused your situation in the first place? If he can succeed in doing that, he can succeed in saving your life." He walked across the cell, and standing on tiptoe, tried to see out of the small barred window. He turned back to see her reaction to his words.

Rosina gazed ahead, trying to think. Two vertical lines showed between her coal-black brows. She sought in her mind all she could remember Wellesley saying about the legal system, but not remembering much. Her soul was pained with the meagre knowledge that there was so much heavy machinery against her in the present system, that public opinion, which could easily sway those in the Council of Justice was very much against her, backed by the solid weight of damnation from the Buckleigh family. Berringer saw the struggle on her face.

"It is a very serious problem, isn't it?" he said.

The question was a disquieting one. Her immature feelings of hope were subsiding. She felt coldly depressed at the weight of so much against her. "Yes, sir, it is. But, what is to be done?"

"With Wellesley Gerard you have one of the finest legal brains in England, my dear. Never fear, he'll find a way, if there is one to be found." For a second his face was sombre, then he smiled quickly. "Even though the standards of professional competence in the legal field here are deplorable, and even though, of the members of the Court of Justice, only the President, Mr van de Greef has been overseas for legal education, I still believe Mr Gerard can do something. He intends to show up these defects. But you have to help him by telling him everything you know."

Rosina had been accustomed all her life to follow the

guidance of others – especially Captain Skewthorn. But for the first time in her life, she was having to think for herself now. It was not easy, this forming of her own judgments, especially when it involved making an estimate of a man's character and honesty – a man in whose hands her life now lay. She stared at Mr Berringer's rosy, lined face with its dome of wispy sandy hair, and he, conscious of her scrutiny, turned away uneasily.

Her mind was a whirlpool of thoughts; of loyalties torn every which way. But resolve was beginning to harden her heart. It was not long before a slow resentment against Captain Skewthorn and the men began to inflame her as she sat in the dank, quiet cell with her tutor. She finally allowed herself to admit that she would not be here if it had not been for the wicked deeds committed by the Captain and his men – the knowledge of which had brought about the deaths of old Samuel Leach and then, poor Andrew. It was this which had brought her to the brink of an unfair death, and not one of them, not even the Captain had come to her aid.

All sorts of vague memories were stirring in her mind. She told herself that they would have worse than her death on their souls – that they were cruel and merciless to transport slaves – many of whom had died before and after captivity. Yes, she told herself she *would* have to trust Mr Wellesley Gerard. He was her best hope.

She fought the loneliness of her cell while Gerard was away, coming face to face with time itself when there was nothing more terrifying than to be alone with sheer time, and for weeks she struggled to keep her pride and her sanity. At Gerard's orders, the table now held a pitcher of milk and plates of food from the George Hotel every day, but apart from Thomas Berringer, there was no one else to talk to. Soon the damp and stale cell became like a small universe suspended in time and space, and she could no longer vouch that a world existed beyond the prison walls, where slaves were still sold in Greenmarket Square, plays were held in the Theatre in town, and where even further afield, so Mr Berringer had informed her, Napoleon had been disastrously defeated in Russia where his army had been dying on its feet long before it reached Moscow, where hunger and disease had thinned its ranks as it retreated ignominiously back across the desolate plains. Now British ships of the line ruthlessly tightened their stranglehold about continental ports, and Wellington in Spain threatened France.

Life was going on all around her, yet she was not a part of it. It was a torture. She found the silence inside almost unendurable; her life had been spent surrounded by others, by being busy for hours on end; being free to roam the small inlets and dabble in the rock pools, tend the animals and climb the hill. Now she was effectively cut off from all communication with the world except through Mr Berringer and Wellesley Gerard. And she was frightened. She was panicky with the desire to get away, and in her panic she plunged into the books Mr Berringer brought, for it was her closest link with Wellesley Gerard and that outside world at the moment. She wondered what Mr Gerard had found out . . . would he change his mind when he returned, believing he could no longer prove her innocent? Would he leave her life as everyone else had?

Before climbing on the cot each night, she knelt down, her head on the blanket and tried to beg God to help her, to fill her with strength and determination. But the words would not come; there was only the image of the dark gallows, and it filled her with a fear the like of which she had never known. She wanted most passionately to live.

She thought again and again of the dead Andrew. She resolved also, if she survived, to avenge his death. And lastly each night, she thought of Wellesley Gerard's tall, lean immaculately dressed figure, his clever, penetrating eyes.

She thought of the play of light and shade on his attractive, strong-boned face when they had last met. And with that shifting pattern in her mind's eye she finally fell asleep, utterly worn out.

Chapter Twenty

It was the beginning of winter. North-western gales howled through the town and battered against the walls of the prison, driving everyone indoors. Heavy rain turned the streets to churning mud. The bay was lashed by storms; the mountain was bleak with cloud. One night, as the British fleet lay at anchor, a north wind came up, and at daylight veered viciously to the west. The guards coming in with the morning meal told Rosina how the ships keels had plunged and reared during the storm, and above the clamour of the wind she could hear a boom and a throb as guns at sea fired signals of distress.

She remembered other nights of disaster at Cape Agulhas, when all that could be done for those in peril on the sea was the lighting of pitch hoops and the kindling of bonfires, to guide the survivors to safety. That night she learned that the ships were helpless, that every cable had been torn from its anchor, and by midnight no lights had been left at sea.

Next morning one of the guards maliciously told her that seven tall ships of the line lay spent and broken on the sands, mutilated parts tossing and drifting on the waves, the beach strewn with cargo. Rosina shuddered as the guard described with relish how four men who had been found stealing wreckage had been hanged, that they had been strung up in turn on the gallows raised at the water's edge, to kick and writhe for an agonising moment and then dangle limp, for the gulls to peck at, until they fell apart.

Rosina immediately set her mind and with controlled cool deliberation turned her back to the man. She soon turned back around, however, as she heard a familiar voice coming towards her cell. Her heart leapt as Wellesley Gerard strode inside the cell, which was now warmed by a small stove, though the chill of the day still soaked in.

"Damn, Rosina!" he said, with a bow, as the cell door was closed. Rivulets of rain trickled from the beaver-brimmed hat in his hand as he walked forward, a dripping greatcoat whipping about his boot tops. "They've cut your hair! You look unrecognisable, dear girl – it will grow soon, won't it?"

She put down the broom she had requested against the wall, and stood staring up at him, her short, cropped dark hair tousled about her head.

"It was the lice. There was nothing else they could do."

"Well, you've put on a little weight. But that hair! What are we going to do about it? You can't go to court looking like a shorn sheep, now can you?"

Rosina could not help smiling mischievously. "It'll grow, sir – never to worry. But, meanwhile – at the time of my trial – it can be hidden 'neath a bonnet, wouldn't you say?"

He looked at her, smiling, "Tis good to see you still have some humour left, even in these grim walls. Besides, it looks rather fetching – different. Now let me bring you up to date with my findings, such as they are."

She let out her breath in a rush as his amused, curving lips seemed to draw her closer, and nervously she stepped backward as if burned by the intensity of his eyes. He did not appear to notice as, divested of his greatcoat, he proceeded to present the facts as economically as possible.

Rosina sat listening with brave composure. Most of the legal details she could not grasp. But her resentment at her situation and determination to seek justice were in full flood. Her battle had been fought during the long weeks of Gerard's absence: she had shaken herself free, and made up her mind that just as he was using her to prove points, she would use him to achieve revenge for Andrew's death and to gain her own freedom.

"Captain Skewthorn and most of his men were still away at sea," Gerard continued. "But I managed to find this Haas Maarten skulking in a farmhouse near Mossel Bay, and force some of the truth out of him."

Rosina looked at him, startled. "You found Maarten? But 'twas he who accused me . . ."

"I know – but it seems that he was upset about the death of an old seaman – Samuel Leach, who was stabbed in the barn. He suspected Andrew Buckleigh of the murder because Buckleigh had apparently been with the old man earlier. He also saw you with Buckleigh near the barn later, when two of the men had a fight. Is that so?"

His eyes were steady and intent, his face concentrated; his mouth unsmiling, and she suddenly felt drained of all strength. She had managed to remain calm and detached up until then; now she felt all that suppressed emotion overwhelm her. She closed her eyes in prayer for strength, protection. When she opened them, he

162

gave no other sign of having studied her than a faint curl of his lips.

Though Rosina had now decided on her course of action, she had spent all her life – until recent months – under the overriding influence of Captain Skewthorn. He had not merely been a man, but also the leader of the settlement – the only home she had known and the powerful captain of an armed ship. He had therefore had the right to order and organise the lives of those under him, Rosina included. She had always abided by his judgment, until she had met Andrew. But now she had to find the courage to go against the Captain: she was consumed by a fever for action to avenge Andrew's murder, and to save herself from also dying an unjust death . . .

"Yes, I was there with Andrew. But he had nothing to do with old Sam's murder. He was most angry when he discovered the old man was dead. His only reason for being near the barn later was to try to discover who the culprit was. I went to help him, that's all."

Gerard's eyes were on her, silently assessing her explanation. Then he shrugged, taking his time. "Haas Maarten believed that Buckleigh had the death to hide, and that you were helping him to cover it up. Though when asked, he couldn't come up with a reason as to why Buckleigh would have wanted the old man dead."

She looked full at him, and took a deep breath. "That is not how it was, sir – not at all. Old Sam was killed because he told Andrew Buckleigh about the Captain's smuggling of slaves— " Rosina bit her lip. This was the moment of truth. "And p'rhaps because of – of the danger that Andrew would talk when he left. But Andrew never killed the old man. As you say, what reason would he have?"

163

Her unusually fierce dark eyes met his cool amber ones in a long look that spoke volumes, then he nodded his head. "Yes, yes, I know all about the slave smuggling. I found that out at Cape Agulhas, and I saw Struisbaai where the brig is careened and caulked and anchored, out of sight." He paused, then continued, "Do you think then, that the same person committed both murders?"

Rosina sighed, clenching her hands tightly in her lap, her brain a battleground of memories. "I don't know, sir – but it had crossed my mind."

She was suddenly aware of a short silence, and looked up to find him looking at her quizzically. "Then why do you think that the first body was buried quickly in the middle of the night, Buckleigh's body was left in his bed until the following morning? Do you think that perhaps it could have been to make all the evidence of the second murder point to you? Do you think whoever it was, intentionally used your scissors so that it would look as if you had done it?"

Rosina pursed her lips, suddenly frozen with new shock and fear. Whatever happened, she would need all her strength and nerve, she could see that. All of a sudden she found herself fighting for air. "I – I never thought of that, sir – I don't know who would do such a thing to an innocent person."

He paced up and down again. "But it is a possibility, is it not? Someone so afraid of being found out, that he would do anything – even throw suspicion on an innocent victim to save himself?" He suddenly whirled about and faced her, his eyes narrowed into slits of concentration. "Who do you think would be the most likely to do that, Rosina?"

Rosina sat up, aghast and white. She thought of Robert Blaine's sneering, contemptuous face, and his bitterness when he discovered Andrew's body. She thought of Israel Wilkins and his crafty eyes, and the squint-eyed Abraham Dance, the ship's doctor Makepeace Trelawney, mute and deformed Henry Mostyn, old Tom Harding – but they had all been horrified and angry when Andrew's body was found. They had all thought she had done it – except Haas Maarten: it had been he who had run away so suddenly with the story that she had committed the murder . . .

Her haggard face whitened with anger. "The only one I can think of – the only one – is Maarten, sir. He'd been watching me for weeks— "

Wellesley stopped pacing. "You think that possibly he left the settlement and threw the suspicion on you, to cover himself?" He spoke in a strange voice, his eyes brilliant once more. "He was entering the deceased's room, wasn't he, when he saw you. Why did he come in just then? Why was he there at all? No one else seems to have been there."

There was a long silence, as they stared at each other, the elegant, sophisticated and educated man from a background of wealth and accomplishment and the young woman, haggard and drawn from months of imprisonment, alone and condemned.

"But what about the others, Rosina? We must not jump to conclusions to, relying also on circumstantial evidence. Those smugglers and pirates – they are *all* ruthless and cruel, even though you've known most of them all your life." There was a short silence, then he resumed, "Now, at the time of Samuel Leach's death, not all of the men were in Agulhas, am I right? Fine. Now we're getting somewhere, narrowing the gaps. Give me a list of the names of those who were there when both men were killed."

165

Rosina made a gesture of resignation. "Well, there was old Tom Harding, and Henry Mostyn – but he – he could never have done it. Then there was Maarten and . . ." she listed several others, ". . . and the slaves – oh, yes, and there was Israel Wilkins, he stayed behind 'cos of fever."

He looked at her with a quizzing interest. "It could've been one of them, but there again, it could have been two separate murders committed by two different persons. We mustn't overlook that possibility and leave someone, possibly a guilty party out."

She stood up suddenly, her hands clenched at her sides, and took a step forward. "One of them killed Andrew, and p'raps old Sam too. He has also been involved in taking fellow human beings and selling them to strangers. I should not be made to suffer when someone else is guilty – someone who does not care whether I live or die. That man must be brought to justice. You must see that it is done, Mr Gerard."

Without thinking, she put her hand on his arm with a pleading gesture. Gerard immediately covered that thin, pale hand with his own strong fingers, and pressed it.

"I shall do all in my power to see that it is done, Rosina – for that is what is needed to set you free." Then he kissed her hand, and left in a swirl of dark cloak and sandalwood.

Chapter Twenty-One

Wellesley Gerard's mind was already hard at work on his new strategy, busily anticipating the time soon to come when he would escort Rosina before the High Court of Justice. There were long memorials written between him and the President, Mr van de Greef concerning the trial, and Mr van de Greef, in consultation with the Governor, had finally agreed to the calling of certain prosecution witnesses, whom Wellesley could cross-examine.

Never before had such a trial taken place in the colony, and it became the talk of the easy-going town. The ships might still bring news of Napoleon's defeats and the growing success of the British blockade, but the news paled as placards appeared everywhere, about the impending trial. It was discussed during the spring and early summer evenings in the local habit of sitting with wine, coffee and konfyts in the manor houses on the mountain slopes, on the shaded high stoeps of the solid houses of the town, with their teak-framed windows and white walls. It was gossiped about during the day along the unpaved, dusty Heerengracht, on the Parade where redcoats exercised their horses, and the townsfolk walked; before the massive walls of the castle, in the shops, and even among the slaves collecting water at the pump in Greenmarket Square, or at the fountain on the Parade.

Interest was heightened at the procession for the public execution of the Swellendam guard who had gone beserk, and many said that the next one would be that of the white murderess.

Rosina closed her ears as she heard the beat of the drums draped in black cloth, as the unfortunate man was marched from the gaol to Gallows Hill, at the foot of the Lion's Rump, his limp form left dangling on the gallows, to show the power of the law.

Justice, in a colony in transition between the old Dutch rule and that of the British was vengeful. Although the second British occupation had begun in 1806, formal cession to Britain had occurred only in 1814, and the system of Roman-Dutch law had not been immediately replaced. It was into this transition that Rosina's trial emerged; into the glaring hostility of public opinion in a court that was not independent, and where favoured individuals were appointed as judges, able to continue their former occupations.

Even although Jan la Motte was now allowed at intervals to visit her briefly, and bring her food and other small comforts, the days were still terrible for Rosina. There were frightening days when she felt her resolution waver, so that she clung mentally and emotionally to Jan with a new urgency, and he, marvellously understood, and soothed and comforted her.

There was more stress due to the fact that the trial was delayed, owing to the difficulty of bringing key witnesses – Captain Skewthorn and most of his crew – to the town, and exacerbated by the departure of Sir John Cradock and the arrival of the new Governor, Lord Charles Somerset, in April 1814.

Under a serene autumn sky, Rosina could hear the bells ringing as the new Governor made his oath of allegiance. The trumpets sounded then the musket salvoes fired, as did the cannons from the castle ramparts and from the ships at anchor. And it was so still that evening that she could hear the thin drift of music from the castle where the new governorship was being celebrated, and across the water, the note of a flute, from one of the ships, where the harbour's blackness was pricked by the lanterns of anchored ships.

During those hours she was constantly thinking, sometimes with hope, but sometimes with terror, of her trial; moods that every now and then she wanted to confess to Wellesley Gerard. But then she shrank from confiding in him. To tell him her fears might make him lose faith in her. On the other hand, how could she endure any longer her anguished hopes, her terrible fears that it all might go so dreadfully wrong, and her deepest sense of outrage at the injustice which had been meted out to her?

Towards the early summer, at the end of Rosina's twentieth year, Wellesley finally succeeded in making Mr van de Greef realise that it was not fair to leave Rosina waiting in gaol. The trial finally went ahead, and Wellesley sent boxes of clothes around to the gaol from a stylish dressmaker in Long Street, for her to wear during the sessions.

On a windy early-summer day, her hair, still too short to be convincingly tonged and curled into the prevailing fashion of ringlets, was secured back off her face and hidden under a pretty bonnet, a maid sent around for the occasion.

Food arrived in covered dishes: scrambled eggs, sausages, oat cakes, peach and plum preserves and a dish full of butter. She swallowed, looked at the array of dishes, the delicious spread before her, and shook her head. She put on the new dress with shaking fingers, afraid to think of what she must look like. Then, on impulse she decided to wear the fine gold chain set with blood garnets Henry Mostyn had given her long ago. She unwrapped it, and gasped for lying beside the chain was the brass buckle she had picked up outside her room at Agulhas. She had forgotten all about it. Was it a vital piece of evidence she should give to Wellesley Gerard?

Pulling on a pair of silk mittens she suddenly recognised the buckle. It came from the only pair of shoes Abel had owned, and the buckles had been given to him by one of the men from smuggled cargo. It had an unusual design, and he had worn them only on special occasions. So – it had been Abel who had come to her door. But why?

She remembered that it had been after his thrashing by Captain Skewthorn. Why had the Captain been so insanely angry with the young boy? Had Abel come to tell her something he knew, but was afraid to admit?

She drew a deep breath as the battle raging in her breast exploded to a din near bursting. Then taking her emotions in a firm grip, she calmly followed the guards outside where a closed carriage pulled by two horses, was waiting. Dressed unrecognisably in a plain gown of soft, white Indian muslin, frilled round the neck with scalloped lace, a close mantle of twilled sarsenet and a matching poke-bonnet of basket willow with striped blue and pink ribbons, she finally walked into the open, wind-swept morning, overcome with giddiness, and trembling with apprehension. The mere breath of clean sea air swirling around her made her lightheaded, almost drunk.

The castle walls loomed forbiddingly above the low roofs of the town; the square in front of it was filled with a milling crowd. At first, she heard nothing in the warm snugness of the carriage but the nervous panic inside her. Whatever sounds of footsteps or carriage wheels or hurrying there was, did not disturb her, so absorbed was she in her own deeply intense thoughts. Then, as she forced herself to calm down a little, she became aware of many voices outside and restlessly she leaned forward and glanced out of the window. She saw young boys loitering at one of the sluices of the brick-walled canal where other children played. The water was low and the canal foul-smelling. The children paid no attention to the dirt and smell as they launched twig boats and trotted alongside to see whose would sail the farthest. Then, stunned with shock she saw that further on, the street was crowded with people, shoulder to shoulder, looking at her with strangely malevolent and angry eyes. The excitement mounted, as a narrow furrow opened in the crowd to allow the carriage to pass. The violence in the air was such that when they arrived at the entrance of the Court of Justice, the crowd shouted and shook their fists at the pale, startled face inside the carriage. What was she to do? Could she go through with it, against all this opposition? No voice gave the answers she sought. There was only the steady clop of iron-shod shoes and the harness clinking bringing her ever closer to her trial.

The carriage drew to a shivering halt. She could see the official building with its row of beautiful windows; with its pediment whose curve lent grace to its array of pure straight lines and angles, in which a clock was set and was now striking the hour. Closing her eyes for a moment, Rosina tried to draw strength from within herself.

171

"Down with the whore! Death to the murderess!" A hoarse shout was heard, to be taken up by another, then another, in both English and Dutch, until the air was filled with shouts and curses against her. She sat back on the cushions, full of mounting fear and foreboding. It was all starting again. Would it never stop? Would the judges of the High Court listen to them . . . and not to her?

With the help of a constable, she stepped down and, head bent, began to make her way up the steps. She was booed, cursed and struck on the back of the head with a cabbage. It sent two more armed guards charging towards her. Then Jan was there, shouldering his way through the crowds.

For a moment, he could not trust himself to speak. The transformation in her was so complete, notwithstanding her loss of weight and suffering, and her new womanhood which was full of character and vitality, brought home to him the starvation of his long and forced celibacy. It had been two years since she had left Agulhas, still very much a girl. But now she stood there, before everyone, a graceful young woman of stunning beauty. He felt a great temptation to gently run his fingers along the cheekbones blooming now with colour as he looked down at her upturned face. Her eyes stared back at him, open, yet as unfathomable as any dark liquid he had ever gazed into. The soft pink lips were tantalizing and gracefully curved, and now slightly trembling. With a will of iron, Jan clamped a grip on himself and held his silence.

Rosina looked up at him, and into the two fine dark honest eyes fixed on her with such devotion that the face, never remarkably handsome, seemed to her the most wonderful and familiar she had ever seen.

Then they were jostled as they were about to

make their way inside, surrounded by constables and Hottentot soldiers, and they found themselves holding each other's hands and looking into each other's eyes, each of them suddenly sensing what was in the other's mind.

A bar of silence vibrated between them, then Jan said hoarsely, "You'll be all right, Rosina. Gerard's a good man. I don't know about the new President of the Court, but *ach*, he cannot be much different from the one before."

Rosina nodded, comforted by the strength of his large hands, and his expressive, determined voice.

"I know, Jan," she said. "I'm sure it will be all right."

Confronted with the earnest need to remain controlled they had reached an understanding without difficulty. They would share all the danger, and he would stand by her side, when everything seemed so against her. Suddenly she could not endure the thought of being parted from this big, strong man.

As they entered the building, Wellesley came at once towards her, immaculately clad in a black single-breasted coat, grey-striped waistcoat, spotless cravat of white muslin, black breeches, and shining Hessians with little gold tassels. Over this he had donned his barrister's black robe and wig. With his ironic eye upon her, she blushed as he bowed and said in his most expressionless voice, "You are unrecognisable, Miss Webb – soon no one will be able to distinguish you from the ladies of society. I had no idea there would be such a hostile crowd – and they're all to be let into court."

"Let in?" Rosina gasped, "But 'tis surely against the law?"

Wellesley hesitated for an instant. Then he said in a

low voice: "It was, Rosina – up until last year when the law for open courts was passed. Unfortunately, although it's a step forward in the law of the colony, yours is to be the first open court case ever."

His attractive face softened somewhat, and having exchanged a word of greeting with Jan, he held out his hand to her. There was unsuspected strength in the elegantly-gloved hand taking hers with such seeming casualness, and leading her through the door to the courtroom lying before them. It was an oval of perfect dimensions, the masterpiece of Louis Thibault, the Government Land Surveyor, and gifted architect. Mr van de Greef, the President of the High Court, a large, powerfully built man with the astute demeanour of a wealthy land-owning gentleman, was there in his most formal coat, freshly powdered wig and hat, along with a full bench of judges and officials in buckled shoes and high cravats. Mr Boschoff, the fiscal in his role as Public Prosecutor was there, formally dressed in high-collared frock-coat and carefully tied cravat, with a short bob wig on his head, watching her entry as curiously as the crowd outside. The only movement was her own, with that of Wellesley beside her. She and he alone seemed to have life in that chamber of seated statues.

He led her to a table where she was seated, and for a second, seeing the coldly fierce eyes on her of the President and his judges and officials, she quailed.

"'Tis normal to feel fear in such a situation, Rosina. The absence of fear is not," Wellesley said softly. "Keeping your nerve in spite of fear, is courage. We are going to win this case."

She coloured, then taking a deep breath, she straightened her shoulders and looked directly at her judges. Mr van de Greef's handsome but plethoric face looked

174

with curiosity at the accused, trying conscientiously not to see her as she was now, but as she might have looked at Cape Agulhas. He tried to discount the elegantly arranged coal-black hair under the becoming bonnet, and the fine dark eyes, shadowed by sleepless and anxious nights, and told himself that it was undeniably a beautifully unusual face of spirit and intelligence, with a decided air of resolution in the curve of the mouth. For all its youth, it was a face of suffering, yet something burned in it, he could not deny.

The fashionable clothes she was dressed in added drama to her striking appearance. Mr van de Greef sat back in his chair. This all made the case more interesting; it was not the simple case of murder he had anticipated. Perhaps there might be something in her defence after all.

When finally the crowd was admitted through the heavy brass reinforced doors, they poured in and there was not enough room for them all. Many had to be content with standing outside, where they would have to rely on messages relayed from the doorway to follow the proceedings.

In the crowded courtroom, the spectators stood discussing names. Who was the lawyer defending the notorious woman? Again and again Gerard's name was whispered among them.

Then the proceedings began, with the prosecuting officer stating the case against the accused, the details of which most in the courtroom were already fully aware, pointing out the evidence of her presence in the room of the deceased soon after his murder with her scissors.

"Miss Webb," he suddenly said, turning cold eyes towards her, "Did you think it was right to sin with Lieutenant Buckleigh? Did you not know it was wrong?"

175

There was a murmur of approval.

Rosina paled, but faced him squarely. "I didn't think it was wrong, sir."

"Shame! Disgraceful!" came a chorus of discordant voices which were stopped by a sharp command for silence from Mr van de Greef.

"Then why," Mr Boschoff thundered, "Were you afraid of Captain Skewthorn finding out – if it wasn't wrong?"

Sudden tears filmed her eyes, but she kept her head held high, as she falteringly answered, "I knew the Captain would be angry, sir – because he had said so. But otherwise, that between the Lieutenant and myself – I thought it was normal between a man and a woman, sir. I didn't know anything else, sir. I didn't know what the world would think – I just did what was natural, sir."

There was loud laughter from the spectators, and even Wellesley smiled. But the faces of the judges remained unmoved.

"Miss Rosina Webb, you stand convicted of a crime so destructive and so injurious in its consequences to the welfare and good order of society that you have been condemned to death. How say you?"

Rosina took a deep breath, trying to keep her fingers from trembling by clenching them tightly in her lap. "I, Rosina Webb, say I am *not* guilty."

From the other end of the courtroom came a surge of voices, which had to be subdued by the guards, then Mr van de Greef sat back a little, and nodded. "You may proceed, Mr Gerard, with your plea."

The judges and officials turned their heads, to watch the tall, elegant barrister with the noble head, the thick eyebrows that had intimidated so many litigants, and

176

saw Wellesley's resolute expression, the carved firmness of his lips as he took the stand before them. In the courtroom there was a hush as the spectators eyed him with mistrust, observing every movement with suspicion, and sometimes with hostility. There was a stir of conversation, and suddenly a voice could be heard quite audibly from the back, saying, "He's a Jew-boy, you know. The judges had better watch their pockets."

A roar of laughter came from somewhere in the crowd, and the derision of the taunt sounded in Rosina's ears like the clamour of a yelping pack of wild animals as the words were passed on to those outside.

Mr van de Greef, grim and unsmiling put down his quill, and simultaneously Wellesley turned, his face white.

"Would the speaker step forward?" Wellesley said, his voice constricted.

"I want him thrown out immediately," Mr van de Greef said as around them was a surge, a mingling of anxiety and excitement, as spectators craned forward to see what was happening.

But no one came forward. Wellesley quickly searched the faces around him. A few looked away as if they wished to have no part in the scene. Some waited quiet and watchful, while others examined his aggressive stance.

Mr van de Greef looked towards the crowd, and a slight impatience entered his features as if he was eager to dispose of a matter that disquieted him.

"So! Not only do we have a bigot in our midst, we also have a coward," he said, hunching his powerful body over the desk. He had never hesitated to test the law; nor had he shrunk from a challenge when it came to facing

177

up to it. "We do not have all day, ladies and gentlemen. If the guilty party has not the courage to declare himself, I order him to keep his odious opinions to himself, or I'll charge him with contempt." He turned to Wellesley, amidst an excited clamour from the spectators. "Pray, continue, Meneer Gerard with your plea."

The two men faced each other for a second without speaking as Wellesley stood before the dock, waiting for silence. Then he said in his melodious and at the same time resonant voice that rang through the room, "Sirs, there is no one more devoted to honest law and justice, than I. For without it society falls into chaos and anarchy. I respect therefore, just law." He suddenly smiled charmingly at them, and there was an ominous murmur from the spectators. He glanced at Rosina's anxious face, satisfied at the stir he had caused. Then his face changed and was full of disgust and anger. "But when there is a miscarriage of justice I deplore it, along with all just men."

Mr van de Greef frowned. "Never the less, Meneer Gerard, we must uphold the laws of this colony which were agreed to at the handing over from the Dutch."

A great roar of approval rose before him.

Wellesley held up his hand. "I do not argue about the principle of agreement, sir, but with the acknowledgement that certain injustices are contained within, which can be changed – changed to the English system which has evolved over years of wisdom and good sense. Because there are serious flaws, must we adhere to them, even though they endanger the very lives of those they profess to protect? I am fully of the opinion that Miss Webb was a victim of that system, that if she had been a young woman of means, she would not have been subjected to such humiliation and degradation."

The attention of the judges was fully caught. One of them glanced uneasily at Mr van de Greef, before Wellesley, his eyes flashing with confidence and vehemence, resumed: "We should eliminate wrong laws, sir, such as the evil of the very one under which my client was seized and condemned to death."

"Your client was given a fair hearing by the judges of circuit court," Mr Boschoff, the prosecutor declared with contempt, and in a voice of suppressed emotion.

Wellesley drew down his black robe and inspected his cuffs, looking elated. Hostility never gave him the clutch of fear that others sometimes felt. It excited him. If the prosecution wanted an enemy, he was ready.

"No," he said with a calm that contrasted with the suppressed anger of the other man. "Miss Webb was condemned on purely circumstantial evidence based on incomplete facts. Important evidence had been excluded – evidence that was of the utmost importance."

He paused, and looked slowly from each interested face to the next. "She was found guilty under an archaic system," he said, putting his thumbs under the lapels of his coat in the nonchalant gesture that always enraged his critics. "Although she is innocent of the crime. And the men who condemned her are no less guilty for their negligence. Those who are allowed to still use such a law become criminals themselves."

"Beware of treacherous talk," Mr Boschoff muttered, leaning forward. "For you talk against His Excellency and His Majesty's Government."

Wellesley's voice dropped eloquently. "No, sir. His Excellency did not make this law, and neither did His Majesty, the King. They inherited an old and worn-out system in a colony that is itself changing. I speak no word against the government, I only declare

179

that the law should be changed. Look upon this young woman, sirs." He looked towards Rosina, and smiled encouragingly at her.

"Through no fault of her own, she was forced into a situation that was threatening and menacing from the start. Isolated for years on end, she fell in love, which is no crime in itself, but a state commonly known to all of us."

Here there was a titter of amusement.

"She fell in love with a handsome and charming officer of His Majesty's troops; an officer who used this innocent young woman for his own pleasure – not in any intentionally cruel way, but cruel nevertheless, because she was not aware of it."

A great hubbub rose inside the room and at the doors, and there were distant shouts of "Death is too good for the whore! See that justice is done!"

Wellesley waited for the noise to subside. Then he spoke again: "She is a victim of circumstance, sirs, just as we all are victims. She truly loved the deceased, with an innocent and simple love, so innocent and so simple that it is hard to believe it possible in this day and age. But then, she lived an unusually isolated life where she met no one of her own age, and certainly no available and dashing young men. Many would say that she sinned with Andrew Buckleigh, but I would remind you that this sin is not on trial here. We are here for the matter of murder. I am not asking you to forgive her, but to listen to the evidence of the case."

Then he flung out his arms and advanced a step or two towards the judges. "Sirs, she has lost everything in her life that makes life worth living. Her very life hangs in the balance while the real murderer goes free. Where is the justice in that? We still have our lives, you and I. We can still breathe the air, and know that tomorrow we shall breathe it again. We eat today, and know that we shall eat again. But not so for Miss Rosina Webb. She knows that one day soon she may die, she may unjustly forfeit her life, her only life, for a crime she never committed."

His voice, deep and stirring, created an atmosphere of drama and brought about a heightened awareness, as he continued. "Do justice to this young woman. You are honourable men, just men. And what can be more honourable, more just, more noble, than allowing the true course of justice to have its way, and through that course, to make a just and honourable verdict – of freedom for Miss Rosina Webb."

There was a great commotion in the court which died as all heads craned in his direction. What an opening! And what a magnificent voice! Despite all her reservations and resentments against why he was defending her Rosina felt a surge of admiration that only great artists of the theatre could provoke in their audience.

It was obvious that Mr van de Greef and his bench had been profoundly moved by his words. There was a great silence, while they pondered on what he had demanded of them, of the course he was asking them to take.

Then Mr van de Greef spoke: "We have heard what you say, Meneer Gerard." He looked at Rosina, and his face with its striking hooked nose and grey eyes was stern. "You have been accused of being a victim of a worn-out law, a law that has become a danger to the people of this colony. But this law still exists. To your defence counsel I say this law cannot be removed at this time, despite his eloquence." He paused to purse his mouth in a dry smile. "I say this law cannot yet be changed, but that is not to say changes cannot be made in the future, when this colony is ready for it." He looked at her again and said in a sad voice, "However, we are men of justice. We are not removed from understanding the pain of a fellow human being, and we will continue with the proceedings to commence until an impartial verdict is reached."

There was a stir among the crowd, and excited whispers as Mr Boschoff the Public Prosecutor read the depositions from the circuit court judges. When he had finished, he denounced the murder, condemning and driving home each point as so many nails in the coffin of her crime.

This caused muffled murmurs from the crowds, suppressed by the president, with fierce frowns, and a bellow of silence from one of the guards at the door. When he had finished, the first witness for the prosecution, Mr Haas Maarten was called, and Rosina felt such a misery and suffering seep through her, that she felt almost suffocated by it.

Maarten appeared, looking not as dishevelled as usual, his cloud of black hair tamed somewhat into a pigtail. Examined by the prosecutor, he was put through a set of questions, and his answers were given in broken English, but without hesitation. He described how Rosina had visited Buckleigh in his room while the Captain had been away, how she had changed from an innocent girl into a shameless strumpet, not caring what she did. He told how unhappy and miserable she had looked when she was told that Buckleigh was going away – as if she could have killed someone . . .

"Kill someone, Meneer Maarten? Who, in your understanding, did that someone mean?" Mr Boschoff asked, raising an eyebrow.

182

"De Lieutenant . . . Lieutenant Buckleigh."

"Kill a man who had spurned her, so that no one else could have him, would you say, Meneer Maarten?"

Maarten gave a lopsided grin. "Something like dat, ya – that she would do."

Mr Boschoff nodded, rubbing his chin. "And what made you go to the room of the murdered man, Meneer? Why were you in the house at that time of night?"

"Early in da morning I go back to da house for my musket. I had left it in da room vere we ate at dinner. I always keep my musket near me – for safety, you understand? As I come from dat room, I hear somesing from up da stairs, footsteps – but not natural ones. Everythink else, you understand, is quiet – too quiet, but it is very early. I go quietly up da stairs, and I see Miss Rosina going into da room of the lieutenant. I vait, den I sink I must now catch her in the act: I fear she vants to runaway with da lieutenant and I haf my loyalty to da captain – Captain Skewthorn in dis. Ven I enter da room dere she is, bending over da body, and da scissors, it sticks from da heart."

"And how did she act then, Meneer Maarten? Was she scared when she saw you?"

Maarten frowned. "She was very scared, like she saw a ghost. She was white like a sheet. But she knew what she done."

At this Rosina made a movement to stand up, one hand clenched on the table, the other raised, opening her lips as if to deny what he said. But a warning look from Wellesley stopped her.

She heard Maarten say, "It vas da shock dat made her do it – da shock dat he was leaving her. But she vas a traitor – a traitor to da Captain who had looked after her all her life."

This caused a minor sensation among the crowds. Soon afterwards Wellesley was given permission to examine him.

"But how could you tell that Miss Webb had actually killed the deceased, Mr Maarten? She was not in the act of killing him when you entered the room. It is only a conclusion on your part."

Maarten replied with unwavering denial: "Da look on her face when she saw me was a look of guilt and fright."

A sense of frustration came to Rosina, and she stared at her hands in her lap.

"Are you an expert on people's facial expressions, Mr Maarten?" Wellesley asked, in a deceptively disarming way.

Maarten, for the first time, showed some hesitation. "I know people, ya. I haf known many people – and I know guilt ven I see it."

Wellesley smiled coldly and repudiatingly into the tanned, gypsy face of Haas Maarten. He raised his dark brows mockingly. "Guilty as charged, Mr Maarten? Could it have been something else you saw in Miss Webb's face? Shock, perhaps, not at seeing you so much as just discovering the body? Could it have been grief or rage at discovering someone she loved – ruthlessly murdered in his bed? Could it have been a number of feelings, a mix of feelings? Often the expressions on a person's face are not the feelings we think, but what we imagine them to be. Does that make sense?"

Maarten frowned, perplexed, and for the first time, his confidence seemed to waver. "Ja – dat could be. But she looked very guilty to me."

"But you could have imagined you saw guilt because of what you thought she had done, when, in fact, she had not done it at all." Wellesley took a step forward, his thumbs hooked in the pockets of his waistcoat. "Tell me, Mr Maarten, what is the expression on my face?"

Maarten looked at him as if he had misheard him, then seeing that the other man was serious, he clenched his hands and regarded him with open dislike. "You – you scorn me. It's in your eyes, for all the vorld to see."

"But why should I scorn you, Mr Maarten? I hardly know you."

With a deep frown on his face, Maarten silently glared his rage at him, then he burst out, "You scorn me because I am Dutch – because you do not sink I am as good as you, an Englishman – one of those who fights wiv glory against Napoleon!"

Wellesley waited, then, turning to face Mr van de Greef, he said, "You have sadly misjudged me, Mr Maarten. In actuality, I feel suspicious of you – suspicious because I do not know what you are hiding in your mind. I do assure you that I was not thinking myself superior. Not all Englishmen are arrogant pigs."

The prosecutor coughed. "This is highly unusual, sir, Meneer Gerard is not on the stage of the Garrison Theatre. He could have lied about what he was thinking. He could have said one thing while thinking another. He could be deceiving everyone – including himself."

The judges peered at each other furtively, suppressing smiles, then Mr van de Greef, who had listened to the exchange with arched brows, glanced at the public prosecutor with a certain amusement. "Explain your reason for this little drama Meneer Gerard."

Wellesley smiled, then pursed his lips as if restraining an irrepressible amusement. "It was to illustrate, sir, how deceiving expressions can be – and that to base conclusions on anything as deceiving and illusive as this,

185

is dangerous. I could have lied – but who could prove I had or hadn't? It is quite at the mercy of conjecture."

Mr van de Greef nodded, and motioned him to continue. "Given the fury of the act of murder itself, Mr Maarten – where evidence has been stated that there was blood on the bedclothes, on the floor, all over the deceased – Miss Webb might have been expected to leave telling signs behind. A few strands of hair perhaps. At the very least, there should have been bloodstains on her hands and nightdress. Were there such bloodstains, Mr Maarten?"

For a moment Maarten stood silent, his eyes measuring the other man, then he shook his head. "No. I did not see any bloodstains on Miss Rosina."

Wellesley looked at him, then said sharply, "There were no bloodstains on Miss Webb, none at all. You say Mr Maarten that there was no sense of struggle about the deceased – no disorder of the bedclothes. Surely, if Miss Webb had just committed the murder which you claim, she would not have had time to put everything back neatly before you startled her with your entry into the room?"

"She could haf done it before I saw her," Maarten replied doggedly, shuffling his feet restlessly.

"But could she, Mr Maarten? We know that there was blood not only on the body and on the sheets, but also on the floor. Now, such details suggest there was a struggle – but a short one that was quickly ended. But Rosina Webb had no scratches or cuts or bruises on her. If the struggle was quickly ended, it was because someone bigger and stronger than she was the murderer, someone far more powerful. Was Rosina Webb bruised or scratched or cut in any way?"

Maarten took a deep, rasping breath. "No – no, I

did not see anything – not bruises, not cuts, nothing on her."

With a bow and a smile at Mr van de Greef, Wellesley said, "Sir, I have done with this witness."

Chapter Twenty-Two

At the end of the day's proceedings, Wellesley escorted Rosina to the carriage, explaining that after the unnerving experience she had been through with the crowds travelling alone under armed guard that morning, he would accompany her back to the gaol.

A rather more subdued crowd gathered about the carriage, and ugly, distorted faces peered in at her. Then they were off, as the Hottentot driver tried to force his way through. He lashed with his whip at the mob until, taking fright at the trampling horses, they slowly dispersed.

On went the carriage, scattering the rest of the crowd in full flight but not before a shower of small stones was thrown at it, one of them hitting Rosina's bonnet.

Stifling a scream, she pulled her head down as Wellesley pushed her to the floor.

"Damn their eyes!" he cried. "Rosina – are you hurt?"

"No sir," she managed to reply as they left the mob behind.

"Those bloody sods could've blinded you!" he exploded as she sat up again, taking off her bonnet that had been knocked askew. "We'll have to be more careful. I never imagined it would come to this." His voice was suddenly gentle, almost a whisper.

Staring into those concerned amber eyes, Rosina could find no reply or other words to speak for the moment. Taking up her bonnet, she numbly accepted his assistance in donning it. She arranged the ribbons and tied them, carefully covering her hair. At last, she looked up at him, but almost pulled away as his hand rose to touch her. To her surprise he tucked in a stray lock of hair that had fallen free and slowly adjusted the ribbons under her chin. She gazed into his recklessly attractive face, with its magnificent dark brows that curved expressively, and that firm, sensuous mouth. Scarcely breathing, she waited, feeling his nearness yet not daring to move.

He smiled slowly, recovering himself. "We wouldn't want to lose our most important client, now would we?" He paused, and gazed thoughtfully at the slowly passing wagons and carts and a few carriages. The dust was thick everywhere as the smothering and noxious summer stench from the canal, flooded with refuse, followed them.

"It's high time the law stating that the canals have to be cleaned twice a year was strictly enforced," Wellesley commented.

"Perhaps you should try to do something to improve that one too," Rosina replied. Her voice was deceptively mild, but her eyes gleamed as she glanced at him.

He smiled. "First things first, dear girl. Now that brings me back to your case. When you are called upon to speak, Rosina," he turned a singularly penetrating gaze upon her, "you've got to go out there and show those judges how you feel – as if they were you, do you understand? We have to win this case."

For a moment she stiffened. She had almost come to admitting that she had been mistaken about him, that

189

perhaps he did care what happened to her, and now, just as she had warmed towards him, he had reminded her that all he cared about was showing up a bad law; that he cared not a jot for her personally.

As she suddenly looked away from him with downcast eyes and lips pressed tight in resentment, he clasped her wrist in a light hold and said quietly, "Do you dislike me that much? It's a great pity. Try not to let your prejudice lead you into mistrusting me. We have to work together on this." He paused as they neared the castle, and veered away towards the beach. "Look at me!"

Time slipped by on silent wings and she felt suffo- cated by his nearness as all her senses were suddenly completely involved with him. But she was painfully aware of her own inadequacies. And as always, there was a puzzling glimpse just beneath the surface of his attractiveness and sophistication, of something – a hint of sarcasm, a brief flash of insincerity, a strange touch of arrogance: still she was convinced that had he not wanted to prove something to himself, he would not have bothered with her case.

She raised her eyes reluctantly to see him smiling faintly. "Good girl. If you had as much confidence in my integrity as you have in my seeming insensitivity it would be better."

She experienced a brief moment of temptation to hurl a caustic accusation that he would do anything to win the case if it would secure him a personal success. Somewhere the bell at the castle tolled in the late afternoon. The wheels of the carriage thumped against the dust and her heart seemed to match the more rapid pace. Time hung motionless as uncertainty pecked at the outer limits of her mind. A slight twinge of conscience invaded the moment as the carriage drew her ever closer to the gaol. It was no use antagonising the very person she needed for her freedom. There was so much depending on this man. Without him, she was lost forever.

"I know you'll do your best, Mr Gerard," she answered in a low, husky voice. "We're nearly there. Please let me go."

A world of tensions hovered unspoken. The clanking of the chains at her wrists stabbed her awareness as he released her. The sun was breaking through the clouds, shining with a heavy golden slant of late afternoon light as the carriage stopped at the entrance to the gaol, where its bell in the turret was striking the hour.

"It's a damnable position that you work with me so reluctantly," he said deliberately, as he handed her down from the carriage, then turned away and left her staring, surrounded by armed guards.

She was bustled into the sheriff's office, and as the warder took up a candle to light the gloom, Rosina followed him, their footsteps echoing on the stone steps while the candle cast eerie, flickering shadows around them. Familiar swift scurrying sounds in dark corners brought chills and the usual foreboding to her, and she clutched her mantle tighter about her, feeling again the wretchedness of the place. The warder thrust a key into the lock and pulled on the door to her cell. It yielded with a loud creak of rusty hinges.

As she walked inside and the door was closed she finally allowed herself to admit that Wellesley Gerard's attractive masculinity and his protection of her in the carriage was such that it had made her knees feel weak. It had brought home to her the starvation of her long, forced loneliness and hunger since Andrew's death.

There was a need within her to feel loved and to give herself in love.

She coloured hotly and turned away in instant confusion, as a white hot bolt of doubt blasted her new-won confidence, and she was suddenly unsure of her own ability to deal with Wellesley Gerard.

Chapter Twenty-Three

A south-eastern wind whistled and tore across the town, driving the cloud over Table Mountain and dust across the streets the following day as Rosina and Wellesley set out for the courtroom, and arrived to face a crowd mercifully reduced by the weather. The wind whipped up whitecaps on the bay and caused the townsfolk to clutch their hats and stagger head-on at street corners. A pair of horses, panicked by a loose sheet of the *Government Gazette* blown into their eyes, bolted down the Buitengracht and galloped madly away.

Old Tom Harding had been brought to the town, as had the other witnesses, against Rosina's deepest apprehensions. As she suspected, in his answers to the questions by the prosecution he proceeded to strengthen the case against her. Then Wellesley rose to face him:

"Mr Harding, how long have you known the accused, Miss Rosina Webb?"

"Since she was two, I reckon. Since the shipwreck all those years ago."

"Eighteen years – or shall we say, sixteen, seeing as you haven't seen the accused now for two of those years while she's been in prison. Did those years give you a good understanding of Miss Webb – enough to know, without a reasonable doubt, that she could commit such a dreadful crime of murdering the man she loved?"

Contempt shimmered in Tom's old mahogany face. "Anyone could see 'ow she turned out – a common li'l strumpet, that she was! She flung 'erself at that redcoat like nothin' you ever seen, and she 'ated me for knowin' it, she did."

Wellesley listened to this with arched dark brows and an amused and negligent smile. "All this appears to be from your mind, Mr Harding. There is nothing to substantiate – to prove one word of what you have said. None of the witnesses or yourself can actually describe any scene of intimacy between the accused and the redcoat. They all suspected it, as you did – but not one, not even yourself, actually saw it. Did you ever see any intimacy between the two in question?"

Old Tom, for the first time, was visibly struck. His face tautened. "No, can't say I actally *saw* it. But we – none of us is fools. Sir, anyone wi' any brains could see that— "

"Could see what? You yourself have said you never saw any real intimacy between the two." Wellesley laughed wearily. "You cannot be a hundred per cent sure of that, can you? No one can, unless they actually walked into the room where the said intimacy was in progress. Now, Mr Harding," he said, in a most terrible voice that reached far into the room, and to the doors beyond. "In all your years with Miss Rosina Webb, did you ever see her in a rage, in a temper? Did you ever see her strike anyone – or any thing?"

"No – can't say as I did," Tom replied with dazed bewilderment. "She – she always seemed such a gentle sort – then. But she had never 'ad a man then, see? Never 'ad such a – a goings-on, it stands to reason, don't it?"

"No, Mr Harding, it does not stand to reason that a person whom you have admitted was "a gentle sort"

194

should suddenly change unrecognisably and behave in a most uncharacteristic manner. You say she never had temper tantrums or rages, that she never struck anyone or any thing in all those years you knew her. In fact, she cared for wounded wild animals and nurtured them in enclosures in the back yard, am I correct?"

"Yeah, she 'ad animals. Went mad about 'em all those years, ever since she be a small urchin."

"So, a person who has all her life been gentle and passive; who loves animals so much that she cared for them in their most vulnerable state could surely not have lifted her hand in murderous violence to the man she loved, no matter what the circumstances?"

The muttering of the crowd was a constant murmur in the background, until many of them were thrown out of the courtroom.

Finally Wellesley looked at Tom again and the golden glow of his eyes was like a flaring flame.

"Admit it, Mr Harding, you have no proof beyond reasonable doubt that the accused, Miss Rosina Webb is a murderess. You have nothing at all, except your own vivid imagination. All you do know is that she visited the redcoat in his room, that she talked with him, that she was happy in his company. Now, is that such a crime? All you know is that she was in the room with the deceased sometime after the murder. You do not know that she touched the murder weapon at all. You do not even know how long *after* the murder she was found in the room. It could have happened some hours before. You were not there. It is only your word against hers."

He concluded in a compelling voice. "The accused, sir, has been condemned by the prefabrications of fallible human beings, who, because of their own

195

feelings of fear or whatever, jumped to conclusions about her conduct, conclusions which can never be proved."

He turned to Tom. "Did the accused ever, in your presence, say that she hated Lieutenant Buckleigh and that was unhappy about his leaving?"

"She – she was a quiet wench. She never said nothin' to nobody."

"Did she ever show she was angry when she heard he was leaving? Did she do anything to show her anger – the anger that you believe led to the murder?"

Wellesley walked towards him, and halted before him. The silence became intense as all eyes watched the confrontation. And old Tom Harding looked up into his amber eyes and read them. He pulled his mouth into a grim thin line, and sniffed loudly.

"Not really. If my memory serves me correct – she jus looked shocked – kinda in a daze. Then she left the room, like. But I never did see her again arter that – until the redcoat was dead."

Wellesley lifted his arm and smiled a little with ironic and sombre humour. "So you never saw her again until after the murder. You never saw her reaction, never knew what she felt, and yet you are convinced only she could have committed the crime. I find that hard to believe, especially as there was another murder committed in the barn of one Samuel Leach, retired seaman, only weeks before. Do you think that Rosina committed that grisly crime as well?"

There was a shocked silence in the room as Wellesley uttered these words, and he lifted his head in time to see the swift expression of fury on Tom Harding's lined face.

"Is this other murder relevant to the case, Meneer

Gerard?" Mr van de Greef asked, with a withering look in his face. "If so, please explain in what connection."

"Sir, it has every relevance – which I shall explain. It was a murder committed because of certain knowledge the deceased had gained concerning the activities of one Captain Skewthorn and his crewmen – illegal activities of a highly suspicious nature. I contend, sir, that there is no concrete evidence against Miss Webb; that the murder of Samuel Leach and that of Andrew Buckleigh was committed either by the same hand or by two different persons for the same reason: that he knew too much about the illegal smuggling of slaves into the colony by Captain Skewthorn, a renegade English sea captain. I contend that Rosina Webb had nothing to do with either murder; that she has been used as a scapegoat in something far more sinister than was previously thought. I argue that there is insufficient proof of her guilt."

Mr van de Greef leaned forward, raising an eyeglass on the end of a gold stick attached to a ribbon round his neck. "And where is this Captain Skewthorn? Should he not be here, to give evidence for his ward, for as I understand it, that is what Mejuffrou Webb is?"

"He cannot be found, sir. His brig, the *Leviathan* was sighted in the Atlantic on the way to Rio de Janeiro and was given chase but eluded all pursuers. I contend, sir, that Miss Webb should be set free at once, and when Captain Skewthorn and his crew have been found that they be tried for the illegal smuggling of slaves and for the murder of Samuel Leach *and* Lieutenant Andrew Buckleigh."

Tom Harding's face darkened with the fire of his inner fear and rage, and he said, "That wench, she murdered the redcoat, I tell ye – 'twas she did it and no one else!"

197

"Empty words, Mr Harding, without a shred of solid evidence." Wellesley bowed to the president and his bench, smiling at Tom with disdain.

And when he left the court later with Rosina, the crowds looked at her, but did not move against her.

Chapter Twenty-Four

That night, Rosina lay on her cot, sleepless, at midnight. Her eyes were dry with strain and exhaustion. The faintest moonlight fell from the small window far above her and lay on the opposite wall. She watched it without awareness. Then it seemed to brighten and become sharper, until it was a face. The features became clearer and it was young Abel's face as she had seen him two years ago. The apparition seemed to smile at her, and shadowy arms seemed to lift as if pleading. Then it disappeared.

She came to herself with a violent start and found she was wet with sweat. The faint moonlight still lingered on the wall, and she shivered, thinking she had been dreaming. She rose and lit the candle she was now allowed on the table. She remembered Abel's buckle . . . what did he want to tell her? What had happened to him? Was he in trouble? It was so long since she had last seen him. It was almost as if he had been asking for her help . . . and for the first time in months, she felt the shock of sorrow, and lowering her head into her hands, she wished there was something she could do for him.

A sudden thought struck her. Perhaps Wellesley could help to find him . . . But would he? She doubted it, for what interest would he have in one young poor, forgotten slave boy. But if she told him about the buckle

. . . would he regard that as important information or not?

She had not been able to pray for many months, but suddenly she stood with a wave of remorse and guilt, and fear sweeping over her. She could not understand how it was that the God she had worshipped since childhood had not sent his powerful lightning to destroy her. She thought back over the past weeks. When she had been at her lowest and most desperate, He had sent Wellesley Gerard, for all his selfishness. He had sent Jan la Motte to comfort her, and Mr Berringer who had taught her to be as close to a lady as she would ever be, and to understand more about the law and what was happening to her. He had sent *her* help. But what about poor Abel?

She hurriedly bent her knees, clasped her hands, bowed her head and prayed in a passion of gratefulness and remorse. After some moments, she lifted her face, her cheeks wet with tears. She asked for forgiveness for her own shameful behaviour with Andrew Buckleigh, suspecting for the first time that what she had felt for him might have had less to do with real, pure and selfless love, than with a handsome male's overwhelming masculinity; that perhaps the physical passion they had shared in its delicious frenzy, had not been spiritual love at all. And she had neglected Abel in her own selfishness.

She made no attempt to promise good behaviour in the future for forgiveness of the past, for she did not know what that future held, if anything at all. She could only beg forgiveness as a favour from a stern and angry God about whom she had been taught. She was torn with misery. She could not tell if she had been forgiven or not, and she did not know how much she would

200

have to suffer on account of all her sins. She was quite panic-stricken with new doubts and fear as she violently clasped her hands together.

She could no longer think of her relationship with Andrew in anything other than shocked horror. She had lain with a man out of wedlock. She could not bear to think of what she had done with that man in wanton shamelessness, and enjoyed it. She took courage finally from the fact that she had thought she had loved him, and given her whole heart; that in some way she had helped him back to health before his final hours.

Much of her remorse and terror left her in that moment, and she calmed perceptibly. She ended her prayer for Abel in a better frame of mind, and the sudden sincerity of her conviction that if Wellesley could wrest something good from her case, to save others, then it must be right. Hope and confidence came flooding back despite her first agonies of shame, and she knew at last with a certainty of purpose that God would help the poor unfortunates who needed His help.

Chapter Twenty-Five

She was awake the next day as the first sun was striking the highest peaks on the mountains, though the town lower down still fumed with mist and dimness. She was dressed and ready to leave for the court long before time, and paced up and down with nervous restlessness. Finally, not able to wait any longer, she left with Wellesley in the carriage, and impatiently entered the courtroom, amidst another even larger crowd of spectators.

There were only two more witnesses that could be called, and Jan la Motte was one of them. Wellesley asked Jan to describe the last time he had seen Rosina at Cape Agulhas before the murder. Once it was established that Rosina had seemed strangely quiet and frightened, instead of using it as extra evidence to show that she was deeply unhappy and bitter that Andrew was tired of her and was restless to move on, Wellesley used it to show that Rosina was afraid of something else – of the murderer of Samuel Leach. She was afraid that the murderer would strike again – at Andrew, the man she loved who knew too much about the illegal transactions in the settlement.

"Sir," Wellesley said in a gentle and reasonable voice, eyeing Mr van de Greef, "how could this quiet and gentle woman have killed the man she loved in such a vicious and mutilating manner, striking him not once but many times. This woman loved her fellow creatures with such deep and intense feeling; even saving them and restoring them to wholeness. Her entire life has been spent in service to her fellow man and fellow creatures; it is totally out of character for her to have committed such a crime of violence and hatred."

He used his enormous talent to drive wedges of doubt into the case for the prosecution, and was prepared to use everything he had to the best advantage on the foundation of uncertainty he had built. His compelling eyes fixed themselves on the judges.

"How does one measure courage, sirs? One can only measure it by oneself. Courage is a shining thing, a glorious reflection of the one who possesses it, and I put it to you that Miss Rosina Webb possesses that courage, that dignity of the truly innocent; that she loved a man with such a purity of love that is unusual, if not extraordinary in this world of today; that she selflessly served that man, a man who did not appreciate the fullness of that pure and simple giving. I put it to you, that she has courageously loved, and stood up against all the hatred and bitter accusations with a dignity and a simple conviction of her innocence which has been little less than noble. If she is guilty, she is guilty only of having loved too much."

All eyes looked at him standing in the centre of that lovely room, tall, strong, a confident man with a firm, resolute face and eyes like changing weather.

He struck his chest with his clenched fist, his eyes raking every face in that room like lightning. "This young woman before you has suffered the most inhumane indignities, yet not once in all that time has she ever behaved in any manner that has been cowardly or undignified. She met her fate the first time, with courage, even although she knew that she was innocent. Her only weakness was that she believed that her innocence would be seen at once by those so-called experts in whose hands she was held prisoner. Those judges and the system have failed her, but let us, and it, not fail her again."

"But why has the prosecution fetched Henry Mostyn as a witness?" Rosina burst out later, facing Wellesley across the flagged floor of her cell. "He is a mute!"

Fragrant with sandalwood, he clasped his hands behind the back of his fine, dark blue coat, and pursed his lips. Near and distant shouts, laughter and heavy voices were borne on the air from the noisy, smelly fishmarket on the beach and gulls uttered their plaintive cries overhead.

He stared at her pale and haggard face, at the dark shadows under her eyes, at the white exhaustion of her mouth.

"Because, dear girl, from the evidence about his behaviour after the murder – the uncharacteristic heavy drinking and the withdrawal into himself – they think there is more he knows than anyone suspected. He was never questioned because he is mute. 'Tis a strange thing, but when one is so handicapped, human nature jumps to the erroneous conclusion that all other senses are also impaired. I saw Mr Mostyn in Algulhas, and he is a deeply unhappy man."

Rosina shook her head in great confusion, her heart suddenly pounding against the walls of her chest like a hammer. "But poor Henry – he can't give public evidence – his deformed body, his lack of speech – I could not bear to see him humiliated in public! I

204

know what I've been through, but he – he will be lampooned, his poor twisted body jeered at. I could not bear that!" Her face was flushed, and her breath rasped in her throat. "He began to drink and behave strange after Captain Skewthorn thrashed Abel."

"Abel? Is that the slave who ran away soon afterwards?" He took a step nearer to her, holding her with the power of his clever eyes. "Rosina, this could be important. This may be the evidence we need."

She raised her hands as if to strike something, then let them fall impotently at her sides. Finally, she held out the buckle to him. "I found this outside my room when the field-cornet came to fetch me. It's from Abel's shoe. I heard him outside my door the night before. I think, mayhap, he wanted to tell me something."

He looked at her, a question on his lips, but it died as his eyes fell on the buckle in her hand. He took it, and after studying it closely for a moment, turned and stared at the window high up in the wall, an edge of its barred grillwork throwing a pattern across his eyes. He seemed, unfamiliarly, to be searching for thoughts. "Why did you not tell me about this sooner?" He turned back towards her. "It may have saved much trouble if you had."

Rosina's features drew together. "I forgot about it, and when I remembered it, I did not think it that important."

"One thing I've learned about cases, dear girl, is that nothing can be treated as unimportant, especially not in one as serious as this one. Why do you think young Abel ran away after being thrashed by the Captain? Is it because he knew something the Captain did not want him to know? Was he causing some kind of trouble?"

"I don't know! Really I don't know!" Rosina's world

had again turned dark and menacing. A bitter bile of fear rose in her throat, and her mind was filled with chaotic visions, and rising to the fore was her face twisted with terror and forever frozen as she stood with a rope around her neck . . .

"Rosina, listen to me!" Wellesley took a step towards her, but she shook her head frantically, unable to extricate herself from her fear.

"We have to find Abel, Rosina! Don't you see? There is no other way. I will look for him and find him, no matter where he is, believe me!" He stood close, his breath falling softly against her hair, her head filled with the subtle scent of sandalwood. There was a need in her to feel the warm strength of his maleness, to be swept into his arms, but she was painfully aware that he regarded her as a client, a poor, unlessoned girl and that as soon as they heard the verdict of the case, he would depart, as Andrew had intended to do, to the wider, more exciting outside world . . . She wanted to believe him, she wanted to believe all the fine and noble things he had said about her in the courtroom, as if he had meant every word, but she knew he was acting out a role, that she was merely another actor on his stage.

He placed a hand on her arm, but, drawing a ragged breath and by an extreme effort of will she turned angrily, slashing her hands sideways with a gesture that cut off any words.

"I – I can't take much more of this, do you understand? I just can't – this not knowing from day to day, week to week – not knowing if I am going to live or die! And I can't take poor Henry's humiliation!"

"Rosina, dear girl, there is something missing and I am going to find it!"

"And if you can't?" Her voice suddenly broke as the

tears streamed down her cheeks. She began to cry, helplessly, worn out.

Then he reached out and took one of her trembling hands, and before she could argue with him, he pulled her to him.

"I can't bear to see you like this," he whispered huskily as he twined his fingers into her dark hair. "I will fight for you as if my own life depends on it, I promise you." Then he kissed her slowly and lingeringly on the lips, and she felt the silence of the cell engulf her. Her whole world careened crazily as his mouth moved upon hers, insistent, demanding, and she was caught up in the heat of a battle she could not win. She should have fought against him, but it was wildly exciting, and she was aware of the heavy thudding of his heart while her own throbbed in a new frantic rhythm. Her head whirled in an ever quickening eddy, but finally she gave up her struggle against the intoxication of his kiss.

Slowly his face retreated. With trembling effort she collected herself, and, as he stared down at her, she drew a deep, ragged breath.

"You are using, me, sir – you take advantage," she said unsteadily.

"I agree, 'tis most unseemly between counsel and client. It shall not happen again. 'Tis far too compromising, and if ever found out, will only weaken our case. Please accept my apologies."

She moved away, and sat down at the table, her legs trembling with new awakened feelings, feelings she knew would betray her again. She wanted him. No matter if he was insincere and selfish. There was a growing need for her to be with him, to share with him what lay ahead . . . but sadly she knew it would not last, that he was as unattainable as he ever would be.

Chapter Twenty-Six

Rosina sat nervously in her seat in the High Court, dressed in a gown which seemed to float around her in a pale blue cloud under its twilled mantle. A high, frothy ruffle at her neck rose from the high-waisted bodice, appearing almost prim to a fault, but calculated by Wellesley down to the last detail. The crowd pressed into the room were breathless with anticipation, for today was the day when Henry Mostyn, the deformed mute would give his unusual evidence. Wellesley waited in the centre of the tessellated floor as the room grew silent.

Suddenly there was a commotion, and a special messenger of the court hurried forward, his face as white as death. He spoke first to Mr van de Greef, then to the prosecutor, Mr Boschoff, then to Wellesley, and finally Mr van de Greef rose with a face like stone.

"It is my duty to inform the court that the witness Mr Henry Mostyn has been found in his lodging room, hanged with his own leather belt," he said, the words rumbling through his heavy frame. "I call a recess until tomorrow when Miss Rosina Webb shall speak in her own defence."

There was an immediate outcry in the court, the buzzing of sound heightening alarmingly as Mr van de Greef called for order. Rosina sat in her seat, her hands in her lap, her eyes wide with shock. She looked desperately at Wellesley, as with a rumble of seats and a hubbub of voices the court rose. Her mind went back wildly through the years. Henry had been the kindest, gentlest of them all. He had been the only one who cared. She had to tear herself away from the memories to bring herself back to the courtroom . . . Wellesley was taking off his wig and handing it to his groom, when suddenly his tall, elegant figure became indistinct and all the voices around her faded away in an uncomprehending babble.

She became aware of her surroundings and Wellesley bending over her with smelling salts in his hand. Jan was behind him, his face lined deeply with concern. Then she remembered. Henry was dead. That poor, dear man had either killed himself or had been killed because he could not bear the publicity, or because he had known too much. She pushed all help away and tried to rise, the sudden movement causing the room to dip and swirl once more. She saw the men come forward, but she forced herself to walk unsteadily to the door, unsupported, closing her eyes against the sickening loss of balance. She stumbled, and the room swooped into another confusing orbit, then she was lifted clear off the floor, and the next thing she had known she was back in her cell, and Wellesley was bending over her again, wiping her forehead with a damp cloth.

The moment he had gone from her cell, the powers of darkness rushed back into the void. The horror was all around her. She felt she could touch it: something living, palpable. But there were only shadows in the cell, dancing with the thin flickers of late sunlight on the ceiling. She stared unseeingly at the walls of her cell, as outside the sun was lying on the horizon in a fiery bed of cloud. She sat for a long time, clutching the gold chain

Henry had given her, biting back the tears as she faced the future, to discover that it was a blank emptiness. She had been cut off from her past and set adrift in a void.

The following day Wellesley returned with the news that he had managed to get her defence postponed to give her time to get over her grief, and to have time to find the whereabouts of Abel. After he had gone, Rosina did not know how long she had sat staring at the walls, unaware of hunger or bodily needs, as the night drew in again around the gaol. The sounds of the dark swelled up around her, and outside, the monotonous pendulum of the surf.

As the days went by, her imagination failed her as she tried to imagine where Abel would be found. She missed the rich voice of Wellesley, and his absence made the hours somehow lacking. The time wore on, and even with visits from Jan, she was beset with loneliness. Her gaze was ever drawn to the door and footsteps beyond that may be Wellesley's. But she knew what she had to do. She had to go over the speech for her defence which Wellesley had dictated and rehearsed with her, and which she had to learn by heart. She lay awake many nights going over it, until the day arrived for her to make it. There had been no sign of Abel, and Wellesley, deeply disappointed was forced to take her to court without the final evidence.

Rosina was well aware that this was going to be the hardest few hours of her life. She put on the pale mauve silk dress with long sleeves that Wellesley had sent around the day before. It was severely plain, with no more than two rows of silver buttons adorning it, but the cravat round her throat was deeply edged with lace, its ends thrust through a buttonhole.

The news ran like lightning through the town that

Rosina Webb was finally to speak in her own defence, and again the court was filled to capacity, rows upon rows of faces, even to the sills of the long windows. The members of the High Court sat on one side of the dias; Rosina faced them in the dock opposite. The heat lay over them all like a pall, stifling, even though the long sash windows were open. Hot sunlight streamed through the high windows and flies flitted through the dancing sheaves of dust.

The Secretary of the Court waited until the excitement in the room had died down and a hush fell, then he said, in a loud and sonorous voice: "I call upon the accused, Miss Rosina Webb to take the stand in her own defence."

Standing upright in the dock, Rosina rose with a fast beating heart, knowing that she must not let fear run away with her. Silently she fought for inner control, wishing desperately that she had Wellesley's confidence and eloquence, and knowing that this was her last chance to prove her innocence beyond all doubt.

She cast an uncertain glance at Wellesley, at the almost insolent grace and assurance that were as familiar as the strong face; at the well-shaped hands clasped lightly on the table not far away. With a small shock she met his unswerving gaze. Her heart lurched with frantic beating as a flame was set burning within her, and she trembled almost uncontrollably. She knew this case was important to him to show up the gross defects in the colonial legal system; that it had become a crusade against wrongs he wanted to redress, not only here, but everywhere; that his own family had suffered in certain ways from bigotry against Jews. And she remembered all he had done to win this case. Suddenly all her prejudice against his intentions were swept away in something much larger, and she understood. It took her several seconds to gain control of herself, and then it happened.

Without warning, something flared up within her, something bewildering but irresistible. Before anyone could say anything, she faced the sea of faces and spoke:

"I am here today, sirs, because of a mistake, a misunderstanding. A man was murdered whom I truly loved – a man I helped to heal, to bring back to strength so that he could go back to his world as a soldier and fight for his king and country against the tyrant, Napoleon. I cherished that man, and I truly cared for him in every way. When he made preparation to return to his calling, I was very cast down, but I accepted his decision because it would have been wrong to keep him from doing what was right: to fight for England and to put the tyrant to flight forever. Lieutenant Buckleigh had a duty to fight, and I knew that."

She paused, and took a deep breath. "I prepared some food for his journey and took it to him in the early hours of the morning. There, in his room, I found that he had been cruelly murdered. My poor darling was dead, and there was nothing I could do for him – nothing!" She lowered her head to catch her breath and then continued. "I was in a state of shock – of anger – of pain when Mr Haas Maarten came into the room and saw me there, beside the body with my scissors sticking out of Lieutenant Buckleigh's heart." She lifted her head and gazed directly at the judges. "He said he had caught me in the act, so to speak, and I denied it, but he did not believe me. I was so shocked, I ran out of the room and away to think on my own. No one believed me – everyone said I did it with my scissors, but I could never have raised a hand to the man I loved with all my heart. I would rather have suffered myself than do that to him, or to anyone. I could not live with the weight of the guilt of it all."

She went on with surprising directness to explain about the murder of Sam Leach, and how shocked she had been, not only at the murder, but at the cover-up of it afterwards, and she described the noise of the cart carrying the body late at night while she was cowering in her bed. Then she said, with a touch of defiance, "The reason I could not explain these things before the circuit court is because I did not know how, but through the support of others, books and lessons, I have learned. And it's all true as the way I see it." At the end, thoroughly exhausted, she sat down, her head bowed, her hands tensely clasped in her lap.

For a long time there was total silence, then there was a resounding noise from the spectators as first one, then another and another clapped and cheered for over a minute, until they were silenced by Mr Boschoff, the public prosecutor who rose and stood facing Mr van de Greef across the floor.

"The accused has spoken eloquently and with apparent sincerity," he said in his clear, concise, Dutch accented voice, as soon as silence fell. "That is to be greatly admired. But she has been coached admirably by our respected and learned advocate, Mr Gerard."

Rosina started. She looked at him with incredulous anger. Mr Boschoff continued, looking at the judges. "The defence counsel has coached and dressed a wayward girl who could not speak in her own defence in Swellendam, and now, two years later, speaks as if she was educated in the best schools in England. It is too much to believe that this dramatic change could

213

suddenly bring about the truth. We have only her word and Mr Gerard's that she did not murder the deceased Lieutenant Buckleigh. We have only to look upon the accused to see that she is a clever young woman who learns quickly and in her desperate situation, to use every ruse she can to sway the court in her favour. How do we know that she was not involved with the first murder, with her – lover, if I may be so bold as to use that term. We do not know. She may, in fact be guilty of not one, but two murders, sirs!"

In a profound and ominous silence he concluded, "We have heard the accused and the accusers, sirs. Meneer Gerard's words have merit, as do his client's, but we have the irrefutable evidence that the accused was in the room soon after the murder, that her scissors were projecting from the heart of the deceased, and that she was evidently shocked on being discovered. I leave it to you, sirs, and we await your judgment."

Wellesley asked if he might address the court for the last time, and after a few minutes deliberation, Mr van de Greef nodded.

For a moment he paused to look around the crowded, oak-lined room, which still rustled with his name; at the spectators, many of whom had throughout the trial become less hostile, at the clerks and the judges at the table, and the long windows that cocooned them all.

"We have, sirs, as I have said before, many gaps in the evidence for this trial," he exclaimed, looking from face to face, turned attentively to him, his own was full of cold and forbidding annoyance. "Too many to convict the accused. There is nothing to prove she killed the deceased beyond any reasonable doubt. There are witnesses missing, who cannot be found at this time, and she has spoken with sincerity, from the heart – a young woman who could not face a court nearly three years ago has now with struggle and determination, won over her handicaps to learn to speak eloquently in her own defence because she does not want to die an unjust death! And when you make your judgment, sirs, do not make it to appease the conscience of the community!"

A loud cheer came from behind him, as he flung himself into his chair.

Light fell from the long windows, and large though the chamber was, the heat was even more oppressive, as the judges left the room to deliberate in one of the offices next door. Rosina was led by Wellesley to an adjoining room, where he had food and drink brought in. Once they were left alone, she had difficulty maintaining even an outward show of composure. Her heart hammered in her breast as he filled her glass, and offered her food. But she shook her head, and rose to pace restlessly about the room, lacing and unlacing her fingers.

"You were magnificent, Rosina," Wellesley said, taking a glass of white wine laced with aloes for bitters. "You did more than I dared hope or expect. The spectators for the most part are now on your side. From total hostility they have turned in your favour."

She faced him and searched his face. "Tis all very well, but tis what the judges decide that matters. Please tell me what you think . . . about the verdict."

He put his glass down and went to stand before her, staring down at her troubled face. He reached out a hand and gently smoothed an errant strand of hair from her cheeks. Then he stepped away. "We have a good chance – there's too much missing for them to convict you on what they have. Public opinion might well swing the verdict in your favour now. 'Tis a fickle fact of life."

"I wish it was all over." Turning away, Rosina pressed

215

her fingers against her temples and shook her head with frustration. "It's been so long now. If the verdict goes against me, what will you do?"

Wellesley strode over to the long windows, and looked out. After deliberation, he swung round to face her, and sat down at the table. "I shall appeal to the Governor and his two assessors."

"And that is the last step, then?" Her voice was barely a whisper in the room.

Her mind suddenly screamed until her skull ached with the pain of it, but her voice was gone, and her hands were clenched at her sides. She stared mutely at him, as he plunged his fork into the pie which a serving girl had hurriedly placed before him. "We can, of course appeal to the King-in-Council, seeing that you are a British subject in a British colony, but that is a costly and extreme measure, very rarely used." A slow smile touched his lips. "Though somehow, dear girl, I do not think we will have to resort to such drastic measures. If the worst does come, then we will fight all the way to the King, believe me. I really do think you should eat something. It may make you feel better."

At her refusal, he nonchalantly leaned back in his chair, putting a table napkin to his lips. "Do you mind if I smoke?"

She felt steadily braver as she shook her head and returned his smile, then she grew serious, her smile fading. "If I am set free, I want to fight for a world without slavery."

Wellesley smoked a cigarillo, the new fashion brought from Spain and raised his thick dark brows. "But my dear girl, you can't be serious, here you are, still fighting for your own life and yet, you are more concerned about the slaves!"

216

She shook her head. "If I don't think about it, I shall go mad . . . and I have seen too much of the cruelty and the degradation of it." She gave him a smile that had an odd finality about it. "The thing is, I'm never free of it. I'm always reminded that I'm not free and nor are they – it's in the gaol, everywhere. To me, that is the horror of it. This is why I want to do it. I understand their pain. Besides, isn't that what you're doing? Fighting against an unjust system here, in this colony?"

He looked at her thoughtfully, seeing her as if for the first time, and not just as a beautiful, unusual young woman who needed his help. There was about her face, the erectness of her body, the way she held her neck, a surprising dignity and strength, considering the circumstances. And the hat she wore made her look strangely audacious, one side of the brim almost obscuring the vision of one fine eye.

As their eyes met, time trembled to a halt. She stood very still, almost hungrily searching his face for some sign.

"Yes," he said softly, "That is what I have always tried to do – to fight against injustice – to defend those who are alienated by society in some way." He cleared his throat. "There are so many prejudices, envies, maliciousness. It's a wonder we have all survived this long."

"I heard what you were called – that first day in court. I'm sorry. I never knew about – prejudice before – religious prejudice that is. In the settlement I never learned about it. We never had any Jews there, you see."

"I have become so used to abuse through the years, dear Rosina, that it has become a bore. I even fought a duel against someone calling me, to quote: 'a direct descendant of the thief on the Cross.' Those who think

217

as he did, are, without knowing it, influenced by the darkest superstitions of the darkest ages, I'm afraid. They don't seem to mind the ancient Hebrews of the Bible, but fail to see that the Jews of today are no different. But with patience and endurance it will all be overcome."

He held his cigarillo lightly between two fingers of one hand as he gestured briefly with the other. "My simple desire is to gain a seat in parliament and to fight for the principle of religious liberty – the right of every citizen to worship freely and to have full civic rights. That it will be very unpopular, I need hardly say. But I seem to attract what others call lost causes."

Rosina tried to smile into his probing eyes, but the effort was a failure. Awkwardly she plucked at the ends of her cravat, and her fingers twirled it restlessly. "Mr Berringer once told me that Jews are not allowed to sit in parliament – why is that?"

"Under the existing law practising Jews cannot take the Oath of Allegiance on what is called the 'true faith as a christian,' and are therefore debarred from any seats," he replied matter-of-factly. He was watching her face, and secretly admiring her courage. She seemed to be taking the situation stoically. He reached for his glass of wine. "But this fight against slavery that you speak of – it is much, much more than fine words."

"I know!" Her reply came out too sudden, and too clipped. She nodded her head, her lips tightly clenched, then the words burst from her in a half sob. "I know what slavery means. I've been a part of it all my life, and I know that it is my responsibility to see that it does not go on. I want to learn all I can how to fight it. I want to know and read all about Mr Wilberforce and those who help him." She stood with a pained frown marring her beautiful face, twisting her hands together and licking suddenly dry lips.

"I have learned painfully, Mr Gerard, that language is the most powerful thing in this life – because language can make people understand. It can make all the difference between success and failure. I heard you use it and I saw the way everyone listened to what you said. I admired that most and I want to learn to speak like that – both in English and in Dutch."

She turned away, not wanting to meet his gaze again. He watched her closely for a long moment, somewhat bemused. He could not know how her pulse raced when he looked at her, how keenly she felt his presence in every nerve of her body, how much she wanted him to kiss her again, and yet feared it because of his power over her, of the way she found herself comparing all other men with him, even dear Jan. And he could never know that beside him everyone else seemed lacking. She was afraid to even question the significance of this, fearful she might then have to admit things she refused to let herself think about.

"I am most shamed by my past." Her hand pressed tightly across her quivering lips, and her eyes squeezed shut as she fought against the emotions that washed against her every resolve. Then she said, "I want to find Abel." The words sounded bare and heavy as she spoke them, not strong and determined as she had intended.

"I think you really mean what you say," he said finally. Her eyes flew open and saw a glint of fire in his. "We will search every corner of this colony until he is found, I promise you that. But first, we must hear the verdict."

It was four hours later that they were called back into the courtroom, and where the Secretary, in his most formal full-skirted coat, freshly powdered wig and three-cornered hat, read out the sonorous preface: "Justice in the name of the High and Mighty King George of England, Scotland, Wales, Ireland and the Cape of Good Hope has been done this day. The accused, Miss Rosina Webb has been found not guilty by the honourable members of the High Court of Justice of the Cape of Good Hope due to insufficient evidence. She is set free as from this hour to go forward into her former life."

Free! Rosina found herself weak at the knees, with such an aching, overwhelming relief that made her feel suddenly limp. The court remained in motionless silence for what seemed to her an endless time, then cheers swelled in all parts of the room. She felt drained, yet elated. She had no idea what the consequences would be, but she knew that whatever had happened to her in those moments was irrevocable. All those nightmares in which she was hanged and the misery of her disaster that left her heart thudding in the blackness of the night was over.

As the cheers became almost continuous, the prosecutor, Mr Boschoff raised his eyebrows in exaggerated astonishment as Wellesley ripped off his gown and wig with unbecoming speed, and hurried towards her. One emotion followed another in her mind, but despite her feeling of weakness she was conscious of a wild exhilaration. No one could spend nearly three years in gaol and hours waiting for the verdict without exhilaration. There was a sense of achievement which seemed to affect even the usual composure and nonchalance of Wellesley. He was radiant with triumph.

All around them, people were milling, and there were continuous waves of sound. Wellesley smiled and took her arm supportively. Others leaned towards them with their congratulations. Many spectators cheered them and each other in delight. And still the ovation rolled on, marking Rosina's victory in the very place where, only months before, they had shouted abuse at her. Now they had seen and heard her, and judged for themselves that she was innocent.

She walked through the doors and stepped, lips trembling, into the future, emerging into the open where the late afternoon looked pure and precious. Beyond, like a promise, lay the town, golden with the light. After her ordeal, it looked inexpressibly beautiful, and the smell of roasting meats that wafted through the late afternoon air in thin grey layers was something she would never forget, as long as she lived.

Then somebody was cheering again. Many voices were cheering. This was freedom. Rosina stood awkwardly on the steps in the afternoon sunlight. She tried to smile, but she knew her smile to be wooden: she was nearer tears than smiles.

She suddenly felt weak and ill. The wonderful feeling of relief faded against the emptiness of reality as she visibly braced herself towards a world of shrewd daily business which had not ceased while she had been in gaol, and she shivered. What was she to do now? Where was she to go? She was more alone than she had ever been, and for the first time in her life, forced to make her own way in the world. It was a terrifying prospect, and one which she had never allowed herself to contemplate in gaol, not knowing what the verdict would be.

As she gazed ahead of her, memory flashed vivid pictures into her mind: Captain Skewthorn's face contorted with rage, his thrashing of Abel, the men's overwhelming hostility. Doubt and fear returned to torture her mind as she knew that freedom was an illusion – that she would never be truly free until he and his men were caught, until the real murderer or murderers were punished, and until then, she would be haunted by them every waking minute of the days that followed.

"Rosina, you must come and stay with my sister, Coenradina and her husband, Andre Combrink, until you decide what to do now that there is nothing left for you at Cape Agulhas."

Rosina closed her eyes as she listened to Jan's pleasant, quiet voice at her side. Then calming her mind, she looked up and smiled for the first time in months, as some of the burden she carried lifted from her soul. "Thank you, Jan."

Their eyes met and she smiled wryly. "Now you are my gaoler, I suppose?"

He shook his head, looking down into her striking face, the wide eyes so dark that the pupils merged with the iris.

"No. Only your protector." He was surprised to see tears in her eyes. It stunned him for a moment, for he had watched this young woman suffer terrible abuse and physical hardship without showing pain. Now he could see that her strength was undermined by vulnerability, as if she was tormented by a secret fear, and he longed to comfort her.

And then, Wellesley stood between them, bowing to Jan. "Permit me to tell you, Rosina, that I have arranged a room for you, at the George Hotel. It's by far the best in town, dear girl."

Rosina caught her breath. "At the George Hotel?" she said in a hollow voice. A vision of maids, housekeepers, grooms, all milling around her, most forcibly struck her mind's eye. Suddenly, even though she was disturbed and attracted to the elegant, clever lawyer, in that moment the home of Jan's sister seemed much more appealing.

"My sister has offered her home, Meneer Gerard," Jan said with an unfamiliar edge to his voice. "I think Rosina will be happier with a family around her, until she knows what she wants to do."

"Surely that is for Rosina herself to decide, Mr la Motte?" Wellesley's voice was unusually clipped, his handsome face suddenly cold.

Staring into his eyes, Rosina noticed anew, their most unusual colour, and for a moment she could find no reply. She had not expected this. But even in her predicament, she could not help admiring the fine figure he made. Now Jan was looking at her too, and she cringed inside. They were asking her to make a choice.

She considered the question carefully, noting the challege in Wellesley's eyes. "I think it best for me to go to Jan's sister's house for a while." Her words stumbled out awkwardly. There was a look of timeless regret on her face as she said, softly, "'Tis more private there."

Wellesley's face was inscrutable, but something flickered in his eyes. "Then so be it," he said, forcing a smile.

Quickly he stretched out a hand, covering her slender fingers with his own for a brief moment before he drew them away. His bold gaze stirred something deep within her, and the sensation was intensely disturbing. Then as she forced her mind to concentrate, he strode away into the crowd and disappeared.

Chapter Twenty-Seven

The whole town buzzed with excitement as the verdict was discussed everywhere. There were those who were still against it, but they could not deny its impact or that of the trial itself; of the fact that Wellesley Gerard had swayed many over to Rosina's side; that her own speech had captured many more waverers. But no matter if opinions were for or against her, it was an undeniable fact that an innocent young woman had been saved from the hangman's noose, revealing all too clearly the glaring anomalies and weaknesses in the colonial legal system, and dissatisfaction would grow, leading to the first important change in the introduction of the jury system for the first time in 1819. But that was still in the future.

Daily, ordinary life in Cape Town went on, blandly, regardless of history. The ships might bring news that in the outside world events were moving swiftly, that Spain had fallen to Wellington, France had been invaded by Britain and her allies who had entered Paris, and Louis, brother of the last king, a witty, gout-ridden, fat old man sat on the French throne; word might come from the outposts on the Eastern frontier of the continuous friction between the black tribes across the Fish River and the Dutch farmers, but as yet Cape Town could still only hear distantly the drums that were throbbing on the other side of the colony and the pace of life in the Peninsula went its leisurely way. The British were now entrenched, having formally taken over the Cape, and the Dutch power that had held the halfway house on the way to the East seemed no more than a memory.

February was well on its way, and it was on a Friday afternoon that Rosina was called to the sitting room in the two-storeyed house in Bree Street of Jan's brother-in-law, Andre Combrink where she was staying. She swiftly descended the stairs to the hallway and the sitting room on one side of the entrance, admiring again, the front door of teak, flanked by teak-shuttered windows, set so faultlessly that its plain flat facade, devoid of orna-ment, had the authority of a picture by a master's hand. The yellowwood floors and the stinkwood furniture had the patina of age and the hand's slow, frequent rubbing. Its white walls, washed with repeated coats of lime, had a bloom, a quality that lent softness to both the light and shadows that fell on it. She admired the skills that had built the house, had put kists and armoires together with dovetailing and little bolts of wood, had polished these and the floors, and burnished to a dazzling brilliancy the silver hasps and escutcheons, the copper kettles and moulds and saucepans in the kitchen, the brass ewer and basin that stood in every bedroom.

She paused a moment in the entrance hall as all the memories of her weeks in this place of refuge came flooding back. It had been a time of catching up, of being reunited with Clara, Achmat, Abdoul and the other slaves brought safely to Cape Town, where they were housed temporarily by Jan and Andre and found suitable work. The joy at seeing Clara coming towards her in voluminous skirts after so long, and gazing into her dark-skinned face, creased with smiles, had been

225

overwhelming. Clara, who had been afraid she would be sold to some unfamiliar and unknown master was pleased to cook for Jan and his old mother, and it was not long before she was comforting the small little Jacques, charming away his tears. Rosina's animals had been set free into the bush once more as there was no one to care for them, and she knew with a deep sadness that there was nothing in Cape Agulhas for her to return to.

Her mind was abruptly brought back to the present as she found herself in the doorway to the sitting room. Wellesley Gerard stood looking out of the long, narrow windows, and turned immediately on hearing her step on the gleaming yellowwood floor. His driving-coat was thrown over a chair, and he was dressed in a close-fitting coat of blue cloth, neat white breeches and shining Hessians. His waistcoat was of the same cloth as his coat and white like the shirt. Ruffles and fancy stitchery very noticeably absent.

He came across the room and bowed gracefully, smiling slightly.

"I'll come to the point at once, Rosina. I come to tell you that I am to search for Abel tomorrow before dawn, on Table Mountain. I have discovered that he lives in a cave with a gang of other runaways."

Taken completely by surprise, Rosina stopped and stared at him. Then, at the thought of Abel, she felt her brain reeling. "But you can't go without me!" she breathed in a tight, strained voice. "I must go with you."

Instant amazement flashed across Wellesley's face, then vanished as his amber eyes scanned her face. "Dear girl, be sensible – tis far too dangerous for a young woman climb that rock face!"

A moment of silence passed as Rosina struggled with

226

her own emotions. "I must go with you!" she gasped. "Jan's sister was telling me only yesterday that in 1798 one of Sir James Craig's officers rode up the sides of the mountain on horseback. And if you're worried about those runaway slaves that once lived in the caves and stoned climbers to death, most of them went at the end of last century! I must try! I climbed the hill at the settlement many times, just like a boy!"

"No, Rosina." The golden eyes glinted suddenly like hard metal. "There's no way I'm taking the responsibility for your life in this way. You will stay here, and that's an order."

"An order? How dare you! You do not own me. I am no longer under your authority. That ended the day I walked out of the gaol a free woman!" She found her wrist seized in a merciless grip.

"By God, young woman," he said with unusual harshness, his eyes seeming to probe her being. "You will listen."

His hands clamped tightly about her narrow waist, and she was seized from the floor as if she were a child and set down on a chair. Frantically she struggled, her slender fingers pushing against the strong, muscled chest that seemed to fill her entire vision. He gave her a sharp shake, and she stilled, staring into his scathing eyes.

"That's better," he said and loosened his painful grip only slightly. "Now listen to some sense. You cannot go with me, and that's that."

"I must go! I owe it to Abel! I will go! And you won't stop me!"

"We'll see about that."

The colour drained fom her cheeks at the finality of his words. With a choked sob she renewed her efforts to escape, then writhed in silent agony as his fingers clenched again in a cruel vice.

"Be still," he commanded, and she had no choice, though she still trembled violently with anger.

"If you don't turn me loose I'll scream!" Her mind flew aimlessly in ever-widening circles as she strained against him, feeling the hardness of his body, and remembering only too clearly his mouth, hot and sweet, caressing and practised in a kiss that had bruised her lips . . .

He raised a thick dark brow and considered her flushed cheeks and the soft, trembling mouth. "I s'ppose you will at that."

Beneath his steady regard, she could not control her rapid breathing, then his eyes narrowed in warning. "'Tis not good sense for you to come with me, Rosina – no one in their right mind would let you, and you've been in quite enough trouble already, wouldn't you say?" His hands dropped away, and he rose and reached out for his coat. "I take it, you see the recklessness of your idea?"

She wanted to stop him with words, to somehow force him to let her go with him. But she could not. There was about him, as always, an aura of power – an authority which left her no choice but to respond. Daring no further words, but with turbulent emotions roiling within her and darkening even more the brown of her eyes, she came to her feet and ran from the room.

Chapter Twenty-Eight

In the drowsy afternoon, Rosina sat with Jan on the high stoep of Andre's house, shaded by a grapevine, that was raised and pleasantly out of reach of the dusty street. There was a sleepiness over everything, the drugged siesta silence when the whole town was abed till three in the afternoon, many of the ladies disrobing entirely to climb comfortably into their four-posters in nightgowns and caps. There were no people, no voices, but their own. Jan sat back easily in a riempie-backed chair, smoking his long clay pipe, the wreaths of smoke curling about his head.

"Do you suppose there will be wind tomorrow?" Rosina inquired, staring out across the street lined with serene white houses, shaded by oaks and firs, and upwards towards Table Mountain, the line of its summit reaching across the sky, which had never known the touch of desecration. She could hear the profound silence of the street pressing down on her, as she sat there. Her gaze returned to the stoep where she idly watched a chameleon perching on a flower, its body spotted like a vivid pink and green bead bracelet.

Jan blew a puff of smoke and shook his head. "*Ach,* but I don't think so. I am counting on it not to, because I am considering a shipment of moleskins and trouser cloths that have come in one of the ships, also birch and hair brooms, quills and wax dolls." He puffed at his pipe and watched the shadows broaden on the mountain. Facing the bay, it was bathed in full light until late in the afternoon, when lumious shadows gathered behind its crags.

"Have you noticed that when the wind blows here we get a whiff of the brewing of Meneer Dyckelmans? Did you know that since the English invaded our town, he is also manufacturing snuff? *Ach*, but I will never touch the stuff myself. It is for the English – and the French with their fancy manners, but for a true Dutchman like myself, I will stick to my old pipe that has served me well all these years." His eyes were suddenly amused, impish, darkly twinkling. "Do you take the stuff, Rosina?"

Rosina's eyes gleamed with humour as she stared at him from beneath lowered lids. "No, Jan – 'tis only for men. Besides it makes me sneeze."

There was a silence, somehow isolating them. Far above them the mountain tops towered into the sky and from somewhere she could hear the sound of a fountain dribbling water.

"There are new trades and new shops opening everywhere now, and most of them are English," Jan marvelled suddenly. "And English merchants by the dozen – dealing in everything under the sun – from horses to violin strings! My God, but we have never seen such restless energy." She watched his face break into a broad smile as he regarded the long pipe in his hands. "But I am not complaining – business is very good these days."

"Jan! You keep Rosina from her siesta. Come you in and have tea." Jan's sister, Coenradina appeared in the doorway. She was a Dutch woman of great pleasantness, soft-armed, amiable, with drowsy dignity.

In Market Square the fruit and vegetable sellers, the sellers of butter and eggs began furling their umbrellas and loading their unsold wares into handcarts and wagons, and slaves who had brought their owners' supplies in baskets slung from yokes across their shoulders were lifting these and wandering off as Coenradina joined them and the conversation turned to the new Governor.

"*Ach*, but that man has had such an influence in the fashions of this place already. All the young men copy his wardrobe, and the ladies tear the trimmings from their bonnets to imitate the fountain of feathers on the top of Lady Somerset's tall velvet hat that she wore to church on her first Sunday." Coenradina bathed them both in her drowsy, amiable smile.

"I hear that His Excellency is vigorous and handsome though in his middle-age," Rosina said mischievously, a smile flitting across her face. "And that his nankeens are glove-tight and his cravat so high he can barely turn his head."

"*Ach, ja,* and there is an upward trend in the sale of curling irons as his Lordship's ringlets over the temple and forehead are copied everywhere." Coenradina giggled. "But then that is good for business. Come now, the cakes and waffles and konfyt are laid on the dining room table. We have also oblietjies with cinnamon and white wine – a recipe from our Huguenot grandmother. They are rolled wafer tea cakes, Rosina." She paused, beaming broadly at Jan. "There is also a nice cake – Elsje has got a light hand with a sponge cake, if the stove is burning good. Rosina, have you now heard about these new stoves that will burn coal? If the government can get coals from Europe I think perhaps people like us also can." She turned to Jan. "What think you, Jan la

231

Motte? Now that Napoleon has been put away on that island somewhere in Europe, perhaps we can."

She stood for a moment, beaming at them fondly.

Genially Jan smiled at Rosina and then with gravity looked at his sister. "*Ach, ja*, Coenradina, he's been exiled on the island of Elba. But there are some who say his faith in his own destiny is not yet finished, that he may yet rise again. The world holds its breath after so many years of war."

Coenradina looked straight into his eyes. "I hope he does not rise again, my brother. But then, what does it really affect us here, in this place so far away? We just do not know from one year to the next which government we are having next."

She left them then, and Jan cast a glance at Rosina's preoccupied expression, then looked down at the pipe in his hand.

"Rosina, there is a matter of importance that I wish to ask you about before we go in and join the others."

Rosina smoothed her skirt and made a small shrug. "What is it, Jan, that is of such importance to delay your tea?" She paused, smiling and glanced up to see his lips pursed as if he was lost in thought.

He gazed out across the street for a long time, where ghosts of smoke rose from the chimneys, before withdrawing from his reverie and looking squarely into her eyes. He came abruptly to the point: His gruff and firm voice seemed to reverberate within her very soul as he announced quietly, "In the absence of the Captain, I want to ask you to be my wife."

Rosina coloured hotly and turned away in sudden confusion, wondering what she should say next.

"I can offer you a good life, Rosina," he laboured further, "a comfortable home, the means to live well,

232

the companionship of my family and myself. And my deepest love and respect."

In the late afternoon light his dark eyes shone softly as he gazed into hers. At another time she would have been attracted by him. But now, when she reached inside herself she could find no emotions, no desire . . . No life, she realized with surprise. With trembling effort she collected herself, and as he stared at her, she drew a deep, ragged breath.

"Oh, Jan, I hardly know what to say. You're – I'm so much younger than you – I would hardly know where to start," she said hesitantly.

"*Ach*, Rosina – but I would show you. Besides, it would be my pleasure to look after you after all you've been through. Think about it – it is a serious matter between a man and a woman after all."

His voice was low and husky in the deepening shadows.

The late afternoon was warm, the air heavy with the smell of sugar bush and heath; and as they sat for a few minutes in silence, Rosina had to dip deeply into her reservoir of willpower to dispel the slow numbing of her defences. She had nowhere else to go. She had no money, no one to support her. And Jan was a good man. He loved her and would look after her well. She would have no fears about the future, he would see to that. She had known him off and on for so long, and he had supported her through her ordeal when others had turned against her.

Then, without warning, the memory of Wellesley's hands holding her in a vice-like grip, his vitality and his exasperating presence suddenly filled her thoughts. Was it another trick of her mind, when, just after the nicest and most suitable man asked for her hand, she felt

233

the disconcerting presence of another who promised her nothing?

Jan's hand reached out towards hers but paused as she withdrew them. He shrugged. "*Ach*, but I have embarrassed you. For that I am sorry, but not for what I've asked of you. Think about it, Rosina. I meant every word of it."

Rosina glanced at him and was silent. When she had first been convicted, she had found in him an ally against the world. During the months in gaol and throughout the trial, the ally had become a friend and protector against her enemies. And now? She looked affectionately at Jan's large, genial, bearded face. Gratitude, she thought, is a form of love. And I am so grateful to you. I do love you, but is that enough?

Chapter Twenty-Nine

The air was heavy, the night was hot. Rosina lay in her bed unable to sleep. The sheet felt damp and finally in the very early hours of the following day, she thrust its clamminess away, and rose, restlessly pacing about the room, her mind full of the plan she had worked out only hours before. She lit a candle, leaving the curtains still pulled against the darkness, and hauled out a pair of old boots, and a pair of borrowed leggings Achmat had secretly brought her, her heart racing with sudden nervous excitement.

It was not long afterwards that Achmat, now working for the Combrinks, guided her to Wellesley's house, through the quiet and barren streets, to the upper parts, removed from the dust and bustle of the town, and looking towards the Lion's Rump. It was a handsome house which he rented from a wealthy Dutch widow, with outer rooms for his cook, body-servant, Lendor, and his groom. From its stoep there was a pleasant view in several directions, south to the Government Offices, the Court of Justice and the oak lined walk running through the public gardens with its large wrought-iron gate at the upper end which kept in deer, tortoises and ostriches, and the mountain beyond; north to the bay with its masts and sails and wheeling gulls and the steep rocks of Rogge Bay.

Achmat left her there, and she made her way round the back, keeping to the dark and shadows, past the coach house and stables, where straw was piled in drifts and there was the rustle of horses, and the cellars where the floors were raised in the old tradition to maintain a cool temperature. She stood for a moment breathing in the sweetness of the vegetation and looked towards the kitchen of the house where light from a candle leaked from the cracks in the shutters. Cautiously she drew near and pulling back a shutter, peered inside, taking care not to betray her presence. For a moment with great embarrassment, she thought Wellesley stood naked as he sponged his shoulders and arms with water from a small basin, but when he moved further into the light, she realized he wore old worn breeches. Steeling herself for the confrontation, she knocked lightly on the door.

It opened instantly and he stood on the threshold, startling her with his immediate action.

"Rosina!" His first word came with surprise, but he quickly recovered, and ruefully rubbed a hand across his freshly shaved chin. "What are you doing here?" Then he tossed his head and stared at her, his amber eyes brittle. "You're not coming with me, if that's what you think! I'm taking you straight back to the Combrinks'. You'd better come in while I finish dressing, though it's no proper way to entertain an unchaperoned young woman."

He stood aside to let her pass into the deep stillness of the kitchen with its brass-bound oak vats standing on the stone-flagged floor, their lids and dippers, and the plain stinkwood Huguenot chest with simple brass fittings used for storing flour. It was a large room, winking with copper saucepans, kettles and konfyt pots all made either in one piece or with bottoms dovetailed in with brass. She turned and faced him, the shafts of flickering candlelight falling along the folds of the borrowed coat and breeches, making her appear more like a dashing boy than a girl.

"I must come with you. I know Abel and he knows me. You will find him quicker if I'm there, believe me."

Her glance flitted hesitantly across his hard, muscled chest and its light furring of hair before her eyes lifted to meet his steady, angry stare. He stood back and leaned against the wall beside her, crossing his arms across his chest. "You're not going, and that's that. Now I'll take you back."

Angry tears stung her eyes. "Will you listen to me! I must come with you. I must see Abel. He won't talk to you! There's no way I be going back to the Combrinks'!" Angrily she slipped back into her old grammar as she raised her voice.

"Shhh." His finger lay across his lips. "You'll wake the neighbourhood then there'll be another big scandal for this less than easy-going town." His voice was flat, hard and biting. "Be a good girl, Rosina, and do as you are told. I'll dress and take you back before they discover you're missing."

Rigid with fury, turbulent tears streaming down her cheeks, she glared at him. "If you won't take me I'll follow you. There's no way I'll be left behind!"

Instantly she was crushed against his naked chest. She tried to raise her hand to slap his face, but his arm encircled her until she could not move.

"Enough, Rosina, enough," he said sharply. "Soon Lendor will be here with the two trackers."

Desire suddenly flamed in his golden eyes, snatching her breath, then his mouth swooped down upon hers, twisting, bruising, rousing, searing her, possessing her.

She struggled weakly, trying to bring some reason from the chaos of her mind, ever aware of the hard, masculine feel of him and the tingling warmth that spread through her body. Ecstasy seeped through the barrier of her own will, and she was answering his demands, not fighting anymore.

Then his arms were gone, and she stumbled free of him, across the room. She tried to feel abused and angered, but he had aroused something much different in her, something like Andrew had, but much, much more intense. All of a sudden she wondered what it would be like to lie against his strong body . . .

Fear rose up inside her then, not of him but of herself, for in spite of her wariness and anger against him, she wanted to draw him down with her on the floor and show him that she wanted him. She had never, not even with Andrew, ever felt this way.

Shaking, she bit back her shock, hoping that he had not seen the sudden naked desire that must shine in her eyes. He turned away, and pulled on a white cambric shirt.

"I can see that your mind is made up, that the only way to keep you quiet is to let you come with us," he said, his voice clipped and cool. "But you are under my orders, is that understood?"

Moments later, Lendor, his manservant from Mocambique arrived in an open cart along with the two Hottentot trackers who knew the mountain.

They passed the shuttered and silent houses, hidden in their rambling secretive gardens, the cart filled with bags of food, rugs, a lantern and guns, and suddenly Rosina felt herself responding with unbearable exhilaration, as an occasional cart jolted passed them in the dim, unpaved and dusty streets. The only other moving figures were a mounted patrol muffled in their long cloaks against the early morning air.

A cluster of small houses pressed in on the dark street as they left all human habitation behind. The cart stopped below a rough footpath leading to Platteklip Gorge, a broad ledge of granite. They quickly dismounted to begin the climb, the two Hottentots and Lendor carrying the bags of food, the rugs and the lantern, moving ahead of them. Rosina's nerves shivered with mingled uncertainty and anticipation as she looked up to find Wellesley watching her. He had discarded his coat and the white cambric shirt was open at the neck to reveal the strong column of neck which accentuated his tall, lean, broad-shouldered frame. A bit of cuff fell over the supple bare wrists, and the old worn breeches with buckskin top boots showed his long, firmly muscled legs. No muscle of his face moved, but a light filled his amber eyes. She tried to stop the sudden racing of her heart, as flushing instantly she bent all her attention on the climb ahead, which was a steady slow slippery one.

Often she had to be helped by him before they stopped at intervals for mugs of water and then went on for hours, the only sound being their laboured breathing and the scrunching and rattling of loose stones above them as Lendor and the Hottentots snaked their way up ahead.

Rosina was determined not to look down as she pulled herself up the rocks, spread with the glorious scarlet flowers of the Red Nerina Lily. Finally, she was helped on to the last jagged shelf of rock, her chest heaving and panting. They were more than three thousand feet above the ground looking down on the town, the valleys and the sea, in an unreal world soaring about them. The air was intensely cold and sharp as a fire was made and they sat wrapped in rugs, drinking coffee and eating bread, butter and biltong, watching the antics of a rock-rabbit a few feet away.

"There is a legend of how Devil's Peak got its name," Wellesley said, watching her as he perched on a shoulder of rock, an unlit cigarillo dangling from his lean, supple fingers. "An old pirate van Hunks lived on the mountain Windberg, spending his days drinking rum and smoking his pipe." A maddening half-smile curved his lips as he punctuated his words by stabbing his cigarillo into the air. Short heavy wisps of dark hair curled slightly about his face, accentuating the lean, striking features. "A stranger visited this old pirate, asking for a fill of tobacco, and, once he had smoked the stuff, he was astonished at its strength. Van Hunks boasted that he could smoke any man senseless, whereupon the stranger took up the challenge to see who would win. They smoked for days and the mountain was covered with black clouds resembling the Cape south-easters." He lowered his voice to an ironic, conspiratorial level, and she strained to hear it. "At last, the stranger fell down exhausted."

"And then?" In spite of herself, her dark eyes widened with curiosity. "Who was he?"

He was observing her with the faintly mocking air that intimidated her, and she knew he was looking at the long tendrils of silky black hair curling about her ears.

"Van Hunks, who had won the wager, bent down and pulled off the stranger's hat to discover the horns of the devil beneath. Hence the name of the mountain was changed from Windberg to Devil's Peak."

There was a short silence, then Rosina looked away. She was even more than ever uncomfortably aware of his nearness, which still unreasonably excited and terrified her. He was so different from Jan and from Andrew, and any other she had known. However often he was felled, he rose to carry on the fight. An insult rebounded from him like a pea catapulted against a muscled chest. And the fight that exhausted others only seemed to stimulate and excite him. Once he had set his mind on something, nothing could divert him from the pursuit of it. And he was deeply passionate; she knew to her cost. He had the power to abuse and humiliate her. She would have to fight to rid herself of the chaotic feelings he aroused in her, feelings which made her far too vulnerable.

Her wonder grew as she studied him and her curiosity grew apace. Her face grew thoughtful, as she tried to imagine what kind of home gave birth to a man such as he and what sort of hand had nurtured him.

She turned away, feeling overwhelmingly stirred by the vista about her. A steep and dangerous wall of granite fell on its downward flight below to the tiny valleys. A puff of smoke drifted from the castle, and some moments later the dull boom of the morning gun reached them, announcing the dawn. The town spread out far below, with its miniature square blocks of houses and few early snail-like market wagons. The bay was a wide grey expanse, speckled with the minute dots of boats and ships. The boats and the water faded and lived with the mists swirling in and out on the surface of the sea. A pale streak of primrose light lit up the east, radiating through the grey pearliness from the jagged humps of the Hottentots' Holland mountains. As the light strengthened, the mists slowly dissolved and the sky was filled with streamers of vivid colour, deep crimson, saffron, darkest purple, cerise, glowing coral to the palest shades of pink. The world was one iridescent mirror of brightness, every cloud, every crevice a fresh miracle of wondrous delight. She gazed down towards the flashing coastline of Table Bay curving away with Robben Island in its midst, her eyes following the sea where it lost itself as it crawled to the horizon like a vast burnished shield.

She gave herself totally to the sun and the air and the aromatic scent of flowering shrub and bush with a sense of life and wellbeing, her recent anxieties and fears completely lifted, feeling in that glorious moment, equal to life and all its deepest problems.

One of the Hottentots came climbing crabwise back down to them and beckoned, pointing to a spot further up, to the right. Immediately they rose and, gathering their things, they climbed up, to where Lendor and the other Hottentot moved silently along a narrow track that appeared to lead nowhere, only deeper into the mountain. Then they came to the mouth of a cave surrounded by a thick undergrowth of bush. Here it was dark and all traces of visible light vanished. Rosina was beginning to feel tired, as if every muscle in her body was aching, but she forced herself to crawl after Wellesley into the thick undergrowth.

"Lendor says the runaway slaves are here," Wellesley said, as they inched slowly forward along a narrow ledge approaching the entrance under an overhanging rock. Rosina hunched her shoulders into the hard crevice of rock, trying to peer through the bush into the cavernous darkness beyond. Wellesley crawled forward on his hands and knees, carefully pulling back the bushes, as she followed close behind.

There was an awful silence about the place, and Rosina tried to relax as her eyes searched for any furtive movements inside. She could see dark ominous shadows, but nothing else. At one spot, she stood rooted, unable to move as her eyes darted along the

242

bushes looping their way around the rocks. She was suddenly afraid that any movement they made might dislodge a rock, or that they would fall thousands of feet to a ghastly death.

"Be careful here, Rosina – there's a jagged piece of rock in our path," Wellesley murmured, jerking her out of her fearful thoughts. He moved back closer, and she felt his hand take hers, and quite instinctively she rested her head against his shoulder. Suddenly it was so reassuring to feel his presence, to know that she was not completely alone, the strong fingers in hers making her feel oddly secure.

Lendor and the trackers remained outside as they went forward. It was so dark they had to feel their way along as they stopped in the mouth of the cave while Wellesley lit the lantern and held it above their heads. On either side there rose a dripping wet wall of jagged rock, excluding all view but a strip of sky behind them. They stood listening to the dripping of water and saw the wet stains stealing down the rocky walls and trickling through the opening. The way before them was a crooked continuation of the great dungeon where they stood, the massive structure at once depressing, gloomy and forbidding. So little sunlight ever found its way to this spot, that it had an earthy deadly smell. Resisting the slow touch of a frozen finger tracing out her spine, Rosina drew back instinctively as bats like blighted fruit hung in clusters from the walls and great spiders ran across them astride their shadows.

"Abel!" she called, her voice echoing eerily around them, "Abel – 'tis Miss Rosina with a friend come to fetch you. There's others outside, but they mean no harm. They brought us here."

They heard a furtive movement from somewhere in

the darker depths of the cave, but they could not be sure.

"Abel! You're safe – we mean you no harm. You can come out now!" she called again. "We know you're here! I'm safe, Abel – I've been cleared of Lieutenant Buckleigh's murder."

Dimly she was aware of a sound nearer by, and suddenly a huge, dark shadow stood over them. With a start, she took a step back, a scream half-born on her lips. Then, the nameless fear that seized her passed in a moment, for to her overwhelming relief, she saw a boy of nearly fifteen years old, sinewy, tough, undersized.

"Abel? Abel? Is that you?"

The figure directed a curious look towards the mouth, then looked all about the cave, as if expecting something else, and then, taking the hat off his head, he slowly came forward, looking at her. He answered in a low voice, "Yes, Missy, it's me, Abel." He frowned as he stared up at Wellesley, and she detected in his eyes some latent fear of him.

Rosina stepped forward, forcing a smile. "'Tis all right, Abel. This is Mr Gerard, a good lawyer who defended me before the judges of the High Court of Justice. He made them set me free. We've brought you some food and drink – here, you see?" She held out a large skin bag.

Intently watchful of Wellesley, Abel took the bag, then, quickly examining the contents, his manner cleared and he replied to her with readiness. "Missy going back to Cape Town with Master Gerard?"

She nodded. "You must come with us. Your mother is with Mr la Motte. Achmat and Abdoul and the others – they're all here. I'll see that nothing happens to you again, I promise."

244

He shook his head. "No, Missy. I not go down there. They sell me to some cruel master – they like half-breeds like me – they sell for high price. I run away from Swellendam, Missy and I walk all the way to Cape Town. It was there, in Simonstown I meet a band of runaway slaves like me. We work as extra hands for the English seamen on the ships, then we come back by different ways to meet here in this cave to sleep. No one catch us here, Missy, no one."

"Abel," Wellesley's deep voice suddenly echoed in the musty depths of the cave, "I will try to help you, if you help us. We want to know why you wanted to talk to Miss Rosina before she left with the soldiers for Swellendam, and why Captain Skewthorn thrashed you so hard after Lieutenant Buckleigh was killed. Did you see something that made you afraid?"

An intense look of terror flashed through Abel's dark eyes for a second. Then it was gone. "I see nothing. Nothing. Now go away from here."

Wellesley frowned as he held the lantern higher. "Abel, there's nothing to be afraid of. We will protect you. I'm not sure of the slave laws in this colony, but I intend to find out, and see what I can do for you. Is there any certificate that registers you as a slave of the Captain? Do you know of anything like that?"

"No, Master, I know nothing. All I have is the cut in my ear." Abel showed him the small triangular cut in his ear lobe, matching those of the other slaves serving the Captain. Then a look of slowly dawning incredulity spread over his face. "You, Master, you got the money? You can buy free?"

Wellesley lowered the lantern. His lips, handsome and sensual yet somehow stern, smiled at him. "I shall try, Abel. If there is nothing to prove who you belong

245

to, then I shall certainly buy you, and give you your freedom. But you have to help me and Miss Rosina. You have to tell me what you know and why, if possible, Mr Mostyn had to die when he was brought to Cape Town to show, by sign-language all he knew about the murder."

Abel released his breath in a great sigh. He squared his shoulders, his eyes bright. "Master will let me say to him, thanks. Abel he will work for you, Master. Even after the Cap'n he is no more, and I don't hope I'll ever see him again. Now not anymore, and then my heart it can be my own." Suddenly he stopped as a new thought struck him. "You say Master Mostyn – he dead?"

"Yes, Abel," Rosina said urgently.

"Now please help us. Do you know about it – the murder? Do you know who did it? Did Mr Mostyn know too?"

A heavy silence fell in the cave, where the sound of dripping water seemed to grow sharper. Then Abel sighed, clutching his hat and the skin bag of food. He looked from one to the other, as if making up his mind he could trust them. Then he spoke, his black eyes prominent and strained:

"Yes, Missy – I know who killed the redcoat soldier." The young man's eyes smouldered and his grip tightened on the twisted hat and the bag in his hands. "I know that why the Cap'n he thrash me, and that Mr Mostyn, he also know and he know why Cap'n thrash me."

"Who was it, Abel? You must tell us because the murderer must be punished." Wellesley spoke sternly, as he crouched nearer to the boy. "Are you afraid of the murderer, Abel?" He suddenly raised his head, and his eyes met Rosina's, his brows gathered in concern. "We'll see that he is caught so that he can no longer harm you, or Miss Rosina, or anyone else."

Abel stared at him a long time, twisting his hat and the bag in his hands. His pain of mind was deeply pitiful to see. It was the mental torture of a frightened young man, oppressed beyond endurance by a fear involving his own life. Then he said, in the low voice in which he had first spoken. "It be Cap'n Skewthorn himself, Master." His voice broke and he stared at a point beyond Wellesley's shoulder.

There was an incredulous silence. "Cap'n Skewthorn!" Rosina burst out, unable to control herself.

Abel cleared his throat, turning his face towards the entrance and peering at it intently. Then he shifted his gaze back with a relieved air. His manner seemed to make the place colder and more menacing to Rosina, but she remained silent as he continued, "I saw him go in the redcoat soldier's room with Missy Rosina's scissors in his hand. I seen him come out again. I tell Mr Mostyn but he shake his head, I must not tell nobody. I tried to tell Missy, but she won't answer the door. Then the Cap'n he sees me. He thrash me to keep me quiet, but I afraid he kill me too, so I run away."

Rosina's teeth chattered uncontrollably. "But why? Why did he ask me why I had done it on the morning after the murder?"

"Perhaps he did not mean why had you killed the man, Rosina, but why you had given yourself to him."

In the light of the lantern, Wellesley stood beside her, gazing down, holding her eyes in a willful vice of amber. His voice was soft, as he continued, but it held a note of determination which in a strange way both frightened and angered her. "Perhaps he killed the redcoat because of his jealousy about you – because you had belonged to another man – a man who had dared to take you in his own house – and not because he was afraid the redcoat would spill the beans about the smuggling."

Rosina stood staring up at him, her eyes dark and bewildered. "But the Captain was not home when old Sam Leach was killed. Then old Sam must have been killed by someone else."

Wellesley nodded, and put a hand on Abel's shoulder. "Come, young Abel – it's all over now. Do you know who killed old Mr Leach?"

Abel glanced at him, as Rosina thought about the Captain. Did he remember the child he had rescued from the sea so long ago? Did he not care about what had almost happened to her?

"Master Wilkins! He did it!" There was a sudden ring in Abel's voice, a tautness in his bearing, which brought her back to the world around her. "I seen him goin' into the barn with his knife. He spy on Mr Maarten for the Cap'n – and on Missy and Lieutenant Buckleigh. I heard the Cap'n tell Master Wilkins to say he had fever."

A disagreeable shudder crept over Rosina, as Abel glanced over his shoulder with hollow eyes. There was a sick feeling in the pit of her stomach, yet near her heart, pounding heavily beneath her breast, there bloomed a sudden odd sense of elation, even a new and fragile sense of freedom. Beneath her swirling thoughts, she knew she had never been truly free until now.

"Now – now Captain Skewthorn and Israel Wilkins can be made to suffer for what they did," she said slowly, "Now everyone can know who murdered Andrew and old Sam."

"It's not as easy as that," Wellesley said, watching her, "It's only Abel's word against theirs – there's no concrete evidence to convict either of them. We have to get them on another charge – a charge that is strong enough, irrefutable enough, to stick. We have to catch them in the act of smuggling slaves into the colony."

She stared up at him, his amber eyes staring down at her almost into her soul. Unable to bear the intense weight of his regard, she turned away. He would never guess the depth of torture he put her through, for beneath her anger and her caution, she still burned with a consuming desire for him. She was ever conscious of him, painfully aware that he would soon leave the colony, forgetting that she had ever existed. But he was a fire burning in her blood, and she could find no way to quench it.

"How can we do that?" she asked abruptly, mortified by her own thoughts, "We don't even know where he is."

"Yes, we do. I've had news recently that the *Leviathan* met with bad weather in the Atlantic and was driven off course. She's been sighted limping towards the coast, badly damaged. The cargo must be in a pitiable state with neither water or food after ten weeks at sea. The Captain can't make for Table Bay, which will refuse him succour and take him in, so he's staying safely out to sea. But he must come in at some point, and then, we'll be ready."

"But why didn't you tell me sooner?" she whispered, transferring her gaze to the silent, watchful Abel standing behind him.

There was an odd look in his eyes as he stared down at her. "I only found out hours before we left to come and fetch Abel, and I didn't know how you would take it then. Remember, you did not know the Captain had murdered Buckleigh, and nor did I."

She gazed back at him helplessly. Suddenly she could

not bear his eyes seeing more into her than she wanted him to know. Her resentment aroused, she said, more sharply than she intended, "I don't see what difference it would have made if I had known! C'mon Abel, we must be getting back now to Mr Combrink's!"

Then she whirled about, as Wellesley, holding up the lantern, followed in her wake, watching her hips as they swayed in the borrowed coat and breeches, with a natural, graceful provocativeness.

Chapter Thirty

Wellesley stood looking down at Rosina on the stoep of Andre Combrink's house, in the heat of a searing bergwind. Down at the beach, the tide was low and the air steamingly oppressive. Four or five tall ships rose at anchor, and the bay was dotted with smacks and dinghies. The noise from the fishmarket could be heard distantly, as the gulls uttered their plaintive cries overhead, some of the more raucous housewives adding their shrill voices to the rest, as prices and sizes of the silver scaled stockfish were shouted and haggled over.

Behind Wellesley, Abel sat proudly in the driver's seat of his phaeton, wearing livery and the conical straw hat of Malay coachmen. The facts of the matter of Abel and the other slaves from the settlement had been put before the Court of Appeal presided over by the Governor, with the Lieutenant-Governor to support him and diligently sifted. As there were no papers registering either Abel or the others as Captain Skewthorn's slaves, the Court's decision was that time and distance had thrown an impenetrable mystery on their past. And as the Captain was indulging in illegal trafficking, Wellesley was allowed to buy Abel and register himself as his owner. Achmat was allowed to work with a cockney blacksmith who paid him well enough, and Abdoul for his cousin, a wagon-maker. The hiring out of slaves had been common practice for generations, and Abel was allowed to put in overtime work where he could find it, and to keep the fees for himself. Wellesley, in his spare time, was teaching him the elements of writing and figuring, and Abel had bought, with his first earnings a small black notebook to keep his accounts, which were painstakingly inscribed with dates and figures.

"The *Leviathan* cannot hold out in the open sea any longer – there are no ports open to her nearby, and the lookouts around the coast have seen her round Cape Point. She is now on the Atlantic side, heading for the only safe anchorage before Cape Town in Hout Bay," Wellesley said, squinting into the light, a shaft of sun candling his eyes. "By law, slave traders have no right to be in any British harbour, and coming into port with prohibited goods is a legitimate cause for seizure. Nor have they the right to call on us for repairs."

Rosina glanced up at him, her eyes pained. "But he must be caught!"

"The military has a plan, Rosina – but it involves you."

"What do you mean?" She stared up at him, her body stiffening.

"A detachment of redcoats intends to ride over the mountains from Cape Town under Captain James Howison to the bay, where they will set up an ambush on the beach. They want to surprise Captain Skewthorn and his men as they step ashore – and they have to make sure they are all ashore. Once they step back into their boats, success will be far more difficult. The plan is for you to go with them to identify the Captain as soon as he steps ashore. But I've extracted a promise from them that you only go if I accompany you – for your own protection."

Her eyes widened in horror, stunned at his suggestion.

"But the Captain is easy enough to identify. He has a wooden leg! They don't need me for that!"

"But that's just it – they want to make absolutely sure, Rosina – he's so damned clever he could do anything – even set up an imposter in his place. He's done that before, in another British harbour, and before the authorities caught on, he'd got clean away. Besides, if he sees you, he will be taken by surprise, which will give the redcoats time to go into action. As a civilian, I've promised not to take any part in the operation. Once your part is done, we must disappear quickly from the scene and let the redcoats take over."

Shocked, Rosina glanced at the trees, whose boughs were swaying and bending in the hot wind. They walked in silence to the carriage, both divorced by the privacy of their thoughts.

A moment passed, then her eyes stung him. "I can't! He has such power in him. I can't!

"But you must, dear girl, if you want him caught, and the others with him. I'll be there to see you're safe, and you can rely on His Majesty's troops." He paused, his eyes narrowing subtly. "Jan la Motte has been given permission to come along."

Rosina froze and stood silently, listening. "He insisted. With all this protection, nothing will happen to you, it's guaranteed."

"I – I'm afraid of the Captain – he's so strong," she gasped, her face white.

"Listen to me, Rosina. 'You have to free yourself. You have to make a choice; a sacrifice. Only you can do that, and this is the way. Will you take the challenge?' His brow arched questioningly, but it seemed more a plea than inquiry he made.

"I so much want the courage to do so— " She brushed

253

the hair from her eyes in a graceful motion, her smooth skin glistening from the heat.

He stared at her a moment, as though making up his mind which words to choose. "Courage is something that comes from within oneself. You have to build it up."

But he was getting to her. He could see it in her eyes, a deepening of awareness behind the fear. They lost their distracted look, and attentive now, she listened to the rich, confident timbre of his voice. She knew that she had been trapped all her life, that it had always seemed that she could not get out. The realisation brought painful memories. But she had to rise above the situation, above all the limitations imposed upon her, that by taking the responsibility and seeing it through, she would succeed. The choice was hers alone.

Holding her head high, she bit her lip, and gave silent assent. "When do we start?"

"Tonight, just after midnight. The ship is due in Hout Bay tomorrow. Jan la Motte has taken it upon himself to fetch you and take you to the place of meeting with the redcoats. I shall meet you there." He paused, his eyes meeting hers, shining enigmatically so close above her. "Why did you send back all the clothes I'd bought you?"

His gaze was now direct, challenging, raking her from her trim and shapely kid slippers showing beneath the hem of her skirts, and passing over the peach coloured muslin Jan had given her so long ago, gathered beneath her firm, round breasts with matching ribbon. The neckline of the dress was demure with a froth of delicate lace ruffles at her throat. It flowed in fluid lines about her body, moulding itself against her, showing the womanly roundness of her breasts and the graceful curve of her hips. Self-consciously she plucked at the lace cuff of one of the sleeves.

"I do not want to live on charity."

"'Twas not charity, my dear girl – but gifts from the heart. Do you still resent me so much?" His face grew serious as he met her gaze. "And as soon as I have served my usefulness, must be gone from your life as quickly as possible?"

"Of course not! I – I – it's just that I have my pride. 'Tis almost like bein' a kept woman, so to speak – with gifts and things – and I want to keep myself now, until— "

His lips spoke no words, but his look touched a quickness in her that made her feel as if she were on fire. It flamed in her cheeks and set her fingers trembling as she stared back at him. His dark hair was tousled by the wind, and he was bathed in a dappled light cast by the late morning sun, aglow with deep golden colours that rippled along his elegant, hard, lean frame. He was the most wonderful sight cast in dappled gold, and she was no less shaken by the sight of him than by his slow, intense perusal.

"Until what?"

Her eyes wavered beneath his direct stare, and her shaking fingers entwined. She was suddenly like a small girl in a fully bloomed woman's body. "I – I have spoken to Mr Combrink about setting myself up as a seamstress in the town. I – I sew tolerably well."

"But that is not what you meant, is it?" He watched her warily, and saw that her lower lip quivered slightly.

"Jan la Motte has asked me to marry him."

"And have you accepted him?" he asked in a controlled voice.

"I am thinking about it. 'Tis a most serious matter."

"Indisputably one of the most serious." She raised her eyes and found herself staring into his. A slow smile spread across his lips, and it bore a strange note

255

of confident knowledge yet, with no threat; no mockery. Just a simple smile that somehow disturbed her more than it should have.

"I ask one thing of you before you commit yourself for life to our worthy Jan. Take back the clothes and trinkets, before you so coldly dismiss me."

"I'll do no such thing!" she snapped, but the colour in her face deepened. "You can give them to your – your fancy women!"

He paused with his foot on the step of his carriage, eyeing her with a twisted grin. "My fancy women? Whatever gave you the idea that I had any?" He chuckled dryly. "Really, there are times when you never cease to amaze me." His smile grew deliberately wicked. "Besides, no woman would want the cast-offs of another."

Rosina's glower was more than piercing as she stared up at his attractive mocking face, her eyes tight with her own frustration and anger.

"You – you're insufferable!" she gasped out, her husky voice rising, then she turned and fled back to the refuge of the stoep.

"Don't forget tonight," she heard him softly laughing, "Come in your horrible old borrowed breeches – it will be easier when riding a horse. Pity you can't shoot. You'll be well covered in any case— "

She turned around on the stoep, her eyes smouldering like dark coals. "I can shoot," she burst out, "Henry – Henry Mostyn taught me when I was but a child!"

With that she disappeared into the shadow of the doorway, as Wellesley shook his head, and turned away to find Abel staring down at him from the phaeton, a grin splitting his mouth from ear to ear.

Chapter Thirty-One

The day aged into evening and a battle still raged within Rosina's mind, which was exhausted by the struggle. Reason and the undenied logic of her own motives waned under overwhelming fatigue, while the multitude of threats raised by her identification of the Captain blugeoned her until she grew numb beneath the onslaught.

She stood, gazing out of the window of her bedroom. In the valley, the far side of every house darkened, its walls to the west radiant in amber light. She could see the beach from where she stood, pleasantly removed from its smells; curves of wet sand gave back tints of opal, and edges of foam creamed and dwindled as the little waves broke and hesitated and withdrew.

She knew with certainty that her new freedom was threatened, that it would only be able to blossom safely when the Captain was behind bars, and even then, she was still not sure. Closing her eyes, she felt again the warmth of Wellesley's breath against her cheeks when he had kissed her in the kitchen of his house, her breasts crushed against his unyielding chest. Her eyes flew open, the memory of her own response seared through her brain, flooding her body with a pulsing warm excitement. And she knew she admired him for his brilliance, his passion, his intense enthusiasm. Always so near, and yet always so impossibly unattainable.

What was the cure for this affliction? Why was she so affected? She watched the stars glimmer through the dusk and thought of Andrew, and her budding feelings of love for him, of how dreadfully he was taken away, and now of Wellesley. Was she one who would ever yearn for men but find satisfaction with none, not even Jan? She had an excellent offer of marriage, yet her mind was still filled with the face of that one who haunted her, and would always elude her.

Listlessly she paced her bedroom, finding any distraction better than surrendering to the fantasies of her mind. Drastic measures would have to be taken to relieve this madness that bound her. She could not sleep. She could not eat. Her life was in a turmoil. The bedroom closed around her, and in every corner she could see Captain Skewthorn's leering, taunting face, and Wellesley's mocking eyes. Retreating from this torture, she returned to her bed and tried once more to sleep before the clock downstairs struck midnight and she would be forced to rise.

The hour of their departure arrived brisk and clear, and after riding for some hours, by the early hours they were placed behind the green-capped sand dunes and the scrubby bush to the west of Hout Bay.

While Captain Howison and some of the redcoats checked and primed their muskets and kept watch, crouching at the stone breastwork, its iron cannon directed across the bay, Wellesley with Jan and Rosina, dressed in borrowed men's clothing, hid behind a large dune with the rest of the redcoats looking directly on to the beach. The attack plan called for Rosina, covered by the muskets of the redcoats, to proceed down

258

to shoreline as soon as Captain Skewthorn stepped ashore, and to identify him by bowing before him. At the appropriate moment, when she replaced her hat on her head, the redcoats would emerge from the dunes, while she disappeared as quickly as possible, and the soldiers at the breastwork would proceed to fire on the ship and disable it but not destroy it so that the slaves in the hold could be released. They gambled on the idea that the Captain would never fire on a woman, especially if Rosina identified herself at once.

Rosina held her breath, her face hidden beneath a low, broad-brimmed hat, listening to the men stir impatiently about her, their guns glistening in the moonlight. She glanced back towards the mountains towering in the darkness above the bay. Silence fell like a shroud over the scene, and they could hear quite clearly the rasping cough of a wary leopard on the prowl somewhere in the bush, and the loud 'hu-hooo, hu-hooo' of a Spotted Eagle Owl.

At dawn the fog hung low on the water as the mild, warm onshore breeze set it stirring. Mists rose in streamers from the oily surface as the men began to awaken.

"The fog can last till almost ten o'clock at this time of year – it doesn't burn off easily," Jan said in a low voice, scratching thoughtfully at his beard as he squinted at the shadows hovering in the bushes around them. "Any ship out there on the open sea will have to wait till it lifts."

It was well into the morning when the fog drifted up to leave a broad pathway open beneath it, but still clung reluctantly about the mountain peaks. When it finally vanished, Rosina looked about her, from her place wedged in between Wellesley and Jan. A half ring of mountains thrust upwards beyond thick scrubby

259

bush and sand dunes which came close to the water's edge along the pale strand of beach which separated the living bush from the tumbling surf that licked the naked shore with white-crested tongues of foam. A wide, wooded valley spread out behind the dunes and the bush, fertile and rich. Down the centre were one or two farmhouses, and to the north-west, enormous sand dunes spilled down from the mountains.

"Look!" Jan kept his voice low, speaking into his beard, as the bay brightened in the morning sunlight. "A ship comes, at last."

Rosina sensed Wellesley's body tense beside her and glanced up. He was gazing across the bay, where a small dot had suddenly appeared. It was the *Leviathan*.

"You've waited a long time for this, Rosina, and so have we all . . ." He seemed to lose words as his hand caught hers for a moment, and she felt the strong warmth of his fingers. She lowered her eyes as she caught Jan eyeing them, feeling embarrassed by that impulsive display.

Suddenly there was a shout from the breastwork, and they paused to look up. Around them the light dappled the mountains and the surf sparkled myriads of diamonds. Behind them and to the right, were the redcoats in the dunes and at the breastworks to the right, a deadly group of grim-faced men.

"The brig's limping badly, but thank God, she's been forced into the bay at last," Jan gasped, holding his musket with white-knuckled tension. "They couldn't hide safely at Struisbaai because the whole coast there is bristling with redcoats. Good God – I see the reason for the hurry! Look out there!"

Propping himself up on an elbow, he motioned to a point out to sea. Rosina's face was in shock, as Wellesley shoved his pistol in his belt and pushed himself up on to his haunches.

"It's a British warship, by God! It's been chasing him, totally ignorant about us," said Wellesley, trembling with suppressed passion. "This will complicate Captain Howison's plan in no uncertain way. But a ship that size can never anchor in the bay, the draught's too great."

Headed towards the bay, guns run out, was a British warship, the Union Jack fluttering from her mast. It had grown much brighter now as the *Leviathan* came in close, her sun-bleached sails gleaming white in the gold of the light, as she moved closer to her goal, between the long encircling mountains of the sheltered bay. To the west, Sentinel Rock reared its distinct triangular head to guard the entrance.

Rosina lay, propped on her elbows, staring at the ship, her mind churning, as the crewmen swarmed in the rigging to secure the sails as the brig was warped closer to an anchorage. Already a long boat was being launched as she anxiously scanned the horizon.

"The warship's taken up a blockading position at the entrance of the bay, and the men on board will be rolling out the guns – whatever are we to do? The original plan will not work any longer," Jan said, his bearded face hard and strained in the sunlight, as they stared at a line of longboats leaving the ship and gliding across the tips of the waves.

"Are they out for an attack?" Wellesley narrowed his eyes to the point Jan was observing. "They must know there are slaves on board."

Jan paused and studied the boats. "From here I'd say some are headed for the shore on the far side, and the others will board the brig." He grinned suddenly, with satisfaction. "*Ach*, but perhaps it is not so bad after all – it's possible they will take attention away from us when the time comes. And Rosina won't have to expose herself more than is necessary."

"For a peace-loving man, you look very comfortable in this precarious position, Jan." Wellesley glanced at the big man from beneath his brows.

Something strange came into Jan's eyes, a veiling, a shadow. "There comes a time when a man must stand up and be counted, Meneer," he said, clearing his throat, and they both glanced quickly at Rosina. Slowly she looked from one to the other, becoming aware of the strain and discomfort between the two men.

Now excited voices from the brig began to filter up, faint in the morning air, and they could hear the sound of cannon trucks rolling over the deck as the guns were being set.

"Some of them are going to make a run for it – into the bush and up the mountainside, while the others look as if they'll fight it out with the man-o-war." Wellesley was studying the wide and sandy beach. "Once the shore party have disappeared into the bush, it'll be the devil to find them. If we are to make a move, it must be now."

Rosina's heart raced with sick apprehension as her eyes searched the longboat for the Captain.

Captain Skewthorn was taller than most of the men around him, and his shoulders were broad, his body square. For a moment she watched as the longboat touched the sands and he climbed out, with the familiar stumping of his wooden leg, the hem of his dark cloak whipping about his legs. He carried his weight surprisingly easily, and despite his handicap, there was still a great strength in him. She could see the tall, strong figure of Israel Wilkins getting ready to climb out, and Robert Blaine's long thin face.

A deafening explosion sounded from the ship, then a second and a third. Black smoke boiled up as a yell arose in the direction of the warship. Its guns had been fired. Shouts rose up, as men began to scatter and in moments a battle had begun.

"There are orders for you to go now, Rosina," Wellesley urged suddenly, a spyglass to his eyes. "Those on the ship won't notice – their whole attention is taken up with the warship. There won't be another shore party from the brig for a while yet during the firing. You'll be covered every step of the way."

"And, Rosina," Jan interrupted tensely, "God be with you!"

Chapter Thirty-Two

For a moment Rosina lay unmoving, dreading the prospect of having to face the Captain and the others. The dunes sounded with the clicks of powder flasks being opened and hammers being readied. Then, whipping the hat from her head, she rose from the dune, and proceeded to crawl away until she could walk upright away from the spot of ambush. Helplessly she looked back over her shoulder as ragged fear assailed the courage she tried to muster. There was no sign of Wellesley or Jan and the soldiers.

There was little enough for her to do, but she was forced to do it and work to its limit, keeping her timing as precise as possible. As she walked down towards the longboat, covered by the redcoats, still hidden in the dunes, uniformed figures of marines suddenly emerged from the bushes on the far side and began to wade silently towards the longboat, and she knew she had to divert the Captain and his men's attention from them.

She turned to face them, clutching her hat, trying not to think of the danger before her. As soon as he saw her, Captain Skewthorn withdrew a pistol from beneath his coat and slapped the butt against his palm.

"'Tis Rosina, sir, don't shoot!" she called as she approached nearer, her dark hair streaming down her shoulders.

As she faced him, his black eyes widened in aston-ishment to see her, and she bowed before him. "Your servant, sir."

"And what are you doing here, girl?" he roared as he surveyed her as if seeing her anew. "Why are you here – in men's clothing? Is this a trick?" His eyes darted quickly over the deserted beach and up along the line of sand dunes.

Israel Wilkins and Robert Blaine came up behind him, surprised, but instantly hostile.

"'Tis a trick, Cap'n – she's not 'ere alone, you can bet on that!" Robert Blaine snapped as his hand dropped to the pistol in his belt.

"Where are they, girl? Where are your accomplices? Who put you up this, eh? Who?" The Captain barked, turning a silent snarl to her face. He raised the pistol as if he would shoot her. Rosina stared up at him, trying to quell the sickening fear that gripped her. He was insane. He would kill her in outrage at what she was doing, just as he had killed Andrew.

"'Tis dangerous hereabouts, Cap'n – them damned marines will be 'ere in no time! We 'ave no time to waste!" Israel Wilkins rasped, his small, crafty eyes darting to the rest of the longboats steadily approaching along the surface of the sea. "We gotta make a run for it – now!" The scar across his ruthless face seemed more livid than she remembered it, and the twisted grin displaying uneven, blackened teeth in the fleshy, tanned face more sinister now that she knew about old Sam. In that moment of nightmarish terror, it seemed as if the devil had taken human form.

As the Captain's dark eyes watched her with angry suspicion, she straightened and met his gaze squarely, realising that the attack would have to come quickly

265

now. Suddenly, tears came. She knew she had to go back quickly, but somehow it seemed vitally important for her to make him understand the whole truth.

"Cap'n Skewthorn, sir – I know now 'twas you who killed Lieutenant Buckleigh, and Israel Wilkins who killed old Sam Leach. You used me as a pawn, sir and your just end is come for the foul deeds you have done."

Israel Wilkins fleshy jaw sagged as he realized the full implication of what she said. His hand came to rest upon his pistol as a horrified expression crept over his ruthless features. "I told ye – we should'a put this wench away for good when we had the chance! Now there's 'er and them marines upon us! We done for!"

"Oh, no, we're not! We've still got time, Wilkins – we haven't come this far to be taken that easily."

As Rosina opened her mouth to reply, the Captain threw out an arm and grabbed her in a strangling headhold, yanking her head back. "You come with us, wench. No one can help you now!" he warned close to her ear.

It was then that there came a burst of shouts from the other men who had climbed out of the longboat and were clustering around the Captain as Wellesley burst upon the scene, with a pistol aimed. He stopped and stared at the knot of startled, watchful men.

"Let the girl go, Captain Skewthorn! You are under arrest for the illegal smuggling of slaves into this colony. You are surrounded by His Majesty's troops. You cannot get away this time. Mark my words, there'll come a day when slavers will be a blot on the name of England and the world." Wellesley's eyes raked the malevolent faces of the men, who had all to a man, a gun in their hands.

266

"Who says so?" Outraged, Captain Skewthorn rasped, "What goes on here does not concern the likes of you! Throw down your gun, Mister! If you don't I'll kill the girl!" He roughly tightened his arm about Rosina's neck, and aimed his gun at her head.

Rosina felt fear sweep over her, as she felt the cold metal of the muzzle pressed close to her face. Her breath almost stopped as she braced for the approaching storm.

"I said, drop your gun, Mister and raise your arms! You are outnumbered. If you come any closer, Rosina will die. 'Tis her doing!" The Captain snarled, "She betrayed me, just like her mother before her!" He leaned forward, as if he would hurl himself at Wellesley, who realising he was on the defence, dropped his pistol on the sand, and raised his arms. Rosina felt a strange cold chill creep up her back. She lifted her eyes to Wellesley's.

His eyes were shining with a light that seemed to come from somewhere in the depth of them. "She was one of your own, Captain – since a child she lived with you. But where were you when she needed you? You left her to suffer for a crime you committed!"

Captain Skewthorn looked at him with a strange, triumphant expression, his fingers biting into Rosina's shoulder in calculated cruelty. "I'll tell you why before you die! She's her mother in looks, in manner, in her gross deceit – both weak women of the flesh – and she the only child of my loins!"

For a moment Rosina was shocked, her features frozen.

"No! My father!" she choked out in horror. She twisted in his grasp, but he held her fast.

"No! It can't be true!" A coldness coursed in her veins and she stared up at him. Everything fell away; the men, the ships, the whole world, leaving her suspended in emptiness with two black eyes staring down at her. Now everything began to make some kind of insane sense. She recalled the blades in Andrew's body; the angry, gaping wounds, and she felt nauseated with the vision of the younger man trying to fight for his life beneath the first cruel blow at his throat.

"Your daughter?" Wellesley burst out incredulously, "Whatever do you mean?"

Rosina considered pulling loose and flinging herself away, but even as the thought came, Captain Skewthorn's hand caught a hold of her hair and twisted her head painfully to one side, prodding her with the muzzle of his gun.

"Her mother had my child before she wed, without a word to me!" The Captain's nostrils flared as he glared down at Rosina, and his face became a twisted mask of rage. "And I was away at sea when she ran away and married that devil Horatio Webb who took her as his own. When he left her, I took her to sea. She deserved to die. And so does her daughter!"

"But I never did you any harm, sir!" Rosina's words were little more than a whisper, but they seemed to enrage the Captain, and he made his first mistake. In trying to face her in a glowering rage, he let her go for an instant, and it was then that Wellesley dived forward to snatch his gun. The men were completely taken by surprise as the weapon shot upward and sailed in a neat arc into a nearby bush, as there was a barrage of firing from the dunes behind them, and with loud curses, they turned to stare. A volley of cannon fire exploded from the direction of the breastwork on to the ship, and from behind the dunes and the bushes a line of redcoats emerged, all bearing long-barrelled muskets. The beach

268

erupted as another round of cannon shot crashed from the ship, and the soldiers began shooting. Robert Blaine immediately cocked his pistol and returned fire with incredible speed, bringing down a redcoat, as Captain Skewthorn yelled for his men to find cover. In moments the morning air had grown opaque with dark smoke, as the crewmen, now milling about in confusion, ran for the bushes up the one side of the beach and began piling up makeshift barricades of brush.

Rosina gripped Wellesley's arm tight as he picked up his pistol from the sand and cocked it. He turned to her for a second, their eyes locked in silent exchange, then he pushed her away. "Run, Rosina – run for your life! Get out of here before it's too late. A damnable skirmish has started." His voice was low and hoarse, his face tense, as the tall, bulky form of the Captain veered sharply to one side, and wheeled about, out of the range of fire, and disappeared into the smoke. "Good God, he's getting away!"

Even as he spoke, another round of cannon shot slammed into the front of the stone breastwork to their right, shaking the redcoats firing the cannon, and there was an explosion aboard the *Leviathan* as she was fired on by the warship.

Wellesley began to sprint across the sand, headed for the bushes where Captain Skewthorn had disappeared when suddenly there were shouts from the ship. The man-o-war's boarding party had reached the brig and was boarding with grappling irons. Rosina paused an instant, coughing from the smoke, then ducked and bolted.

Chapter Thirty-Three

She ran. Only a few more feet remained and she reached the nearest dune, and threw herself down, so that she could lift her head and watch the proceedings. While the redcoats at the breastworks fired grapeshot from the cannon at the ship, and the boarding party from the warship grappled with the brig's crew, a musket battle between the redcoats and the shore party from the brig raged across the dunes.

By now the air was dense with smoke, as the redcoats and the marines closed in upon the bushes where the crewmen had entrenched themselves. It was then that Jan emerged through the bushes. Rosina froze when she saw him. He was raising his musket, preparing to fire when his body suddenly jerked back and lay on the sand. She pressed back into the dune, her knuckles gripping white, her mouth clamped to a lipless line, her eyes shut.

Then her eyes shot open, flashing. Desperately she crawled over to him, her mind tumbling over itself with shock. Jan dead! What a terrible tragedy for his mother to bear, and his small son without a father.

He lay face down in a shallow depression in the sand. A pool of blood stained the sand near his heart. One hand still clutched his musket. The other was stretched out, his fingers buried in the sand in a last desperate convulsive effort. She stared at him, her mind filled with the sight of another man who had died an ugly and untimely death, and all because of her. She struggled against the outrage and shock that engulfed her, and through the mad buzzing in her ears, she heard a distant shouting. She was disturbed by a barrage of firing from the soldiers in front of her, and shaking her head to free herself from the shock, some sanity returned. The soldiers had reached the barricades of brush, and the marines were kneeling in ranks, methodically firing into the bushes.

Men were running all over in the bushes now. With sickening horror congealed in her chest, she realized that of Wellesley there was no sign, but she knew that he was in the midst of the fighting – fighting, as Jan had done, against her enemies! Closing her eyes, her breath frozen in her throat, she remembered golden eyes gazing down into hers, the smile that could taunt, anger, please or soothe, the vitality of his presence, the swift intelligence of his mind, his wit.

I love you, Wellesley Gerard. 'Tis love, pure and simple, there's no denying it anymore, she thought wildly, tears welling up within her eyes.

Suddenly her mind was clear. She stared at Jan's body, then she prized the musket from his fingers and grabbing the powder flask and shot, she rose, her shirt and breeches torn and stained from his blood, and, half crawled, half climbed a fairly steep dune directly above the barricades to where she could see the tall, fleshy form of Israel Wilkins cocking the gun in his hand.

The image of Jan and old Sam Leach rose before her eyes as she felt her palm grow moist against the wood of the stock, and for a moment she thought she could smell the stench of her own fear. Then, trembling violently,

271

she rose onto her knees to get a better aim, when he looked up and saw her. He hesitated a second, startled. Suddenly he recognised her and started to aim his pistol. She lifted her musket and cocked it, forgetting her fear in the danger of the moment. She pulled the trigger, and the hammer of the musket fell. The stock kicked her shoulder and a burst of smoke momentarily blinded her. The air flashed with an explosion as the shot crackled out, the ball whistling down the dune. A split second later, Israel Wilkins flung wide his arms, and falling to his knees, his large body crashed to the sand, in a pool of his own blood.

Just then, with the smell of gunpowder strong in her nostrils, and her eyes still smarting from the wisps of grey smoke trailing from the muzzle in her hand, she turned her head, and saw Abel, crawling up towards her, his shirt torn and stained from the underbrush. Her eyes, wide with incredulity, suddenly narrowed as she saw that he carried a musket.

"Abel!" she hissed. "What are you doing here? Get back at once! 'Tis too dangerous for the likes of you here."

"But not dangerous for you, a woman, Missy? Then 'tis not too dangerous for a man like me." Abel crawled to where she crouched, and halted beside her. "Master Gerard, he buy me free, Missy." His sing-song voice was unwavering. "The Captain is no longer my master, and Master Gerard, he has given me my freedom. You know what the Malay Imam, Achmat van Arabia say? He say "He who redeems a slave, has taken a man out of the fire." I hear him say that in the mosque in Vreedenburg street. Now I free to fight the Captain."

He moved beside her, gripping the handle of his

272

musket. "I learn to shoot when I runaway – I go to help the redcoats!"

"Abel! you've got to stay out of it, d'you hear me?" Rosina shifted her musket and seized his arm and started to pull him down behind the shelter of the dune, but he ducked and ran down, his feet disappearing into the sand as it flew up in clouds after him.

Before she had time to think any more about him, she saw Wellesley launch himself from somewhere in the smoke, at the figure of Captain Skewthorn who was pawing for pistols which were no longer in his hands, but lay in the underbursh. A howl of rage broke from him as Wellesley attacked, and with a thud the two men locked their arms in a test of strength. The Captain tried to dive to one side, in order to gain hold of his pistol which had fallen a few steps away, but Wellesley held on and they crashed to the ground in a cloud of sand, and to Rosina's eyes, became a thrashing confusion of twisting arms and legs. Shaking with her own emotion and her anxiety for Wellesley, she reloaded the musket as quickly as she could, and crawled forward, knowing that she dared not shoot in case she hit Wellesley and not the Captain. She wondered desperately what to do.

"Oh, no, you don't, you treacherous wench!"

She gasped and whirled, seeing the long, thin face of Robert Blaine, as he came up behind her, aiming a pistol up at her head.

Then he let out a sudden scream, and fell backwards, his body tumbling down the sand dune as a shot was fired from somewhere behind him. As he fell and lay deadly still, half buried in the sand, the thin, undersized figure of Abel crawled up the dune, the smoking musket in his hands.

"See, Missy – you need me to save your life," he said

273

simply, and she had never felt so pleased to see anyone as she was to see him in that moment. Then her attention was drawn back to the two men rising on their knees as Wellesley thrust his head beneath the Captain's chin, hugging him with his arms until the older man's spine was bent to the breaking point. The Captain growled, then suddenly twisted aside, and the hold was broken. They fell again obscured in a cloud of sand.

The Captain's hand touched one of the pistols, which he snatched, as he rolled above Wellesley and brought the gun up. Wellesley caught the gun, and the tendons stood out in his neck and arms as he strained to deflect the gun from aiming at him.

Rosina urgently turned to Abel. "Stay here, Abel, and don't move. Cover me while I go to help Master Gerard."

As he nodded vigorously and reloaded his musket, she crawled quickly down the dune and into the bushes on the one side, realising that Captain Skewthorn was still a very powerful opponent, and an extremely dangerous one. She crept forward, pushing the bushes out of her way with one trembling hand, until she came out at a spot behind the two men, unseen by the others who were busy reloading and firing their guns in a state of frenzied desperation.

She saw Wellesley heave, hurling the Captain over his head and away from him. She gasped as Captain Skewthorn shifted the pistol in his hand, while grabbing the other one lying further away as Wellesley scrambled to his feet. As the Captain aimed for Wellesley's heart, and Wellesley leaped back to avoid it, Rosina, with the full awareness of her feelings and fiercely protective of the life of the man she loved, rose from the underbrush, cocked her musket and aimed.

The Captain's triumph was ended in a shriek of pain and he stumbled backwards across the sand, reeling from the shot which caught him in the chest.

"Rosina! You shoot remarkably well, dear girl! You've just saved my life!" Wellesley gasped, knowing in that second that the memory of her face, scratched and streaked with sand and blood, and her cool, strong courage would stay with him through the measure of his days.

"Oh, Wellesley!" she cried throwing down the musket, and running towards him. "You're safe!" Stepping before him, she suddenly pulled his face close to hers and kissed his lips until he took her in his arms and lifted her against him in a fierce, crushing embrace.

Chapter Thirty-Four

Sunset was gathering over the mountains and the placid white beach, where the shiny surface of the sea reflected the light of the waning sun, as Wellesley sat propped up against a dune, holding still while Rosina applied a cool wet cloth to his forehead, where a shot had grazed it. Jan's body had been taken back to Cape Town for burial, as were the bodies of the Captain and the men who had been killed during the fighting. Before the cargo of slaves could be freed of their shackles, the surviving seamen were rounded up, in chains before the mounted redcoats. The only one missing was the Abraham Dance, the ship's cook who had managed to escape in a long boat, but not empty-handed. He had managed to remove a sack of coins from the hold.

A hundred and forty of the slaves were saved, and eighteen more were given burial, but seven of the rescued ones had already died from sheer weakness. Rosina and Wellesley had watched with growing sorrow the naked strings of men and women emerge slowly and shakily from the hold, their feet and hands still secured with individual chains. As each struggled outside, he or she would stare into the blinding sun for a confused moment, then turned in bewilderment to gaze at the mountains and bush beyond, before they were assembled in longboats and taken ashore.

After sternly admonishing Rosina and Wellesley for the deviation in the original plan against the Captain and his men, Captain Howison, a burly, red-faced man, stepped between the heaps of wreckage from the ship, and gave orders to have the slaves carried to the hospital of the new Slave lodge in the Gardens. There were a hundred men, thirty-three women, weak from exposure, hunger and disease. After that, he said, Lord Charles Somerset would have to decide what was to be done with them.

They both now sat in silence. The moment of danger had passed, and the battered ship before them proclaimed their victory, the epitaph to Rosina's season of fear and submission. Frowning with the glare of the fiery sunset and the misery which overcast their achievement, they both looked across at the brig. It was not the fact of death that kept them in silence; for that was the price of justice. What both of them could see was the body of Jan and the others lying on the sand before they had been taken away, and the pathetic lines of slaves walking dejectedly after the last of the redcoats.

"Oh, Wellesley," she cried. "I don't want to live, with all the shame— " She burst out into sobbing, and said, "Jan, Andrew – your part in it all – all because of me."

"It was all because of your father," he said breathing heavily, his face composed. "He was an evil man."

"I know – but he was my father and nothing will ever change that."

"But you can rise above it – by doing something worthwhile for those who suffer, can't you see that?"

Wellesley winced as Rosina's fingers touched his forehead, gently probing at the welling knot. His shirt ripped and torn, he shook his head as if pained. "Emanicipation will become the right of every slave

277

throughout the Empire. Those scurrilous slavers like Captain Skewthorn and his ilk will be defeated and wiped out to a man." His lips became a thin, angry line as his eyes sparked with odd, piercing lights. "From what I've seen here, as elsewhere, the slaves, even those who have been well-treated have too little part in the heritage of their country; too little reward for their labours. There is already much work being done to this end, but I feel it now my responsibility to join the body of emancipationists and add my voice to theirs."

Rosina raised her eyes as she finished the task of cleaning his wound, admiring the hard ripple of his chest, the long, muscular legs. Her dark eyes caught his, and for a long moment the two gazes held unwaveringly.

"But what about your fight for religious freedom? You feel so deeply about that too."

When he spoke again, his tone was certain, as he directed his words to her, his amber eyes suddenly brilliant with conviction. "The religious issue will always be there – I will never turn my back on it, but this problem is gaining ground, and must be accomplished soon. It's too urgent to postpone. I feel I must speak up about it. I will also write about it – and you must help me, because you have seen and experienced what few speak, though it lies in front of them. We will speak of it so that there will be deep shame, and then more deeds to end the suffering. That must be our task – to join Mr Wilberforce and his body of courageous, right-minded men and women."

Rosina regarded him for a long moment. He had not only vision but the gift of eloquence and a beautiful voice, and she had learned that these were formidable weapons for any man, and in that of a man passionately sincere they were invincible. Slowly she turned her face away, her eyes filled with tears.

278

"What is it, Rosina? Have I said anything to upset you? Surely you agree with me. It was you, after all, who wanted to fight for the slaves."

He sat watching her with a suddenly impassive expression, though he felt as if every part of him, his heart, his entrails and his lungs, had turned as pale as her face.

He moved away from her, and folding his arms across his chest, he looked straight ahead, his expression pre-occupied. "Are you still in love with Jan?"

She gazed out across the sea, watching the evening flood the sky, the water, and the mountain-tops with gold and crimson. The mountains ranging all around, were dimmed by a bluish haze that clung to the high, jag-ged peaks. The sheer beauty of the place was awesome. She stared at the land from left to right gilded with dark copper tints where the dying sun touched it with fingers of bright golds and brass. Then she returned her gaze to him, her eyes searching the golden flames smouldering in his eyes.

"Yes, but not in the way you think – he was a friend, nothing more – the brother I never had."

She fell silent, and he moved nearer and stroked the hair that was falling down her shoulders, his compassion strong even as he felt within him the knife of jealousy. Quite suddenly, he could understand why Jan had lost his life for her. She had been, for him, a new life, new hopes, and new dreams. He could understand what it meant to draw youth and vitality from her like warming oneself before an open fire on a cold night. Jan could not resist that – and nor could he. Beneath his fingers, her hair tumbled to freedom as he inhaled the fresh fragrance that wafted from it.

"I love you, Rosina," he said softly, "I love you and I want to marry you as soon as possible."

Rosina looked at him incredulously. "You do? Why didn't you tell me before?"

Wellesley gave an odd, half-crooked smile. "Remember when you said that you thought I was using you to show up the legal system? That was true," he said, smiling as her cheeks flamed at the memory. "But afterwards, as I learned to know you, I fell in love with you, and I wanted you to love me for what I am. But, I thought you loved Jan."

Her heart thumped with a sweet wildness that stirred her very soul. "I love you, too, Wellesley – only I was unsure of your feelings," she whispered. Then, suddenly she cringed like a frightened child. "But I am no woman for you – your world – I am ordinary and down to earth and – they would laugh at me— "

He had thought there was little any more in the world that could stir her to such fright. She had shown such courage in the face of alarming difficulties.

"Shh." he said, looking at her in mingled love and respect. Even in the dying light, with her hair tousled and her clothes dusty and stained with blood, she wore a sensuality and a simple strength that stirred his heart to burgeoning pride. "I will help you every step of the way through the new mazes of your life, and my family will love you. My father is a gentle scholar and poet, my mother quietly devoted to him, my sister Rachel is my strongest ally and my two brothers are amiable enough." He placed an arm about her shoulders, holding her trembling form close. "You are everything I want," he said, and thought with surprise that this was the truth.

At the beginning when he had taken on her case to prove his own point, he had regarded her as an unfortunate, poor wretch in need of help, an unlessoned, naive girl. But after the months spent with her, working with her, helping her, providing protection for her, he had realized how strong she was, how courageous, and intelligent, and in her own suffering from persecution, he had shared with her, his own. "You are not only beautiful, you are also courageous and strong, and from all reports, a wonderful housekeeper. And to think I was determined to marry for money!" A smile slowly spread across his face, showing his even, white teeth, his eyes twinkling with tiny golden lights of amusement.

She held her breath while he gazed at her, his eyes touching her everywhere. A full rush of visions filled her mind, each brighter than the next, as the full measure of pleasure burst within her. I'll be beside him in the fight against injustice . . . I'll share his brilliance, his enthusiasm, his hopes . . . He'll be in my life, my bed. I'll have his children!

He put both his arms around her, and she said, "I need your help. I knew so little before we met. You must educate me to fight for the slaves."

He did not answer immediately, as she clung to him, and after the buffeting and rejections she had endured he seemed to her like a secure and sheltering anchorage.

"No one must ever hurt you as you've been hurt," he said, stroking her face beneath the curls at the side of her cheeks. "You must come back to England with me, and tell them just what you've seen here, and what you've suffered – tell them all about the slaves."

"But I couldn't leave Abel and Clara behind – they – I must help them here all I can."

"Clara wants to stay here, she says she's too old to move. She's happy with old Mrs la Motte and the boy Jacques. They'll need her all the more now. Abel – he's keen to ply a trade, with some help, which I've offered." Slowly his head lowered, and his lips parted as they met hers. A warm tide of tingling excitement flooded her as her lips answered his in hungry impatience.

Time seemed to verge on eternity before he raised his head, his amber eyes holding her softly as he whispered, "Is that agreeable to you, my darling?"

Her cheek against his sturdy shoulder, she stared up at him and could not bring forth the words to express her joy, now that her vulnerability and deep mistrust had been overcome, that the barrier she had erected against him, had crumbled.

Suddenly a rattle of hooves at the edge of the sand dunes drew their attention. For a moment the black flank of Wellesley's horse and the dark brown of Abel, its youthful rider were visible across the sand. Her spirit thrilled with the sight, and briefly her eyes blurred with joyful tears. She smiled up at Wellesley, feeling a sense of growing freedom within herself, of unfettered love, and her voice was choked and broken as she whispered, "'Tis far beyond what I ever dreamed, my dearest Wellesley. Far beyond my wildest dreams."